SPARK OF TRUTH

BOOK THREE OF THE HIDDEN WIZARD

VAUGHAN W. SMITH

FAIR FOLIO

ISBN: 978-0-6481931-1-1

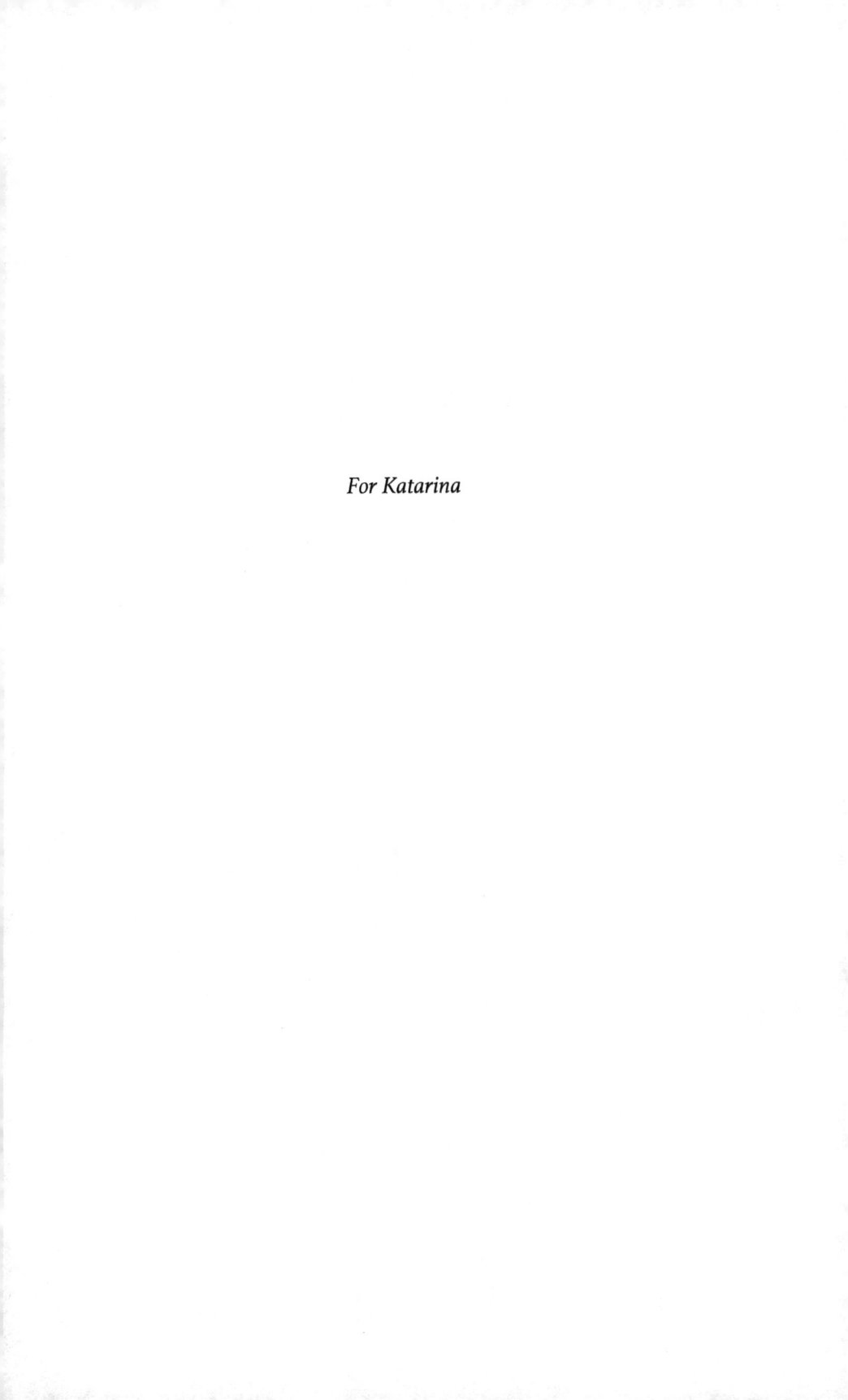

For Katarina

1

A NEW BATTLE

Alyx stumbled through the brush, narrowly avoiding a Blighter.

"Classy," she told herself, and leaned back against a nearby tree. The thick branches were a steadying force, although the leaves bristled in an uncomfortable way. The stench of Blighters was all around her and it caused her stomach to turn. She checked her hair, ensuring that it was still reliably tied up. With care, she looked around and noticed that the vile creatures were scattered everywhere.

Why are they in this forest? Nobody was tracking me.

By force of habit she checked for weapons. All she had was a short sword strapped to her lower back. It was useful, but it was not the sword that she had carried her entire life. Not that she ever really got much use out of it. But it was a comfort and reminder of her father, and now it was gone.

She crouched down and slowly approached the nearest Blighter. She winced as a twig snapped, but the Blighter didn't react. She pulled back her arm, tensed her muscles, and dived in with a deadly swipe. The Blighter dropped quickly and quietly, folding into the nearby bushes. Movement caught her eye, and she looked over. Another Blighter had entered the area and had witnessed her kill.

It looked at her blankly, and turned its head to go somewhere else.

It ignored me? Impossible!

Blighters acted on instinct alone. Or under the direct supervision of a powerful force. But she had already taken out the biggest threat around here.

"If they're not here for me, who is controlling them? And for what?" she said to herself. Her body ached, and her limbs felt stiff. But her curiosity was sparked. She had to investigate.

Sticking to the cover of the trees, Alyx stalked the Blighter that had ignored her. It seemed like a good plan, since it hadn't reacted to her at all. And it was more likely to lead her to whatever it was looking for. More accurately, whatever it was being targeted at.

She spotted more Blighters around, each behaving the same way. Like they were combing the forest for something important. Watching their movements, she noticed a pattern. They seemed to be converging on something.

This I have to see.

She knew she should leave this alone, and she should be recovering. She had done the impossible, and had earned a rest. She had fulfilled her life's purpose.

Weren't you supposed to just ride off into the sunset? Not find another problem to solve?

She pushed those thoughts aside and focused on the problem at hand. It was time to see what these Blighters were up to.

She tracked them with care, ignoring the complaints of her body. Light was fading, gloom rising around her and fewer shafts of sunlight pierced through the thick canopy. Everything was building towards something. But what?

She sensed something shift, and the Blighters started moving with purpose. They increased their speed and their snarls started to fill the forest.

"It's beginning," Alyx whispered, and increased her speed. She didn't worry about making noise now. She had to get to the bottom of what was happening.

Some of the Blighters were stalled, as if waiting for something. Alyx couldn't help herself, since they were easy targets. She ended each with a quick slash and kept her pace.

Never a bad time to put down some Blighters.

As she progressed, she started seeing larger and larger groups. It was unheard of for them to group up in such confined spaces, which further fuelled her curiosity. If there were any doubts left in her mind, they were completely dispelled now. She was committed to whatever this was.

A burst of sunlight startled her, as she emerged into a large clearing. There was a campsite, and in the middle, were three people. Each had weapons drawn, and they were facing off against the hordes of Blighters.

In a few seconds Alyx had appraised the group.

Fighter, thief, and civilian with a sword, she thought. They needed her help. And in return they could explain why they were such Blight magnets. Alyx stepped forward with confidence; the firm ground underfoot provided a good place to make a stand. She headed directly for the small group, pausing only to cut down Blighters in her path. There was a clear trail of bodies in her wake, and the group ahead noticed her approach.

"I don't know who you are, but thanks for the help," the fighter said.

"You stand with me, the others can support from behind," Alyx said. The fighter nodded and accepted her suggestion. A dagger whizzed past her face and embedded itself into a nearby Blighter.

"Don't mind me, just supporting from behind," the thief said, her voice dripping with sarcasm. Alyx understood the gesture and gave her a respectful nod. It was important to have them all on side. She then turned to fight.

Blighters were converging from all locations. Alyx moved next to the fighter, and readied herself.

"In case anything happens, I'm Alyx," she said as she pivoted to slash at an encroaching Blighter. Her name came out with a grunt, less eloquently than she had hoped.

"I'm Vincent. Nice to meet you." He stepped forward and tripped a Blighter, slicing through the other just behind it. Alyx finished off the Blighter that stumbled towards her and took a moment to glance at Vincent's sword.

Unbelievable. He noticed her gaze.

"Yes, it's Runesteel. You can take a better look when we aren't being killed."

"Sounds good." Alyx eyed the next group. Sweat started to drip down her face. She shouldn't be this tired, but her body was weary. She hadn't had a chance to recover from her previous fight, and had landed herself in a surprisingly large battle.

No rest for a weapon, she thought and prepared for the next assault. She pointed into the heart of the group with her weapon, and Vincent nodded. Alyx launched herself in, ignoring the strained cries of her legs as she pushed them even harder. She accepted none of the pain, focusing on the impending attack. With two quick slashes she took down a Blighter and wounded another. The thickly packed group dispersed immediately. While their attention was kept by Alyx, Vincent swept in and whirled through the rest, his sword flashing as he advanced.

Alyx stole another glance of admiration at the Runesteel sword, then retreated back with Vincent.

"Nice job up there, but they aren't slowing down," the thief said.

"That's Lara," Vincent said.

"And the master swordsman over there with the angry face is Alrion," Lara said. She smirked at him and he grunted at the comment.

"Alyx here. Do you have an escape plan? I don't like our chances if this continues."

"No. They cornered us here over several days," Lara said. She gestured at the clearing. There were Blighters surrounding the perimeter.

"Fine. We stand together for now, and if we get overwhelmed I'll create an opening for you," Alyx said. She didn't take her eyes off the approaching Blighters.

Why am I offering myself up for these people? she thought. But then she answered herself quickly.

I am a discarded weapon. I no longer have a purpose.

"I'm sorry how useless I am. Lara and I have taken on more than this just by ourselves," Alrion said. The frustration in his voice was obvious, and Alyx could sense that something must have happened to him. Clearly the sword was not his preferred weapon.

"Never mind that, focus on the task at hand," Vincent said. He pointed at the encroaching group and Alyx joined him in advancing.

Wave after wave of Blighters poured into the clearing. Each time Vincent and Alyx moved together, picking apart the Blighters with relative ease. Vincent and his Runesteel opened them up, and Alyx finished off the rest. Lara and Alrion stayed back, Lara providing some spotting and long-range assistance while Alrion just scowled. As the fight wore on he grew angrier and angrier.

Alyx could hear bits of conversation and noticed that Lara was trying to calm Alrion down. But she didn't focus on it; the battle carried her full attention. As it continued, her hair tumbled free. Her long flowing brown locks swayed just above her shoulder line. She had never fought with her hair loose, and enjoyed the carefree nature of it. Although it did restrict her head movements to ensure her vision wasn't obstructed.

Vincent was proving to be a capable fighter, as she had initially assessed. He was clearly older and not as fast as her, but he was strong and sure. His blade more than compensated for any lack in his speed and technique, and the Blighters were not enough to trouble him in capability. But the vast number and constant stream were wearing him down too.

The clearing was now full of Blighters. Every time Alyx cut one down, another was right there, ready and eager. She had never seen Blighters in this volume or with such intensity before.

"There's no end to them," she said.

"There is, but it may take a while," Vincent said. He kicked over a Blighter and slashed at another that was approaching. He looked slower. Alyx was worried. She chanced a look behind and saw that Alrion and Lara were in the thick of it too. Lara was dancing around, dodging, slashing, and harrying. Alrion was using slow and deliberate strikes to finish off any Blighters that were still standing.

Good pairing to make the most of this, but they can't continue for much longer.

She still couldn't believe what she had gotten herself into. It was time to make a difference. She remembered the path she had taken to reach them. It had been narrow, and would provide them a reprieve. If they could get there. But she would see to it.

"I'm going to advance, stick with me and let's make it through to a better place," she said. Alyx summoned the last of her reserve strength and made a final push forward. The first few Blighters were taken by surprise, falling before they could react. The next layer stepped back, unsure of what to do. Alyx dashed into the space, Vincent sticking with her. She couldn't risk turning back, to check on the others. But she knew that Lara would do the right thing.

The thief has good instincts. She's a survivor. She looks familiar somehow, Alyx thought. But she pushed the thoughts away. She had an impossible mission to complete. One she had set herself, but one she would still achieve.

Her left foot slipped and threw her balance off. But she compensated and lurched forward. She stabbed at a Blighter with her sword and grabbed another to steady herself. Before it could lunge in to bite her Vincent cut it down in a smooth motion. Working together they made slow progress, but more and more incidents threatened to end their battle prematurely.

Swaying on her feet, Alyx spun around and changed her approach. Gesturing behind her, the group readjusted their position. She had reached the edge of the clearing, and was shielding their retreat.

"There's Blighters on the path," Lara shouted.

"Less than here. And it's tighter," Alyx shouted back. She missed a Blighter, and it lunged for the advantage. Desperately she kicked it away, and managed to inflict a slight cut with her sword. Vincent finished it off, and stepped in front of her.

"You've done enough. You won't survive any longer," he said.

"It doesn't matter now. This is a fitting end for a weapon like me," Alyx said. She shoved Vincent aside, and ran into the thick of the remaining Blighters. Vincent swore, and started to follow. But he hesitated.

"Pull back," he said. Alyx smiled. At least he understood what lay ahead. Now all she had to do was make sure it was a fitting death. She ignored defence and focused all her energy on attack. The Blighters shrunk back, confused, and frightened by this new approach. Alyx let loose, years of discipline and training and focus falling away. She could be free, and let her cares go. And this horde of Blighters would be a thrilling final stand.

There were too many. Her muscles started to cramp up and freeze. Her movements became stiff and the Blighters grew bolder. They started to surge forward, tripping over each other in their eagerness. Despite her best efforts, she was starting to get nicks and scratches from their claws and rudimentary blades.

Death by a thousand cuts. How ironic.

She laughed to herself. However, she didn't notice one particular Blighter that wasn't dead. It jumped up from the ground and went in for the bite. Alyx threw her arm up at the last instant to shield her face, but couldn't stop the bite. Its fangs sank in deep and her arm felt hot and cold at the same time.

No! Not like this!

She kicked the Blighter away and threw down her weapon, hoping they would kill her outright. She closed her eyes and waited for the end. But around her she only heard death and mayhem.

Cautiously she opened her eyes and looked around. Vincent and Alrion had joined the fight, and were finishing off the final few Blighters. Lara was holding off those trying to join in from the path.

"I don't understand," she said as they approached her.

"I couldn't stand by and watch you sacrifice yourself," Alrion said. She could see a strange mix of anger and sadness in his expression.

She knelt and retrieved her sword. She also used the movement to cover her arm. It didn't feel right to reveal her situation just yet.

"What do I do now?" she whispered. She had let go and accepted her fate. But now, a new path was showing itself. But how long could she last before succumbing to the infection?

2

A KINDRED SPIRIT

"I'd love to complete the introductions, but I've had enough of Blighter innards for one day," Lara said. She surveyed the area around them in disgust. What had originally been a simple camping spot was now a Blighter graveyard of horrors.

"Agreed. Do you know this forest well?" Alrion said to Alyx.

"Relatively. There's no other spot like this, but I can lead us somewhere we can stop and rest a little," she said. Lara could see the exhaustion on the warrior's face, as much as she tried to ignore it. She couldn't help wondering why this stranger had risked her life to help them.

I'll keep an eye on her. If she's hiding something, I'll find it.

She stuck close to Alyx as they picked their way through the battlefield. She looked over at Alrion and saw him lost in thought.

Something is troubling him. Something more than just his condition. I'll have to figure that out later, she thought. Another thing to take care of. Vincent seemed like the practical sort, but Lara wondered how they would fare without her. Alrion was in his own world more days than not, and this was dangerous country. Especially with the horde of Blighters they had just encountered. She hoped it wasn't a sign of things to come.

Soon the clearing was behind them, and they continued along a narrow trail. The vegetation was thick and lush, suggesting the path had not been used in a while. Alyx was out front, stepping slowly but surely. She held her sword out, but only slashed at the most troublesome plants. Lara wasn't sure if it was due to respect for nature or lack of energy. Either option seemed equally likely. She glanced over at Vincent to gauge his reaction.

He didn't seem any different, just focused on the task ahead of them. He had been checking on Alrion though. So, he must have suspected something too.

I wish I knew more about this infection. There has to be more we can do.

Although it had been progressing slowly, it weighed on her mind every day. Every night she lay awake, listening out for signs of it progressing. Nothing was obvious, but the lack of any signs was in itself troubling. Her greatest fear was that it was progressing silently, and there would be no sign of it until too late.

In time they reached a small area with thinner tree cover. There was still thick vegetation, but also places to sit. Lara threw her pack onto a nearby shrub and sank into the grass. It was hard and slightly damp but she didn't care.

The rest did the same thing. Vincent spoke up first.

"Alyx, we are in your debt. You made the difference today, and I will be forever grateful." He stood and bowed to her. Alyx waved him away.

"I accept your thanks, but it is not necessary. I followed my curiosity, and decided I could not stand aside."

"You were ready to die for us! Why?" Alrion said, full of wonder.

"I'd like to know too," Lara said. Unlike Alrion, she gave Alyx a questioning look.

"I am not afraid of death. Especially now that my life's work is done. It seemed like a fitting end, if that were the case. But, here we are. My story is not done yet," Alyx said. She lay back, using one of the bushes behind her as a makeshift pillow.

"Please, share your story. At least some of it," Vincent said.

"Very well. As you know, my name is Alyx. I was the only child to my father, and therefore the only heir to the Warden of the North."

"Your father was Fenkirk?" Lara said. She couldn't hide the surprise in her voice.

"That is correct. You may be aware, but he was slain by the Skull King when I was only eight years old." Alyx paused. Lara knew of the story, but didn't know Fenkirk had had a daughter. She looked over at Alrion and Vincent and they appeared lost.

"I don't think they are as familiar with the history around here. You may need to explain a little," Lara said.

"The Skull King was one of the Four Generals of the Blight. We can discuss them later. All you need to know, however, is that he was completely evil and his head was all black with only his skull show-ing. He killed my father to prove his dominance, and conquered the rest of the area without opposition," Alyx said. She spat into a nearby shrub. Lara could see the anger boiling up in Alyx. Surprisingly she noticed something similar in Alrion too.

What's happening with him?

"I had no future. No woman can become the Warden. And the title means nothing if you can't provide the people with leadership and safety. So, I took up my family sword, and swore revenge on the Skull King," Alyx said. There was a satisfied look upon her face as she spoke, and Lara thought that perhaps Alyx had succeeded.

"That's a hard life, to take on such a burden at such a young age," Vincent said.

"It's the life I chose, so it is not hard."

"Your family's sword? Wasn't it famous?" Lara said.

"Yes. Both for its size and its legacy. It is called Andrylir." Alyx looked at her hands, despondent for a moment. She quickly recov-ered, but not before Lara noticed.

"What does that mean?" Alrion said.

"It means 'One Strike'."

"Is there a reason for that? Is there a story around it?" Lara said.

"Yes, there is, and the legend is true. One strike from it can kill anything."

"Impossible!" Vincent said.

"Believe what you want. But I took up the giant sword of my father, and turned myself into a living weapon. I thought of nothing else, did nothing else, until I could have my revenge."

"You did it, didn't you?" Lara said. A wicked smile crept along Alyx's face.

"I did. At great cost, but I did. And now I'm here."

"Without your sword and without a purpose," Alrion said. Alyx looked like the wind had been knocked out of her. Lara turned her attention to Alrion.

That was incisive of him, she thought. Wonder and curiosity flowed through her in relation to his words.

"You have me at a loss, but I cannot deny your words. Perhaps there is another purpose for a weapon like me," she said, her voice much quieter now. The pride that had infected it before was gone.

"I also said that I would show you my sword," Vincent said. He stood slowly, taking the opportunity to stretch.

"Allow me. My father made both swords," Alrion said. Before Vincent could react, Alrion unsheathed his sword and offered it to Alyx, pommel first. She grabbed it and Alrion sat back, satisfied.

"This is a beautiful blade," Alyx said, turning it over and admiring it from many angles.

"The stone ..." Lara said, pointing. She almost thought she had imagined it. A quick glow from the diamond in the pommel of the sword. But it wasn't reflected light. There was a pale blue to the glow. She looked over at Alrion and he was looking at Alyx with interest.

"What do you mean?" Alyx said. But Vincent understood immediately. He strode over and examined the diamond while Alyx still held it.

"It's faint but unmistakeable. You were bitten," he said. Alyx shrank back.

"Who are you?" she said.

"The diamond reacts to those tainted by the Blight. If you were a Shade it would be bright blue," Alrion said as he rose. He quietly stepped over to Alyx and retrieved the blade. The stone had a distinct glow to it, stronger than before. But still relatively pale.

"You also?" Alyx said, pointing at the diamond.

"Yes. But it hasn't claimed me yet," Alrion said before returning to his previous seat. He put the sword away, and watched Alyx with a curious gaze. Lara wanted to quiz Alrion, but she decided to wait until later. For now, she had to get to the bottom of this new problem.

"When were you thinking of telling us?" Lara said. She didn't hide the anger in her voice.

"Soon. I didn't want to taint the purity of the gesture you made."

"That's why you threw your sword down," Vincent said.

"Yes, I knew it was over. I am sorry for the confusion. It seemed like a fitting end, that was all."

"It is a fitting end," Lara said.

"It might be, if it was the end. But it won't be. You're coming with us," Alrion said.

"She's infected! This isn't a game!" Lara shouted. She couldn't believe what he was saying.

"She saved us. It's the least I can do."

"No, the least we can do is not harbour a threat like her. No offence, Alyx," Lara said. She had to shut down this idea before it grew any further.

"What is she going to do? Infect me?" Alrion said, laughing. He had to be losing his mind.

"I do appreciate your kindness, but it would not be a kindness travelling with you and knowing that I will succumb to the infection and be a danger to you," Alyx said.

"Would you change your mind if I told you I am going to find a cure," Alrion said. He had a gleam in his eye and stared straight at Alyx. She sat up straighter, giving him all her attention.

"You should not toy with me like this."

"I'm not. I'm on a quest to end the Blight, and I have a lead for how to get cured. The Mystics who live up in the mountains."

"Fairy tales. You shouldn't give yourself false hope," Alyx said. She sank back into the greenery and watched the sky.

"No less of a fairy tale than the Pool of Knowledge. Which I found and drank from. Or the fact that my grandfather cured the Blight from Avaria," Alrion said.

"You did what?" Alyx rose and stood over Alrion.

"I found the Pool and drank from it. It gives me visions of what I need for my quest. It showed me to the monks of the desert, and their secret trial of the Will. And now it is bringing me to the Mystics of the north. I know their power is crucial to cleansing the Blight. I just need to get there."

"Your story is fanciful, yet plausible. But no matter, we will never get there in time."

"How infected do I look?" Alrion said. He rose and stood close to Alyx. She looked him up and down.

"Judging from the mark a few days. But you don't seem to have some of the other signs."

"It's been a week," Alrion said quietly.

"We can't let this happen," Lara said to Vincent. She could sense the conversation turning, and didn't want it to continue.

"I'm seeing both sides here. Alyx is an incredibly effective fighter. We could use the help," Vincent said.

"And when she turns?" Lara said.

"If we don't make it in time, we can deal with her. We just dealt with a whole clearing of Blighters," Vincent said.

"I'm already infected. We just need to keep you two safe. And monitor her progress. The diamond should help," Alrion said.

"I just—" Lara said, but Alrion interrupted.

"There's something you all should know. This whole attack was my fault." Alrion paused and waited. After a few seconds he continued.

"Wraith has been taunting me ever since that day. He's inside my head, whenever he wants. I have been working at blocking him out, but it's exhausting and I'm still learning how to deal with this. The Blight is affecting me too somehow. My emotions surge more, especially what we might consider darker emotions. Like anger. And so earlier today I lost it. And look what happened!" Alrion grew very quiet. Lara tried to speak but choked up. She walked over and gave him a hug.

"Don't beat yourself up, we're here for you remember. Have you been carrying this all by yourself?" she said.

"Yes, I've been trying to be strong. And I've given Alyx a death sentence at the same time. That's why we have to bring her with us. It's her only chance. And we owe her that much."

Alyx closed her eyes and looked down. Vincent walked over to join Alrion too.

"We're with you son, and don't worry Alyx can join us if she's willing. I actually think it's her best chance too. The risk is not too great, and she will be a fine addition to our group," he said.

"I understand why you want her to come and won't stop it. I guess I'll just have to keep my eyes on you," Lara said, looking directly at Alyx. She finally understood what was going on with Alrion.

Why didn't he just say something? They were close enough for that.

"You are all assuming that I want to come," Alyx said finally.

"I know you will," Alrion said. His voice had a confidence that Lara didn't understand.

"How can you know my mind when I haven't even decided?"

"Because you haven't said no yet. And I need to cure you. You are infected because of me, so as soon as I am cured and I have the power to do so myself you will be my first case. That's why you must come."

Alyx rose stiffly from the ground. She walked over to Alrion.

"Please stand," she said. Alrion stood with a little rockiness.

"I, Alyx Vanstar, Warden of the North and Slayer of the Skull King, do hereby pledge my life into the service of Alrion." She completed the gesture by plugging her short sword into the ground in front of her.

"I accept your service. And I hereby pledge that I will cure you from this infection. Once I do so, you will be released to do whatever you wish," Alrion said. He removed her sword and handed it back to her. Alyx bowed and sat back down.

"Now that we're all friends, what's the plan?" Lara said.

"We need to brief Alyx on the way, and continue on our journey."

"Do you know your destination?" Alyx said.

"Not exactly. Just that it's north, at the snowy peaks," Alrion said.

"That helps, there is only one region that could be. But those mountains are vast and treacherous. We will need more guidance."

"It will come."

"Very well. Then I suggest we head to the nearest town and resupply ourselves. We will need much for this journey."

"Agreed. Do you have a place in mind?" Vincent said.

"I do."

"Then let's make a start. We can talk on the way, and the further we get from this mess the better," Vincent said. He started to work through their belongings. Lara approached Alrion with care, putting a hand on his shoulder. He turned to face her.

"You're not alone. Don't carry this burden by yourself," she said softly. Alrion took her hand gingerly, and warmed between his own. Then he returned her hand.

"I must. I can't taint you with it, and weigh you down. You deserve to be free," he said, sadness in his eyes. He blinked away a potential tear and turned to look for his belongings. Lara's heart cried out.

I have to find a way to help him.

3

LEFT BEHIND

Celes had been incredibly patient. She had kept a low profile, avoiding areas of Plynth that would be accessed by the network of Tainted. It was infuriating but she knew it was important. Eventually Vincent would send word and confirm that everything was all right.

Except he hadn't. It had been over a week, and she was tired of waiting.

I just need a way to find them. And I know just the place, she thought. The one place she had been avoiding, was the place she needed to go. Regardless of the outcome of the clash in the desert, she knew that the Tainted would have information and perhaps even instructions on what to do next.

I need to start with Glinda.

It made perfect sense. Glinda was either an ally, or too compromised by the help she had already given them to run to the leaders of the Tainted. If Glinda was still trusted, she might find out something useful.

She will definitely tell me something.

She checked her outfit, and left the small house with confidence.

Her boots echoed noisily on the stone walkway outside. For the first time she wasn't trying to sneak around. She didn't care if she was found.

Celes started by walking around to the barracks near the town gates. She knew Glinda was a guard, so it was the most logical place to look. Acting like she belonged, Celes walked right into the building. There were a few people loitering around, and those that were paid her no attention.

"Head up, you belong here," Celes told herself. After a quick lap around the barracks she saw no sign of Glinda. She stopped beside a guard standing around near the entrance. He was staring off at something else, his mind elsewhere.

"Have you seen Glinda this morning?" Celes said. The guard was initially startled, and ran his hand through his hair.

"Oh, ahh no, I don't think so. She must be on patrol," he said. Celes thought he was very odd.

"Are you new?" she said.

"Yes, how did you know?"

"Oh, I just know most of the faces around here."

"Do you want me to pass on a message?"

"No, that's fine I'll just see her later. Thanks," Celes said. She waved at the guard and left. As helpful as it would have been to leave a message, she didn't trust that guard. And she didn't want to compromise Glinda. There was no knowing how many of the guard were Tainted.

It was a strange position to be in, relying on a Tainted guard. She would never have expected it, but Vincent had been insistent and she had come to realise that there was something different about Glinda. She was Tainted, but trying to live her own life.

Maybe there's a whole lot of people like that out there. Wanting to be different, but trapped by the infection? she thought. It was certainly a perspective she had never considered before. But then again, she had been living another life. Sheltered, and focusing on her family. Tales of the Blight had been fanciful stories to the folk of Hamley.

Celes headed back to the blacksmith shop where Vincent had been working. She found the owner working in the shop, and approached him.

"Hello, I'm sorry I forgot your name. But my husband Will was working here recently," she said.

"Oh, no problem. It's John. Is everything alright?"

"Everything is fine. He had to leave suddenly for family reasons, but I thought he would be back by now. So, I just wanted to stop by and let you know." Celes could see the real concern on the man's face slowly change into relief.

"Oh, great. I was really worried. I never really paid him, and he completed a lot of work. I felt really bad that something had happened, and I never had a chance to properly compensate him!"

"It's all fine, don't worry he was happy enough for the experience. Have you had more trouble with the guards?"

"No, they backed right off after that last incident. It's been very quiet. I managed to get my orders out and it's all been busy. I do miss having Will around though, he's fantastic. I hope everything's all right. I didn't know what to do, I didn't even know where he was staying!" John looked flustered and apologetic. Lara thought it was sweet.

"I feel bad about not coming to see you sooner. For now, assume that he won't be back for a while. I'll make sure he does see you though."

"That would be nice, I need to thank him in person, even if he won't be sticking around. You take care," John said. He waved at Celes then returned to his work.

At least that's taken care of now.

Next, she took the main path between the blacksmith and the council chambers. It was the best next step. She knew Glinda frequented that route in the past. Plus, she expected that the councilman would still be active. All they had done was embarrass him, and probably only to a limited audience.

She spotted several guards as she went, but none paid her any attention. There were market stalls up, and she could smell the spiced meats tempting her in. There were many other handmade goods as well, such as garments, wooden trinkets, and even some blacksmith toys and tools.

Celes stopped suddenly. She picked up a blacksmith puzzle and looked it over carefully. It was so similar to one that Vincent had made for her years ago.

I remember the day so vividly, she thought. It was her test, to see how good he was and how willing he was to work on other things. He had passed with flying colours. Even then she had spotted something special in him.

Just be safe. She put the puzzle back down, smiled at the vendor, and kept walking.

"You're getting too sentimental. Everything is fine," she told herself. Celes quickened her pace and soon saw the council building looming. A shiver went down her spine as she remembered her last encounter there, and what happened after.

I'll just have a quick look, she thought. After a quick glance left and right, she eased into the flow of pedestrians and entered the council building. As before the room was full of people, some bunched together in conversations, others trying to get the attention of officials. Celes wove her way through, heading directly for the passage that led to the council chambers.

It was a risk heading back there, but she needed to investigate. And she felt confident that she could leave quickly if she was spotted. With a sure step she entered the hallway and looked for people. There were some administrators walking around, but few others. Celes carefully navigated down the corridor, heading for the room at the end. Where the councillor worked.

It's safer here, it's more public, she thought, reassuring herself. As she approached she slowed down, ensuring her footsteps were quiet and wouldn't draw attention. She listened out for voices, and only heard the general murmur coming from the main hall. Most of the doors she had passed were closed, which explained the lack of noise.

She crept along, trying not to look too suspicious. The door to the councillor's chamber was half-open. When she couldn't hear anything, she flattened herself next to the wall and listened closely. Nothing.

Next, she peered through the crack in the door hinge, trying to see inside. She didn't see any evidence of people.

Seems empty, I'll take a quick peek.

She quickly entered the room and verified it was empty. Then she reached for the door.

"No, better it's untouched," she told herself. She retracted her arm and looked around the room. It was a simple arrangement, even though each piece of furniture was heavy and expensive. A large desk dominated the space, with the councillor's chair behind. It was larger, more padded, and detailed than the two visitor chairs.

Celes stepped around the ornate desk, skimming her eyes over the stacks of paper. Most were reports or letters, but all were concerned with general council matters. Nothing she could use.

To be expected. They seem to do all their communication another way, she thought. Satisfied that there was nothing useful, she approached the door and glanced out.

"Damn!" she whispered and hid behind the door. There was a guard walking down the hallway. His steps were heavy and loud, and they weren't slowing.

I'll talk my way out.

She started working on her story. The footsteps started to slow, and finally stopped. Celes could see the guard standing in the doorway.

"I know you're in there. Meet me in the laneway behind the chambers, and don't attract any attention," a female voice said. It sounded familiar, so Celes could only assume it was Glinda.

If I keep getting spotted like this, I'll have to hand in my thief card, Celes thought with a laugh. Although, to be fair, she normally operated at night. These daytime infiltrations were a new thing. She retraced her steps, walking through the corridor like she belonged there. Nobody challenged her, although most were busy or behind closed doors.

She emerged into the main room and joined the flow of people.

Well, I found Glinda. Doesn't matter how it happened. Now I can get some answers, she thought as she left the building and walked around looking for the lane access. She turned left into the first cross street, and before long found a lane that extended behind the council chambers.

It was narrow and full of rubbish. Celes could smell that before she saw it. There were plenty of places to hide, which was comforting and risky at the same time. She stepped through carefully, trying to find the guard.

"Over here," a voice said. Celes followed the voice and stepped behind a large crate full of wet paper. She saw Glinda standing there.

"Oh, good it is you. Come here often?" Celes said, gesturing at the lovely surroundings.

"No, which means we will not be spotted together. What are you doing?"

"Looking for leads. Vincent hasn't returned, and the Tainted are my best link to find him."

"There's some sort of upheaval going on. Wraith is mobilising lots of Tainted in the north. But I don't get most of the communication," Glinda said. She sounded tired.

"Is everything alright? Were there any repercussions from when we escaped?"

"Some. I was put on guard duty for the mansion. I had to stand outside for fourteen hours a day. It was my punishment."

"They didn't suspect anything?"

"If they did, they're over it now. By having me there I proved my loyalty since they were able to observe everything. Thanks for backing off."

"Of course. And the councillor?"

"He flew into a terrible rage. But he didn't really have anyone to focus it on. So, we all copped it. I think Wraith was more amused than anything else. It was just a humiliation that passed. All in all, it could have been worse," Glinda said. She had a concerned look on her face and she directed it at Celes.

"So now you're wondering why I'm showing up to cause you more trouble?"

"Exactly."

"Well, I've been hiding out and staying out of sight. But it's been over a week now and I haven't heard anything from Vincent. I was hoping you might have something you can tell me?" Celes really needed something. Glinda was her last hope. Glinda looked around the alley, and stepped in closer. She expertly avoided some trash on the ground.

"There has been some talk. The last thing you heard about was the desert attack, right?"

"Yes. And the damn councillor was so gleeful about it as well."

"I'm not sure what happened, but it didn't end as expected. There's some sort of chase on now."

"That sounds promising. Like they made it away."

"I would assume so. But I have a bad feeling. I can't explain it, but I don't think Wraith achieved nothing. I've heard him before when something completely failed, and he's ruthless. And if something went wrong and it was his fault, he still makes everyone else feel it. But I don't get the same feeling."

"You think he achieved a victory of some kind? Even if there's some sort of chase going on?"

"Yes. I know it's a little vague, but it feels like an important detail," Glinda said with care. Her eyes darted around again, and she crept closer still, leaning in. She whispered in Celes's ear.

"There's something else. They're using some sort of special Trackers. It's a type of Tainted I've never heard of before," she said. As soon as she had spoken she stepped back. Celes's eyes widened and she thought through the implications.

"I need to meet one," she finally said. Glinda nodded.

"I have someone in mind actually. But I'm warning you, he'll want some kind of deal in return for helping you."

"That's fine, I can negotiate that. It's too important to pass up," Celes said. Glinda acknowledged Celes with a slight nod and beckoned her to follow. Celes's mind was running wild with theories and plans. But she solidified it all into one thought.

I'm coming.

4

PATH OF THE SWORD

Alyx led them through the woods and back to a path of sorts. Alrion welcomed the open space. He had felt so confined, especially when the Blighters boxed them in.

It's crowded enough in my head, need a little space out here, he thought, laughing to himself. He appreciated Lara's offer of help, but he couldn't accept it. Not in its current form. He wouldn't burden her with the taunting, the feeling of being weighed down slowly. The weight of a thousand angry, mindless beings trying to pile on him. No, this was better. He just had to watch his temper.

In these times he would almost reach out to his Spark. But he shuddered at the memory of the one time he had. Even the thought of reaching through that murky filth was enough to put him off. There was no reason to keep thinking about it. But he couldn't resist, since it was off limits. He needed to occupy himself. He sped up until he was alongside Alyx.

"How did you learn to fight like that?" he said.

"Years of intense training. And focus. Why?"

"I need to learn something. I'm useless right now without my power. I can't afford to be a liability when the stakes are this high."

"It will help with your anger management too," Alyx said. She turned to look at him again, sizing him up. Alrion felt inadequate, but he didn't know why.

"That sounds like it could help. I need something to focus on, since I can't do any magic. Would you be able to train me?"

"I can. But you must follow my instructions to the letter. There's no point otherwise."

"I can do that." Alrion imagined fighting better. It seemed like a great idea to defend himself without using his power. He could see himself fighting off nearby Blighters with a sword then burning others at range seconds later. He got a little carried away with his imagination, and found himself swinging his right arm. Alyx stifled a small laugh, but Lara didn't hold back at all.

"Practicing, are we?" she joked.

"Just warming up," Alrion said, his cheeks reddening.

Why do I have to be so awkward?

It hurt more with Alyx there. She was so cool and focused and to the point, that he felt like more of a clown in comparison.

"I used to do that kind of thing. You must have inherited it," Vincent said with a chuckle. That made Alrion feel better. His father had a knack for changing the mood.

"I've never trained anyone before, but you seem keen so I'm sure it will work. We will start slow, and ramp it up. I'm afraid my body needs a proper recovery before we get too advanced," Alyx said. Alrion nodded and turned to take in the scenery. The windy road was taking them far away from the forest, and into some sparse plains.

They stopped briefly for a snack, before pushing on.

"It's so exposed here, we need to reach somewhere more sheltered to rest this evening," Alyx said.

"I couldn't agree more," Vincent said. He was looking around at their surroundings and seemed concerned. Alrion was looking forward to a rest, but not the quiet it would bring. He wasn't looking forward to fending off Wraith again. Things were easier during the day when he was occupied and had people around. But at night it was far worse. Sometimes his mind turned to thoughts of Wraith and the Blight unbidden. He found it difficult to think of anything else.

Soon they came upon some rolling hills, and Alyx led them into a dense copse of trees nestled into a hill. It made for a nice sheltered spot, with lots of space around.

"This looks great," Vincent said. He immediately started setting up camp with what they had available.

"I'm just going to do a quick scout around," Lara said. She dropped her bag and took off.

"Don't worry, it's safe here," Alyx said to Alrion.

"Have you used this spot before?"

"A long time ago during a terrible storm. Hopefully we fare better tonight." Alyx slowly seated herself against a tree. She closed her eyes and relaxed.

"How did you become so focused?"

"It's just a state of mind. With practice you can achieve it."

"You sound like the monks I met in the desert," Alrion said, laughing.

"I've heard of them. Capable warriors and strong willed. Didn't you mention some sort of trial there?"

"Yes. I can't talk about it, but it taught me a lot."

"Well, you probably have all the tools you need. It then becomes about throwing away the distractions. For me it was simple."

"Why?"

"I watched my father be murdered in front of me. It was nothing to discard everything else. Too easy, in fact," Alyx said. She stared off into the distance.

"I'm sorry, I didn't mean to bring that up," Alrion said.

"It's fine, it was a long time ago. And he has been avenged."

"What happened to your family sword?"

"Long story. Suffice to say it's gone." She drew her short sword and turned it over in her hands.

"This is not suitable for training. Not ideal for sparring due to its length, not safe enough and won't last long against your Runesteel. Let's skip to real swords. Vincent, can I borrow yours?"

"Sure," he said, handing her the scabbard. Alyx put her sword away on the grass nearby and drew the Runesteel sword.

"Let's see how this works," she said. She strode over to one of the trees nearby with purpose in her step. In one fluid motion she slashed out with her arm. The tree offered no resistance, and after a momentary delay was neatly sliced open. The cut portion tumbled down causing a loud bang.

"Well, now they know where we are!" Lara said with frustration.

"The sound will carry, but not far. Don't worry. The sword has a good balance to it, you are very skilled, Vincent."

"Thank you." Vincent gave her a short bow.

"Alrion we will train with these. You shouldn't be fast enough to injure me, but let's start slow, just in case. I'd rather not lose any limbs."

"Not until I can heal you," Alrion said, trying to make a joke. He thought he saw a partial smile from Alyx, but it was gone in an instant, so he wasn't sure.

"Ready your sword," she said. Alrion shuffled his feet and drew his sword, holding it out. His muscles were tense, awaiting his commands.

"Too stiff, and too forced. You need to be light and reactive. Tension will cause you to move slowly and make mistakes. You will drop your blade." Alyx walked over and shifted Alrion's legs, and adjusted his posture.

"Still too stiff. Imagine that you just had a long hot bath," she said. Alrion gave her a strange look.

Did she really just say that?

"You think that I don't bathe? That's quite insulting," Alyx said. Lara burst out laughing.

"It just seemed like an odd suggestion," Alrion said.

"I think it's quite accurate really. Heat is a great way to relax your muscles," Vincent said. Alrion started to speak again, but stopped himself. He tried to loosen up.

"Better, for now." Alyx walked back until she was several paces away. "Follow my movements," she said, taking him through a simple exercise. Alrion followed along, paying particular attention to allow him to copy her exactly.

~

Hours later they took a break. Alrion was bent over, drawing in deep breaths and leaning on his sword.

"You look tired now," Alyx said.

"I am."

"Good. One final movement. Do the whole sequence," she said. Alrion's arms were heavy, and his shoulders ached. Even his legs were complaining. The day's events, the walking, and now the training had worn him out. But he complied all the same.

He was too tired to worry about the finer movements, letting his sword flow the easiest way.

"Good. Again. Continue," Alyx said. Alrion gathered one final burst of energy, and rather than step away Alyx blocked it. The meeting of the swords rang out through the clearing. With a slight push she sent Alrion tumbling back, and he found himself seated on the ground.

"Now you can rest," Alyx said. She slowly walked over to Vincent to return the sword then eased herself down. Alrion watched her very carefully.

"I see you're sore and tired too!"

"Of course. After two battles, hours of walking and another training session with you. I'm only human after all."

"So you say," Alrion muttered under his breath.

"You did a lot better at the end there. What changed?" Lara said. She quickly dropped down and sat right next to him.

"I was too tired to think about what I was doing. It was part memory, part instinct."

"And that's why it looked more fluid. Don't you think Vincent?" Lara said.

"Definitely. You're making great progress. Maybe you can hang up your wizard robe," Vincent said.

"I wouldn't do that just yet," Alyx said with a smile.

"If you insist. Not that I can do anything right now," Alrion said. He had reminded himself of the infection. He felt around his neck, seeing if there was any change. But there was nothing to feel. The mark had spread, but it was only colouring. It didn't have any dimension to it.

"It seems to have stabilised, well in terms of looks," Lara said.

"I might have to start wearing a scarf."

"It won't look out of place once we get further north," Vincent said.

"True. I think I might turn in," Alrion said. He said his goodnights and found himself a comfortable nook to set up for sleep. As he lay down, he had one last thought.

I'm way too tired to care about anything right now. What a relief.

Alrion rose gingerly, feeling the stiffness and pain throughout his muscles. He hadn't felt like this since the first days of his apprenticeship as a blacksmith.

"You look a little uncomfortable," Lara said. She was perched on a rock nearby watching him.

"I haven't had a workout like that, probably ever." Alrion tried massaging his calf muscles, but they remained the same.

"It gets harder before it gets easier," Alyx said. She approached and tossed him a hunk of bread.

"Eat quickly and get packed. We need to make it to town today, and the sooner the better," she said. Before Alrion could respond she had turned and walked away.

"She looks well-rested," he said.

"I know. Maybe she's not human," Lara said, chuckling.

"Well she did kill the Skull King. That sounds like a big thing."

"Oh, it is. He was known as the face of the Blight. Apart from the obvious reasons, he just seemed to embody everything people hated about it."

"Do you think she will tell us the whole story?"

"Maybe, in time. Less chatting, more packing. You don't want her angry at your next training session," Lara said, winking at Alrion. He sighed and forced his muscles to move. The training was definitely a good thing, even if there was some discomfort. He hadn't heard or thought of Wraith yet. And with luck he wouldn't again for some time.

As usual Vincent was packed and ready, so they set off as soon as Alrion was prepared. Alyx led them with confidence through the hills, and by midday they had stopped at the top of a hill and surveyed the land beyond.

"Do you see that settlement down there?" Alyx said.

"Yes, it looks impressive," Alrion said.

"That's Rolyntide. Nice town, and there's a resident Healer. They say she's incredibly gifted."

"Have you ever used her?" Lara said.

"No, I've just passed through really. Visited the inn, resupplied myself. But it's worth us paying her a visit. Not only for some assistance, but also information."

"You think she knows something?" Vincent said.

"When you talk about Mystics, I think about Healers. There's one in every town, and some of the stories are wild and out there. I'd say this Healer knows something that will help guide us on the way north."

"Sounds plausible," Alrion said. He tried to pick out where in the town the Healer may live. But he didn't know what to look for.

"I suppose we should get going then so we are settled in before dark," Vincent said.

"Definitely. We don't want to stay out here overnight. It's too exposed, and we'll be easy targets if we're being tracked," Alyx said.

"I agree," Lara said. She turned and looked into the distance. Alrion could see the worry on her face.

"Then let's go," Alrion said. He knew that Lara was cautious, but she also had good instincts. He definitely didn't want to risk being caught out. He still wasn't confident he could assist in a fight without being a burden.

5

THE HEALER'S SECRET

The town felt welcoming, and Alrion even thought the single guard looked friendly. He turned his disinterested gaze towards them and started to speak.

"Hello there. State your business," the guard said, a weariness and boredom to his words.

"Just passing through to visit family up north," Alyx said.

"Very well. Staying the night?"

"Yes. We'd like to visit a Healer tomorrow too before we go. You have one here?"

"We do. You'll find her in the middle of town. Not far from the inn."

"Thank you. We'll be good," Alyx said.

"I'm sure you will. I'd hate for you to make work for me," the guard said. He patted his sword and gave them a friendly grin. Alyx waved and continued along the road. Alrion nodded at the guard and kept close.

"I get the feeling that he'd actually be dangerous. He would feel so wronged by having to do something," Alrion said.

"You're right about that. It's easy to keep the peace around here. People like to keep to themselves, don't want to cause trouble. It's only really the Blight," Alyx said. She led them through the town with ease, even though the light was starting to fade.

"You have a favourite place to stay?" Lara said.

"There's only one place to stay. It's the inn we are headed to. Also, if the guard doesn't see us there tonight he will be suspicious. So just remember to be seen and not heard."

"I can do that. Do they do awful puns for the inns around here?" Lara said.

"I'm not sure what you mean. We're almost there," Alyx said. Alrion gave Lara a funny look.

I guess we'll understand when we see it.

The inn loomed large before them, and the sounds of merriment and light spilling out was alluring.

"The Tanked Tankard?" Lara said, barely able to get the words out. She looked at Alrion then at Alyx.

"Yes?" Alyx said.

"That's the worst name. It's terrible." Alrion couldn't help but laugh.

"I know. I thought we had already seen the worst in Brangtur!" Lara managed to say before bursting into laughter herself. Vincent had an amused look on his face but Alyx was just confused.

"I don't get it. It's a perfectly normal name. In my home we have a place called 'Alcoholic Ale'."

"Cultural differences I suppose," Vincent said, opening the door, and ushering everyone in.

It feels good to laugh, Alrion thought as he entered the inn. It made him forget about what was happening, if only for an instant. They walked up to the bar, and Vincent enquired about rooms. Alrion saw something out of the corner of his eye and took another look. It was an extremely polished tankard sitting on the bar. It looked too ornamental to be in everyday use. He picked it up to look it over and caught his reflection. He almost jumped, and managed to put it down with a shaky arm before dropping it completely.

"Everything alright?" Lara said. She had her arm on his shoulder and looked concerned.

"Oh, just a trick of the light. I thought I saw something," Alrion lied. Lara gave him an odd look and nodded.

I'm not sure she bought that, but I'll worry about that later.

He couldn't shake the image from his mind. He had seen his reflection, and the black mark on his neck had grown. And now it had more marks around it. But the thing that scared Alrion the most was his eyes. They looked somehow different. Like he was ill, or hadn't slept.

Both of which are accurate, he thought. But the scariest thing was the fact that his body was changing. It wasn't just a feeling, or an idea. It was really happening. And he felt an intense fear deep down in the pit of his stomach.

"What if I fail?"

"Son, snap out of it. Let's put our things upstairs," Vincent said. Alrion looked up and saw his father gesturing towards the back of the room.

"Sure, let's go." Alrion followed close behind, and made sure he didn't lose them in the crowd.

"Just don't lose it," he told himself. He managed to negotiate the boisterous crowd, dodge a man's dropped drink and ascend the stairs. The hustle and bustle of the inn soon faded away and all he could hear was the sound of footsteps on the wooden floor.

"We're in here; ladies over there. Meet downstairs in a few minutes," Vincent said. He pointed at the two rooms and entered one immediately. Alrion followed closely behind.

"Are you feeling alright?" he said.

"No. I am infected remember?" Alrion said. It came across more sharply than he had intended. But his father didn't seem to react to that.

"I know, which is why I am checking in. I need to know how far things are going."

"About this far," Alrion said. He drew his sword and looked at the diamond. The glow seemed stronger, and had more colour to it. Not the bright blue it would be eventually, but noticeable.

"Still a way to go then. Did you want to talk about Wraith?" Vincent sat down on one of the beds.

"No. It's just a problem I have to deal with. The training helps. When I'm too tired for anything else, I don't worry as much."

"I'm glad the physical activity is helping. But that's just putting off the problem. If you don't find a way to deal with this, it's only going to get worse. You can't ignore it."

"Ignoring it is all I can do. I can't give that thing any of my attention," Alrion said. He didn't even want to say its name. He considered the topic over, and noticed his father standing again.

"That's fine. But I'm here, and we can talk anytime. I'm hungry," Vincent said, walking over to the door. Alrion stayed behind to ensure his things were put away, then walked down by himself.

He's only trying to help. He couldn't understand why his father annoyed him so much.

~

The next morning Alrion was last to rise. He had slept terribly. His dreams were full of images of the Blight, Tainted, and other related scenes and events. He couldn't remember anything concrete, just the feeling that remained.

"Time to visit the Healer," Vincent said.

"I'm ready," Alrion said. He felt dizzy but didn't say anything, and negotiated the stairs with a little more care than normal. Alyx and Lara were waiting outside. Alrion thought he sensed a bit of tension, but everything changed once they noticed him.

"Is it far?" he said.

"No, I had a look earlier. We only need to walk past a few buildings to find the Healer," Alyx said.

"Let's see what she says. I hope there's a lead, like you suggested," Vincent said. Alyx led the way, the rest of them falling in just behind. Alrion almost tripped over a raised cobblestone.

"Still half-asleep?" Lara said.

"Something like that," Alrion said. He decided to concentrate a bit more on his steps. He managed to stay on his feet and they arrived at the Healer's residence within a few minutes.

It was a multi-storey house with a large wooden door, and potted plants everywhere. There were even vines climbing the walls in places.

"It's like a house in the forest," Lara said with wonder. Alrion couldn't have agreed more. It looked out of place in the town, even though it was big.

Alyx opened the door roughly and entered the house with Alrion and the rest following close behind. They stepped into a large foyer with only another large room and a staircase visible. The furnishings were all simple, but were well constructed and maintained. A woman sat at a table, working on some papers, and looked up at them.

"Good morning. Do you have an appointment?"

"No, but we would like to see the Healer."

"Freyda is busy right now. You will need to come back later. I'm sorry," the woman said. She tossed her hair to the side, and returned to her papers.

She doesn't look particularly sorry, Alrion thought. He stepped forward.

"Please let her know that we will be waiting here until she can see us," he said.

"I'm sorry, but that's not how we work," the woman said. Alrion grabbed a chair and sat down.

"That's fine, I'll be here when she's ready. Taking his cue, Alyx grabbed a nearby chair and did the same. Soon they were all seated, watching the woman. She watched them for a short while, then returned to her papers.

Half an hour passed that way, in complete silence. Except for the rustling of the paper as the woman worked through her stack. Nobody else entered or left the room. Finally, the woman put her papers aside and looked up.

"Now that's done, I can explain to you further about why you should leave."

"I'm listening," Alrion said.

"We don't treat Tainted here. If you would please leave that would be appreciated," the woman said. She had a matter-of-fact tone to her voice and pointed at the door.

"Why would you say that?" Alyx said. She rose and started walking over.

"Don't think you can intimidate me. I know Tainted when I see them."

"Why don't you hang back Alyx? We want the Healer to talk to us," Alrion said. He rose from the chair and walked over himself.

"Why do you think it's her?" Alyx said.

"Because she can see we are infected. A normal person wouldn't be able to tell from that distance. Isn't that right?" Alrion held a hand out, beckoning the woman to answer.

"That is correct. Being clever doesn't change my mind. I'll call the guard."

"I'd rather you didn't, Freyda. I bet you can also see that we haven't turned yet, and I'm not a normal infected. Am I?" Alrion said. He was taking a risk with this, but he had a feeling about her. She was definitely different somehow, and not just for recognising Tainted.

"It's true, you are different. Him too." Freyda pointed at Vincent.

"And her?" Alrion said, looking at Alyx.

"Just normal infected. Sorry."

"It's fine," Alyx said, unconcerned.

"Now we've established that you are a Healer, you do have some sort of special power, and you know we're not just an ordinary group. So why are you telling us to leave?" Alrion said. He wasn't going to leave without a straight answer, and he still felt like there was something they could get from this woman. Alyx had been right about the Healers.

We're so lucky we met her.

"You're trouble, too much trouble. And I don't know how long you have." Freyda looked ready to march them straight out.

"Until we turn?" Alyx said.

"That. And until they catch up to you."

"You can sense them?" Alrion said. He hadn't expected that.

"I'm not going to explain myself, but I know that there's a lot of Tainted on the way. The whole area is going crazy." Freyda sighed and sank down into her chair.

"Help us then. We'll leave town and nothing will happen. The mess will just follow us north," Alrion said.

"What do you need from me? I can't cure you."

"Information and directions. We seek the home of the Mystics."

"I don't know what you are talking about," Freyda said. Her body language became incredibly closed off and she folded her arms.

"Is that so?" Alrion said. He walked back and sidled up to Lara.

"I'm no expert, but she's lying, right?" he said.

"Absolutely. Alyx gave us a good tip here," Lara said. She glared at the warrior, but said nothing else. Alrion nodded, and walked back to Freyda.

"We know that you're lying, and I understand. We're just this big bundle of trouble just landed on your doorstep. You probably have truly sick people upstairs that you need to protect. But we're not just any group. My grandfather was Granthion, and I've been charged with taking on his life's work: to cure the Blight. But I can't do that in my current state. I need the help of the Mystics."

"Why do you talk about them like they're fact?" Freyda said. There was a curious tone to her voice.

"Because I've seen one, in a vision. A vision granted to me from the Pool of Knowledge. I know the power they have is the key to my quest. And time is against me. Please, I know you know something. Just tell us what you know, and we'll be on our way!" Alrion had nothing left to lose. If Freyda was going to keep quiet, they had to move. He couldn't lose more time. He felt drawn, and nervous. Like the Tainted were just one step behind. Looking at Freyda, he could see something changing. She had come to a decision at last.

"I can tell you something. The Mystics do exist, I have met them. I don't think they can solve your problem. It's not how they work. But I won't rob you of the opportunity to ask them yourself."

"Thank you. It means a lot to me," Alrion said. Freyda stood and

walked to a cupboard at the back of the room. She opened the doors
and busied herself inside looking for something.

"A-ha!" she said, and closed the doors. She returned holding a
silver amulet with a pure white stone in the middle. She handed it to
Alyx. Alyx held it gingerly in her hand.

"What is this?" she asked.

"It's an amulet that they gave me. It's charged with their power. It
will help you in two ways," Freyda said. She pointed at Alyx's chest.

"It will slow that process down a little bit. And you need as much
time as you can get," she said. Alyx gripped the amulet a little tighter.

"This is an incredible gift," Alyx said.

"You need it more than me. But you must return it."

"I swear. I will return it!" Alyx was incredibly serious and Freyda
looked a little shocked at the intensity.

"There is one other way that it will help you. It is attuned to the
power of the place that they reside. It will help guide you there."

"Have you been there?" Alrion said.

"No. I can't explain how it works, I just know that it does."

"Thank you. You've really helped us. I don't know what else to
say," Alrion said. He looked around at the others.

"Your thanks are enough. Now leave, before you endanger
others." There was no harshness to her voice now, but it was still
direct.

"Sure. Let's go," Alrion said. Lara and Vincent said their goodbyes
and they left the house immediately.

"We will be able to travel quite a distance before it gets mountain-
ous. We need horses."

"Agreed. Do you have something in mind?" Vincent said.

"Yes, follow me," Alyx said. She was still gripping the amulet in
her hand.

"Can I see that for a minute?" Alrion said. She stopped abruptly
and handed it to him. The metal was cold but he could feel some sort
of warm pulsing coming from it. He peered at the stone within then
started to hand it back. He stopped and motioned to Alyx.

"Turn around," he said. He unclasped the amulet and Alyx understood. She moved her hair and Alrion carefully fastened it around her neck.

"That's better," he said. Alyx felt the amulet with her hand then started walking again. Alrion did the same with his own amulet. He had been wearing it so long it just felt like part of him. He hadn't even looked at it properly in a long time.

The black streak in the white stone around his neck looked exactly the same. But it felt different for him now, looking at it. Knowing that the tiny sliver of Blight within that stone was within him also. He felt over the surface of the stone and had a realisation.

This is the same stone as the amulet Alyx was given. What's the connection between the wizards and the Mystics? Alrion thought. It was another question for when he eventually found them.

6

AN UNUSUAL ALLY

C eles stayed close to Glinda. After leaving the alley they stuck to main streets. But Celes had to push hard not to lose the guard in the crowds. Slowly they moved through smaller streets, with fewer people and less wealth. More rubbish, smells, and homeless. Large spaces were vacant, or had temporary residents camping out.

"Where are you taking me?"

"A place nobody likes to go. Which is the perfect place for hiding."

"Hiding from normal people? Or hiding from Tainted?" The distinction was important to her. She needed to know if this man could work with her.

"Both. It's a bit complicated. We're almost there," Glinda said. She entered another seemingly empty yard. But there was a small shack at the back of the property. This one had nobody trying to camp out.

"This is suitably creepy. Even the homeless are avoiding it," Celes said.

"For good reason. Quickly now," Glinda said. She led Celes to the front door. It was old and weathered, hanging at a slight angle. Glinda pulled it roughly and disappeared inside.

"It's me," she said. Celes followed close behind and stopped suddenly. It was very dark in the shack and her eyes needed to adjust. She could make out the outlines of some simple furniture. A chair, a couch, a desk, and some sort of side table. All placed irregularly around the room. There was a figure seated on the couch.

"I know it's you. I just don't know who she is," a raspy voice said from the darkness.

"This is Celes. She needs your help."

"Celes. That name is familiar. I'm Tarren. I have an idea on what you might want from me."

"Nice to meet you. Has Glinda mentioned anything?"

"No. In fact I'm surprised that she brought someone. But she knows me, and my desires. Perhaps there is an overlap in what we want." Tarren shifted on the couch but Celes couldn't see exactly what he was doing.

"I'm looking for my son. I heard that you have specialised tracking skills and could be of assistance," she said.

Tarren laughed, a scratchy grating sound. "I am good at many things. That's why they call us Trackers. That's why I was selected in the first place. Because I knew how to follow trails and find people."

"Selected?"

"I was not born this way, nor did I succumb to an attack by a Blighter or similar. No, I was transformed into this. One of the first I believe."

"I'm sorry. I didn't know that was possible," Celes said. She was glad for the dark, they couldn't see the horrified look on her face.

"It's of benefit to you now. I can probably help you, and I have the freedom to do it. I believe they have since perfected their process."

"That sounds promising," Celes said. She wanted to remain cautious until she found out just what Tarren was after.

"Why don't you take a seat? Glinda, you can wait outside," Tarren said.

"Sure, see you soon," Glinda said, and left quickly. Celes watched her leave, not feeling confident at being left in the dark with Tarren. But this was her best lead; one she had to make the most of. She grabbed the chair and brought it a bit closer to Tarren and sat facing him.

"First, let's discuss your son. Is he infected?" Tarren said.

"Why?"

"Easier to track. Once you're infected you are connected to everyone else. It's part of how the Blight works."

"Not to my knowledge. I hope not."

"That will make it harder to find him. What else can you tell me about him?"

"He's a wizard and his name is Alrion."

"Interesting," Tarren said. "Continue."

"He's on a quest to cure the Blight. There's this wizard who was transformed into a Shade who is after him as well. I think he calls himself Wraith now."

"Oh."

"You're going to have to say something now. Clearly you know something!" Celes was trying hard to restrain herself. She could tell that something she said had triggered a connection for Tarren.

"Wraith has assembled a team of Trackers to chase down a wizard. I get the impression he is infected, but I haven't been told explicitly. It would make him easier to track. From what you've said, there's a good chance it's your son." Tarren went quiet. There wasn't any emotion in his voice. Celes couldn't believe it. Alrion was infected? It didn't make sense. Vincent had rushed there to prevent an issue like this. If Alrion was infected where were they going and why?

"This is a lot to take in. As much as I want you to be wrong, there's too many elements that ring true. Can you track the Trackers? Can we find my son?"

"You're asking a lot. I need to actively work against Wraith. That comes with significant dangers."

"You said something there. You said work against Wraith, not work against the Blight. What's that about?" Celes rose from her chair and stared intently at Tarren.

"While there seems to be this central thread that connects us all, there are factions. And Wraith leads one of them. He didn't create me."

"I'm going to need to know more about that."

"Another time perhaps. Are you ready to hear my price?"

"Fine. What is it?"

"I want to be cured of the Blight." Tarren said the words and just let them hang without any follow up. He stood as well. Celes noticed that he was taller than her. But it was hard to make out the details in the dim light.

"It's not in my power to grant that," she said.

"I know that. But you mentioned your wizard son is on a quest to cure the Blight. You need to guarantee that he will cure me."

"If you help me find him, then I will encourage him to cure you. I can't guarantee it because I don't control him. But I'm confident he will want to help you, especially since you will be helping me. Maybe that's not what you want to hear, but I'd rather you had the truth upfront." Celes was taking a risk, but she couldn't agree to that bargain without a caveat. She couldn't sign up Alrion to something he may not be comfortable doing. Tarren appeared to be looking into the distance.

"There's more chatter. Things are happening. You have played this well. You want me to serve, then I will get my reward. Very well, I accept." Tarren stuck out an arm. Celes was a bit apprehensive about shaking it, having no idea what she was shaking. But a deal was a deal, and she had no other options. She grasped his hand and shook firmly.

"Good, you have strength. I will meet you outside in a moment." Tarren disappeared into a back room. Celes rushed outside and breathed deeply from the fresh air.

"You look a bit spooked," Glinda said.

"It's creepy in there, and his voice ... it's not reassuring. But I agreed to his terms. He will help find Alrion."

"That's good. He's not a bad guy, Celes. That's why I brought you. I figured you could help each other."

"I hope you're right."

"When I'm right, you'll be one step closer to curing us all. That day cannot come soon enough." Glinda turned and watched the door open. Celes watched too, fearful of what would emerge.

Tarren was a tall man, with black hair and a black scarf wrapping around his neck. He wore a dark brown robe, covering all his body with the hood pulled up.

"Is this acceptable?" he said. He looked suspicious but not outright concerning.

"Yes."

"Good. However, I must warn you. Once we leave the city we'll travel lighter than this. My markings will be harder to hide."

"That's fine. We will adjust, as we need to. Where should we be heading?"

"North."

"Not the desert?"

"Not anymore."

"This is where I'll leave you two. Take care and come see me when you return," Glinda said. She came in for a hug, which surprised Celes. She gave the hug and Glinda whispered in her ear.

"He has a good heart. Just try and listen."

"Thank you for introducing us. I'll come find you when I return. Take care of yourself and your daughter," Celes said. Glinda waved and walked off quickly.

"This way," Tarren said. He moved faster than Celes expected. She had to up her pace to stay with him.

"I'm not just a Tracker, which you will find out. Speed is one of my abilities. You'll probably need a horse to keep up."

"That can be arranged."

"No need to fuss. We can get one on the way."

"Are you sure? I don't want to make more trouble for you."

"I have resources at my disposal. It will only be trouble later when they figure out what I am doing," Tarren said. He didn't add any more. They progressed through the dark streets and emerged at a small inn with stables attached.

"Wait here," Tarren said. He quickly entered the stables.

What a strange man. Hopefully he's everything he says he is. I have to at least see where things progress, she thought. Tarren emerged quickly, leading a black horse.

"Here. Keep it to a trot for appearances, but you can ride faster once we are in the wilderness."

"Sure, I'll follow your lead," Celes said. She jumped onto the horse and nudged him forward. Tarren walked alongside without any effort. If anything, he was restraining himself from going faster.

They wound through many tightly packed streets, in an area of the city Celes had not really explored. Finally, they arrived at a small gate.

"Oh, I didn't know there was another gate here," Celes said.

"It's not advertised widely. It's a service entrance. More security too. But we won't be challenged on the way out," Tarren said. Celes nodded and kept pace. The gate was only wide enough to fit a standard wagon through. Two guards maintained watch. When they saw Tarren, one of them walked over to the metal winding mechanism. He grunted and puffed and slowly lifted the gate up in the air. Celes felt a little nervous with such a large weight hanging over them, but put it to one side.

They passed through the gate without incident, and Celes heard it crash back down to the ground moments later.

"We are free of the city. Soon we can start in earnest," Tarren said.

"Do you know exactly where to go?"

"Enough to chart our course. I want to keep our goal as hidden as possible. That way we can travel fast and remain safe."

"That makes sense to me," Celes said. She looked at Tarren more intently, wondering what he was thinking. He didn't seem to be completely focused on the trail in front of them. He suddenly turned and looked exactly at her.

"Everything is fine. I am monitoring communication as we go. Do not be alarmed."

"That's fine, I was just curious."

"Understandably. You will know much more by the time we are

through. But for now, while we need to appear quite normal I will see what information I can glean. Later we will focus on speed."

"Thank you I appreciate that. I'll leave you to it," Celes said. She continued to take in the countryside. She didn't recognise this path, and saw a large cart coming towards them.

I wonder what's inside?

The driver of the cart didn't look at them twice; he just focused on the path ahead. Even though Tarren seemed preoccupied he moved to the side to allow the cart to pass. Celes peeked over and saw stacks of cloth and wool.

Nothing exciting.

But she was sure more illicit things had to come in this way. It was not a coincidence that Tarren was familiar with the service entrance to the city. They continued along the path joining another she was more familiar with. This too had a lot of people on it. It was a major route. She was about to mention that to Tarren but he spoke first.

"We are taking a path just ahead so we can travel faster."

"Of course," Celes said. She kept her eyes open and looked for the other path. There didn't seem to be one, and the path they were on seemed the same as it had been all those years before.

"Here," Tarren said. He veered off onto a dirt track. It was so well disguised that Celes almost missed it. She nudged her horse across and followed close. After a few turns they appeared to be travelling parallel to the main path, but with a lot more tree and vegetation cover.

"This is a safer path. Not as well known, and not as frequently travelled. Plus, we won't be spotted from the road. I will take point and you try and keep up," Tarren said. Celes felt like scoffing at the statement but she held off. Tarren started to stretch his legs then took off like a bolt of lightning. She quickly spurred the horse into action.

I don't know how that works, but he sure is quick, she thought. It was comforting that they could make great progress. But it made her nervous thinking of what else he could do.

7

GENERALS OF THE BLIGHT

Alyx headed for the edge of town. There, they found an older man selling fruit and vegetables out of a wooden cart. He had an old brown hat tipped over his face and Lara thought he was asleep.

"Is this him?" she said.

"Yes, it is. Hey, Wilson!" she shouted.

"Not so loud, I was enjoying the warm sun. There's precious little up here at the best of times. Who is that?"

"It's Alyx. We met on the road before. I helped you out of a sticky situation."

"Oh yes. Those stinking thieves. They never knew what hit 'em," Wilson said, chuckling. He grabbed an apple and threw it to Alyx. She caught it and took a bite out.

"One of my best seasons. What do you think?"

"Delicious," she said. She tossed it over to Alrion. He took a bite and surprise overtook his features. Without saying anything he tossed it to Lara.

It's just an apple, she thought, biting into it. The juices almost dripped down her chin, and it was the perfect blend of sweet and sour.

"Fine, it's pretty good," she said.

"What brings you to my neck of the woods?" Wilson said.

"We're heading up north, and I remembered you lived around here. We're going to need some horses," Alyx said.

"I don't know about that. I've only a few left, and I don't want to part with them."

"Can you spare two at least? Or three?"

"Hmm. I suppose I could let go of two. Would you be needing them long?"

"We would ideally be bringing them back, but we'll buy them all the same. You never know what will happen on the road," Alyx said.

"I doubt you'll run into anything you can't handle. Although, you do seem to be missing that giant sword of yours."

"I do miss it."

"Now that's going to be a story and a half! Tell me when you come back this way. Young man, you push this cart. We'll head back to the farm and I'll give you a deal on two horses," Wilson said. He stood and adjusted his hat, waiting for Alrion to come over and assist with the cart.

～

Hours later Alyx had negotiated a deal and they had the two horses saddled and ready to go.

"I'll go with Alrion. You two share," Lara said.

"Fine by me. You alright with that, Alyx?" Vincent said.

"Of course. Better to distribute the weight for a long ride."

"Here we go," Alrion said. He mounted and helped Lara up.

"Have fun you lot. And bring back my horses and some good stories!" Wilson shouted after them as they left.

They rode hard until noon, maintaining a cracking pace. The countryside was becoming less dense with greenery, and the road became flatter and rougher.

"Let's dismount and give the horses a rest. We can walk them for a while," Alyx said. They dismounted, and Vincent handed out bread to snack on.

"There's something from your story I'd like to hear more about," Alrion said to Alyx. She bit a big chunk of bread and chewed it slowly before responding.

"Some things I will not discuss. But ask."

"You mentioned the four generals of the Blight. What's that all about?"

"That's actually an interesting story. Surely you know it Vincent?"

"I've heard a version, but not sure how accurate it is. You tell it."

"Very well. Many years ago, the last King of Valrytir decided he would put an end to the Blight. This was before your grandfather cured Avaria. Valrytir is a huge kingdom, renowned for its fighting prowess and advanced armour and weaponry. They have the best army, and they can usually avoid outright battle because of their reputation. The King decided to task his four greatest generals with ending the Blight." Alyx glanced over at Lara, and Lara flinched. But she didn't think anyone else noticed.

"Four generals?" Alrion said.

"Yes. Each of them, a specialist in a different way. And each one worth one hundred men in terms of skill and strength."

"Who were they? What exactly did they do?"

"Rindale was an Assassin. Expert at stealth and taking out single targets. Cathar was a skilled warrior. He was incredibly strong and wielded a great sword. He was unmatched in taking on multiple foes due to his speed and reach."

"Cathar, I think I know which one you mean," Vincent said. Alrion looked puzzled but said nothing.

"Yes, well that will be explained soon," Alyx said looking at Alrion. "The next was Darvin. He was a protector, and renowned for his skill with the sword and shield. He could weather any onslaught, and navigate situations too dangerous for anyone else. Finally, there was Fermur. He was an archer without peer, and could scout like nobody else."

"They sound like great warriors. Did they lead an army?" Alrion said. He looked like he was trying to puzzle out what had happened.

"No, they had information on a lead for what was the source of the Blight. So, the four of them went alone to assess and see what they could do. They didn't wish to lead a huge expedition without knowing what they were walking into."

"What's the next part of the story?" Lara said. She was curious to see how much Alyx knew.

"Nobody knows what they encountered. It seems likely that they found the source of the Blight, but failed. Instead of accomplishing their task they returned as changed men. Transformed and corrupted by the Blight. And they took on different names and aspects."

"What are they called now? I assume one of them was the Skull King?" Alrion said.

"Exactly. Cathar became known as the 'Face of the Blight' due to his unique transformation. But he was widely known as the Skull King and actively embraced the name. Rindale was known as the 'Hand of the Blight'. We're not sure what happened to him."

"I can answer part of that," Vincent said quietly. All eyes turned to him instantly. Lara was shocked. But Alrion spoke before she could.

"I don't understand. What did you have to do with him?"

"He was the one that captured me, and infected me with the Blight. He was targeting my father. However, since he was with me he was also healed of the Blight when Avaria was cleansed. Well, that's what I assume. I never did go and check for myself."

"That's quite interesting, I never would have suspected that," Alyx said.

"Wow, I hope your grandfather's spell worked. If it can cure the four generals of the Blight, it can cure anyone!" Lara said.

"I hope so. The fact that nobody has kept track of Rindale since then is a good sign," Vincent said. Alrion nodded, and looked to be thinking over something.

"What about the others?" he said.

"Darvin became known as the 'Heart of the Blight' and is thought to be leading them in some capacity. And finally, we have Fermur, who became the 'Legs of the Blight'. Some believe he is being used as a messenger, since he has been seen all around the country."

"How do you know all this?" Lara said.

"I spent my entire life devoted to one thing; getting revenge on the Skull King. It made sense to track those he was working with."

"There's so much more to this than I knew. How does Wraith factor in?" Alrion said.

"You've mentioned him a few times. What is he exactly?"

"He's a wizard that has drunk from the Pool of Knowledge, as I have. But he's been transformed into a Shade. But he retains his power. So, he's this impossible creature now. All the resilience and danger of a Shade, with the magical power of a wizard."

"I can see why that would be a problem," Alyx said. She looked thoughtful.

"I must say though, I'm not sure how much magic he can actually use. It did seem like he was either holding back, or there's some constraints," Alrion said.

"Hopefully we don't need to find that out," Lara said.

"Oh, we will at some stage. I need to take him out."

"One step at a time," Vincent said.

"You also seem quite knowledgeable about Valrytir. Did you live there?" Alrion said to Alyx.

"Of course. How else did you think I trained to be a living weapon?"

"Sounds like an interesting place.

"It is if you need to learn about battle. All the best smiths work there, and are constantly refining weapons of war. For warriors the training is brutal. Sparring is done with slightly muted versions of real weapons, no wooden swords allowed. Fractures, bruises, and even cuts and slashes are common, and you soon learn to avoid them."

"That sounds intense. Have either of you been there?" Alrion said. He looked at his father and Lara. Lara looked away, not wanting to respond.

"I spent some time there, many years ago. But I decided that I didn't want to create tools of war and revolve my life around that so, I ended up in Brangtur," Vincent said. He looked over at Lara.

"I lived there a long time ago, but didn't really get into all that military stuff. Not my style," she said. She hated that she couldn't really talk about it, and she didn't have the impressive battle experience that Alyx did. It seemed to be important to Alrion. She could understand that, given all they had gone through. And now his power was unavailable, he needed something else to defend himself.

"Wow. It's just me then who hasn't been?" Alrion said.

"I did give you a pretty sheltered life, sorry about that," Vincent said. He chuckled and looked a bit sheepish.

"Well, it sounds like somewhere I should visit. Especially if they know where the source of the Blight is!" Alrion said. He looked at Alyx expectantly.

"I'm not sure there's anyone alive who still knows that. But it could be an option. I must admit I never thought about that myself. Is that somewhere you need to go?"

"I really don't know. I've been relying on the information from the Pool to guide me. Maybe I need to find that place, maybe I don't. It's a bit frustrating, but I have other things to focus on first. Like finding a cure."

"I'd like you to focus on that too."

"Of course! I'm responsible for your infection, and I am taking it seriously," Alrion said.

"Very well. Let us walk a bit further and when we find a suitable spot we should settle in for the night. The horses can rest and we will leave at first light."

"I agree," Vincent said. He started actively looking around, presumably for good places to set up camp.

"Anything coming from that amulet?" Alrion said. Alyx held it up and peered at it.

"I don't see anything special. How about you?" She offered it to Alrion and he took a look as well.

"Doesn't look any different."

"Then we continue on the same way tomorrow. I'll check it peri-odically as we go, see if there's anything we can use."

"I'm happy with the camp," Vincent said. He had settled into a spot leaning against a nearby tree. One of the few around.

"In that case, you need to train some more. I'll just be borrowing this," Alyx said, grabbing Vincent's sword. He gave out a friendly laugh, and watched the two square off. Lara felt a bit left out, so had to find herself something to do.

"I'll just go scout a bit, see what's out there."

"Good idea, take care and don't go too far. We're not familiar with the country here," Vincent said.

"Sure." Lara looked over at Alrion but he was already engrossed in watching Alyx demonstrate a movement.

Typical. Lara took off, heading further ahead and towards the area with the most trees. She was actually curious if they were entering another area, and the way they had come had so little cover it wasn't even worth looking over. Any sign of anyone coming would be obvious a long way away.

Lara pushed forward, the smells of moisture and flowers coming on stronger as she explored. It looked like they were on the boundary of another forest. Before long she was amongst it. She didn't recog-nise the trees, they had a distinctive curled look to their branches and leaves. She plucked one of the leaves off and crushed it in her hand. It gave off a clean, fragrant smell.

I wonder if they use this in medicines, she thought. But her attention was quickly taken by something else.

That was definitely something.

She darted forward towards whatever she spotted, trying not to make too much noise. But she trampled fallen sticks and brushed past some thin branches, causing them to snap or bend noisily.

"Just press on," she told herself. There were definitely signs of movement ahead. Lara pushed through some underbrush, trying to anticipate the direction. She stopped and looked around. Everything was quiet around her. She peered into the distance, trying to figure out where the natural paths were. Then she saw it. It was dark and faint and far away. But a dark shape flitted through her view and deeper into the forest.

What was that? She thought. It could have been nothing. But it did worry her.

It didn't move like a Blighter. Maybe I'll just keep an eye out.

She felt defeated and didn't want to admit that she had let something get away. It seemed fine for now, to just be more watchful.

"I'll find it again and confirm without alarming anyone," she said to herself.

8

HUNTED

Alrion awoke swiftly, forcing his eyes open. It took a moment to reorient himself. It was just before daybreak and they were camped in the forest.

It's fine, just more dreams.

But the feelings lingered. It felt so real. But he couldn't put anything specific to it. Just thoughts of darkness, fear, pain, and more.

"Right on time, let's get ready," Vincent said. He was packed and waiting.

"Do you ever sleep?" Alrion said.

"When I need to. You need less, as you get older. One of the few benefits."

"If you say so. I'll need a minute," Alrion said. He packed as quickly as possible, but his hands were unresponsive and cold. Without the sun the morning was incredibly chilly.

"Get used to that, it's only going to get worse as we travel north," Alyx said. Alrion cupped his hands and blew hot air into them.

"If I only had my Spark," he said, looking at his hands. He could generate as much heat as he wanted if that was the case.

"You'll appreciate it more after this," Vincent said. Alrion could tell his father was trying to lighten the mood a bit. But he wasn't interested. He could hear the traces of whispers in his mind. Which meant that someone was trying to communicate with him. Most likely Wraith, but he had received other messages. He looked over at Alyx and she seemed preoccupied with something. She noticed his look and spoke.

"You did better yesterday. More controlled, better instincts. But you are very inconsistent. You can be making sudden progress then become clumsy."

"Thanks," Alrion said. He knew exactly what she was talking about. It made sense too, he was still figuring out what he was supposed to do. It was a completely different set of activities to what he was used to. Everything he had done had been so slow, precise, and careful. Especially the blacksmithing.

But the sword work had the same demands of precision, with the addition of speed, balance, and agility. But he feared something else was happening. The effects of the infection. It was like his body was starting to get confused, and there was interference from within. But he didn't want to say anything yet. He would keep an eye on it. And also see how Alyx moved. Surely it would affect her too.

"How'd you sleep?" Lara said as she walked over. She was ready to go but looked tired.

"Not well. You too?"

"I was thinking about too many things."

"Same."

"You can tell me if anything else happens. I want to help," she said. Alrion could see the truth in her words. And he knew he could trust her. But something felt off. Like he couldn't share what was happening.

Maybe I don't want to burden her with this? That was probably it. He didn't want to dwell on it.

"Let's get going, I don't want to get caught here," he said. He walked over to the horse and mounted, helping Lara up. She leaned against him as they rode off, and he appreciated the closeness.

Initially the ride was difficult, navigating the poor trails and finding a way through the new forest they had discovered nearby.

Alrion had to concentrate fiercely, to not be ejected from the saddle by an obstacle or on steering the horse into dangerous territory.

Chirps of birds and unknown animals rang out from the forest, and Alrion found the sounds interesting but had no attention for them. He was not just focusing on the horse, but the growing distractions within.

The whispers he had felt before were becoming louder, and occasionally a word sounded within his mind. Often, they were too soft or unintelligible. But every now and then one popped up and he was sure of what it was, but ignored it. He glanced over at Alyx and saw her deep in concentration too.

Maybe she's noticing as well?

Slowly the noise rose, but it didn't become any more understandable. It became loud and annoying, like standing in a room full of people talking but not understanding what they were saying.

Alrion maintained his composure as best he could, but he needed his attention to be on navigating the dense forest. A bump here, a nick there, and quick adjustment of the horse, all these things niggled at him. All the while the cacophony grew inside his mind.

"Just shut up!" he yelled in frustration. Everyone stopped and stared at him. He realised in that instant that he had spoken the words aloud. He noticed a sympathetic look from Alyx, but concern and surprise from Vincent.

"What's happening?" Lara said from behind. She put her hand on his shoulder. He didn't need to turn around to know she was worried.

"Sorry, there's some sort of Blight communication going on. It's so loud and intense, but just noise. I hate it and I can't get rid of it. Please tell me you have it too?" he said, looking at Alyx.

"I do. But perhaps it is louder for you. For me, it's more background noise."

"It's so frustrating. I can't concentrate on anything else. And I can't even understand what they are saying."

"Do you even want to?" Lara said.

"No. But it just makes it all the more infuriating. Have you been in a room full of people shouting in another language?"

"I have. I see what you mean," Lara said with a thoughtful look on her face.

"That does sound infuriating. Has it been happening a lot?" Vincent said.

"On and off. I can usually switch off or ignore it. But something is different. Like it's insistent. That's the only way I can describe it."

"Just do your best. I think we should keep moving," Vincent said.

"Agreed," Alyx said.

"Sure, I'll do what I can," Alrion said. At least the Blight chatter had seemed to die down after his outburst. Although he didn't want to continue that as a strategy. It didn't seem like a good idea. And he had everyone worried.

As they rode on, the distractions started again. He could hear more of the insistent whispers, and almost understood words. But there was a changing intensity to it. Like it was building up to something.

"Hunt. Trap. Go." Alrion heard these words amongst other garbled nonsense. He was sure of it. He looked over at Alyx.

"Did you hear something different?" he said.

"Yes. I heard the word 'hunt' quite clearly. What do you think?"

"I think they're coordinating something. They must be tracking us, hunting us down. I even caught the word trap as well. Is there anything about this area that is special Alyx?"

"I'm not that familiar with it. I think we will be emerging from the forest soon. That could be opportunity to spring an attack."

"Let's just take a few precautions. I suggest we dismount, walk the horses from here. When we reach what we think is an ambush spot, approach carefully on foot," Vincent said.

"You're thinking of springing the trap if there is one, and keeping the horses safe."

"Exactly. If they do this properly the horses won't be able to get us away and could be injured or worse during the fighting. So, let's be cautious."

"That sounds wise. I will be able to point out when we need to leave them," Alyx said. She seemed lost in thought.

"I hope I'm not alarming everyone for no reason, but I think it's significant," Alrion said. He didn't want to ignore a possible sign then get them into trouble later.

They dismounted carefully, and stored all their extra provisions with the horses. Travelling light now, they would be ready to fight in an instant. Alrion grabbed the handle of his sword in anticipation. He felt more comfortable with it, but knew he would still struggle in a fight.

I'll deal with that when it comes up. At least they can't infect me. Can they? He thought. He had to chuckle to himself. There had to be some benefit to being infected, surely. And if they did indeed get attacked, it was good he had some sort of warning.

"Let's tie up the horses now," Alyx said. She gestured to a small space between trees that would do. Looking ahead Alrion could see more light penetrating the trees. It had to be the way out that Alyx had spotted.

Alrion patted his horse, checked that everything was tied up correctly and stood next to his father.

"I'm ready," Alrion said. He was only half-lying.

"Good. Stay close to me. We will let Alyx take the front foot."

"I'm expendable," she said as they walked.

"I didn't mean it like that," Vincent said.

"I did," Alyx replied. She was focused on the path ahead and said nothing more. Within a few moments, she drew her sword and ran forward.

"There must be something ahead, stay calm and follow my lead," Vincent said. He drew his sword and Alrion did the same. He could see a light glow from the diamond, and it didn't seem like it was coming from him. Lara was close behind, scanning the area for any attackers.

"I'll ensure we don't get jumped from behind," she said.

"Good. Let's advance, we don't want Alyx to get overwhelmed," Vincent said. He moved forward at a steady pace and Alrion kept up.

As the forest started to drop away, the scene before them expanded into a mess. The ground was torn up and Alyx was fighting off several Blighters at once. There were more coming, but each group seemed to be paired up with a Tainted.

"They're organised!" she shouted as Vincent approached. He didn't bother replying, instead swinging his sword, and slicing through a Blighter that was trying to attack Alyx from the side.

"Thanks!" Alyx shouted, spinning to cut down another and move on to another angle. Vincent stepped up into the space where she had been, reinforcing her. Alrion hung back a few steps. A Blighter came out directly at him and he froze momentarily. He forced himself to step into one of the moves Alyx showed him and he managed to force the Blighter to stop and dodge.

Being mobile allowed Alrion the opportunity to let his muscles take over. He started to remember the feeling of the sword movement, and let it guide him. He mentally stepped back, allowing the sword form to swing and poke at the Blighter, effectively cutting it down.

I can do this.

Another two Blighters jumped in to replace the fallen one. As the first drew back its arm it fell to the ground, a dagger catching it square in the head.

"Got your back!" Lara shouted. Alrion used the opportunity to press the attack on the other one. The Blighter was distracted and didn't defend itself well, going down quickly. Sweat started to form on Alrion's brow, and he drew in some quick breaths. Looking up he could see more waves of creatures descending upon them. But they were trying to bypass Alyx.

Vincent looked around as he fought, and seemed to be coming to a similar conclusion.

"I'm going to try and draw them over here," he shouted. Vincent pushed forward into the oncoming Blighters, knocking two down but not finishing them off. He was instead carving a path forward. Alyx dropped back a little to be closer to Alrion.

"What's he doing?" Alrion said.

"Giving them an easy target. Or making them think he is trying to flee. Hopefully it works."

"I hope so too," Alrion said. Initially it did seem to make an impact. The two that his father had spared immediately rose and charged after the blacksmith. Fewer Blighters were making the effort to come over and challenge Alyx. But then Alrion noticed something odd in the movements. There was a clump of Blighters moving forward as a formation. Not only that, but they kept looking around for something.

"Look at that group. They seem to be following orders. They're not like the rest," he said. Pointing over at them, he drew Alyx and Lara's attention.

"Lara, you watch them, I'll keep my eyes on the ones closer," Alyx said.

"Sure, don't lose concentration," Lara said. Alrion trusted her with that task too. He needed to keep his focus on the enemies closest. He knew Alyx was good, but it didn't take much for one to slip through in the circumstances.

"I think I have something," Lara said. Alrion looked over at her immediately.

"At the back there's a pair together. They seem to be directing that pack of Blighters. What do you think?" she said. As Alrion turned back to look properly a dagger whizzed past his face and dropped a Blighter right in front of him.

"Got your back, but that doesn't mean you can turn away!" Lara shouted. Alrion knew she was right. He had let his attention be drawn too easily. So, between the intense encounters of the battle, he let his view wander over to the two that Lara had pointed out. One of the two seemed to be a leader of sorts, barking out orders but also pointing and surveying the fight. The one next to him seemed different. As if he was providing advice.

"Wizard," Alrion heard in his mind, amongst the blaring and confusing noise of the Blight communication. He somehow knew that the Tainted one advising the leader had uttered that word. Alrion decided in that instant that he had to move.

"Follow me!" he shouted at Alyx, and started moving. He threw his weight behind a long slice, cutting down a Blighter from behind and moved away into the space behind it. Alyx cursed and dashed over, whirling through another group with a slashing of blades.

"I hope you know what you're doing," she said, kicking another Blighter to force an opening.

"Keep going, they're following!" Lara shouted. Alrion looked up and saw the tight group of Blighters had changed direction again.

"Vincent come back and cut them off!" Alyx bellowed. She stayed one step behind Alrion, keeping the Blighters at bay. Alrion stopped; he had reached a dead end. There was no way further back, he had ventured too far from the forest entry.

"This is as far as we go," he said. He readied his sword, trying to ignore the slight trembling of his wrist.

"We've got this!" Alyx said, pushing forward once more. Alrion was amazed by her intensity, and it seemed to be working. At the same time, he could see his father working his way over. The Blighters didn't know which way to turn, and they struggled to put up much of a fight. Within minutes the fighting started to die down.

"They're sneaking away!" Lara shouted. She pointed to the odd pair of leader and advisor. They were re-entering the forest.

"Come with me. Vincent, you finish up here," Alyx said. She ran off with Lara, barely stopping, avoiding any straggling Blighters. Vincent methodically worked his way back to Alrion's side, and together they fought off the remaining Blighters. Alrion sank down to the ground, exhausted.

"Not here, let's get back to the horses," Vincent said. Alrion nodded, it was too much effort to talk. He hauled himself back up and they made their way back into the forest.

9

A NEW TYPE

Lara was light on her feet, easily getting ahead of Alyx. There was little danger now, and she wasn't concerned about the threat from the two Tainted. Especially since they were fleeing the scene.

What if one of those two spotted me before?

The thought of it made a pit in her stomach. What if her mistake had resulted in that ambush?

I have to catch them!

Lara increased her speed, almost tumbling over when her foot caught on an extended tree root. She staggered forward and regained her balance. But her knee felt the pain of the sharp movement required and she pushed the sensation away.

Where are they? She thought as she continued. She slowly let her speed drop, and instead focused on looking for where they may have gone.

"Lara, come back here!" Alyx shouted. Lara was reluctant to give up the chase, but she could sense the urgency in Alyx's voice. She jogged back, and found Alyx standing where they had left the horses. Only there were no horses.

"They're gone," Alyx said. She sheathed her short sword and looked around.

"I checked those knots, they were tied properly," Lara said. There was no sign of the ropes either.

"Then they must have come and let the horses free. There's no trace of them. Not much in the way of tracks either, it's quite a mess." Alyx bent down and examined the ground. But she just shook her head and stood. She kept her eyes on the area, but looked unimpressed.

"It must have happened earlier, they didn't have time right now. We would have heard something," Lara said.

"Right. Maybe those two did it before, to hedge their bets in case the ambush failed. They did seem familiar with the area. You tracked them pretty quickly, yet they still got away."

"They did," Lara said. She was searching for excuses, but didn't know what to say. She had failed several times now and it felt terrible. She saw Alrion and Vincent approach. Vincent had his usual demeanour, and looked fine albeit a bit tired. Alrion looked completely washed out.

"Horses are gone. Looks like they did it during the fight," Alyx said.

"They've definitely been here before. Even chasing them I lost them," Lara said.

"This is a setback. But we're all intact. Anything valuable in your bags Alrion?" Vincent said.

"I have your ring and my amulet on me. And I was wielding my sword. But the notebook was in there."

"The one with the mysterious wizard messages?" Lara said.

"That's the one. Any messages now will go to them," Alrion said. He let out a sigh and looked around the area.

"Don't worry about it, if it turns up, it turns up. We don't need those messages to move forward," Vincent said. Alrion looked up at him, his face brightening a little.

"Exactly! Everything we need is here. We'll just be slowed down a bit," Lara said. She hoped to cheer him up a bit more.

"Wilson is going to be annoyed. I'll have to explain when I get back," Alyx said.

"If they cut the horses loose, maybe they'll find their way back one way or another," Vincent said.

"Let's go with that theory. So what next?" Lara said.

"We must move forward to a safe location. It is quite a walk I think. It would be unwise to camp on the plains tonight," Alyx said.

"How's everyone doing? Just tired? No injuries?" Vincent said.

"Nothing major," Lara said.

"Nothing here. Muscles are tight though, still not rested enough," Alyx said. Alrion mumbled something but didn't clarify.

"Let's move out then. The sooner we get away from here the better," Vincent said. He shook his head once more and returned to the path.

"I'll go ahead and scout out," Lara said. Before anyone could respond she dashed forward. She just had to do something useful. She thought she could survey the scene of the battle and see if there were any Tainted that had fallen. They might hold clues as to how the ambush had worked, and any planning that had gone into it. But she couldn't shake the image of that shadow she had almost caught before.

What if they were here and I missed it? And even now I was too slow to catch them. Tainted are not stealthy or fast. What's going on here?

Lara slowed to look through the fallen bodies. They were predominantly Blighters, which she found interesting. Usually there were more Tainted to direct and control the Blighters.

Further afield she found what looked like more Tainted. She turned them over gingerly, looking for anything that might help. But she found nothing.

"Typical. But to be expected. They do seem to do a lot of communication by thought," she pondered. It was time to return to the group. They weren't far behind, and Alyx urged them all forward.

"Keep moving," Alyx said.

"Anything there?" Alrion said.

"Nothing of use. But I have an interesting theory."

"Which is?"

"There's a new type of Tainted that we haven't encountered before. One that's fast and stealthy and can even track people," Lara said. It seemed almost silly saying it out loud. But she saw nodding heads and interested looks all around.

"What's your reasoning?" Vincent said. He moved in closer and gave her his full attention.

"Well, look at how they managed to get away. But they also knew where our horses were and made sure the horses were chased away while we were busy with the fighting."

"Agreed, good point about the tactics. Some manner of stealth required there."

"How did they know where our horses were? Have they been watching us?" Alyx said.

"I think so. I saw something last night when scouting. But I couldn't make it out and it disappeared," Lara said. She couldn't keep it to herself any longer, even if it looked bad for her. She felt her cheeks colouring as she said it. Alyx looked angrier than the others and her footsteps were louder and more like stomping.

"What? You saw something and didn't say anything? We could have done more to prepare. I don't understand your silence," Alyx said.

"It was just a shadow, it could have been anyone or anything. I didn't want to alarm anyone. Obviously, I won't do that again, now that we know what we are dealing with."

"I am a bit surprised you didn't mention it," Alrion said. Lara didn't know what to say. She didn't want to try and explain it more, it would just be embarrassing. They wouldn't understand.

"I just made a mistake," she said.

"And another one letting them get away now," Alyx said.

"I think that's a little unfair. Since they got the jump on us, and as you said at least one of them seems a bit different, it makes sense that they could escape," Vincent said. He stepped forward and put a hand on both Alyx and Lara's shoulders. "We need to calm this down a bit before it escalates. The enemy is out there, and we are doing them favours by doubting each other."

"I have something important to add," Alrion said.

"Let's hear it," Vincent said. There was silence until Alrion spoke again.

"When we were trying to distract them away, and those two Tainted directed the Blighters back to me. I heard a word amongst their communication. Wizard." Alrion paused.

"You think they could pinpoint you as the wizard?" Lara said. With each word she grew more incredulous. That was a serious problem if it was true. But it did help explain some of the behaviour.

"There could be something to that." Vincent turned away, deep in thought.

"But how is that even possible? Do you think they have some way of recognising what you look like?" Alyx said.

"It felt like it was more than that. The battle was pretty chaotic, yet they knew exactly where I was. I think there's something going on. What if this theory of a new type of Tainted isn't just one who is fast and stealthy. What if they're actually a Tracker?" Alrion looked around at the group. Lara felt stunned. Of course, that had to be it.

"That would explain how they've tracked so closely behind. But that would mean we can never shake them off," Lara said.

"It's just a theory," Alrion said quickly.

"There's definitely some merit to it. But let's not jump to conclusions. There's always a way around an obstacle," Vincent said.

"Exactly. You can just kill the Trackers," Alyx said.

"Is that your solution for everything? Lara said. It was an easy comment to make, and she felt a bit bad for it. But in a way, it felt like a valid question. Alyx had devoted her entire life to killing the Skull King. And a lot of Tainted and Blighters on the way.

"I won't take offence at that, but when it comes to the Blight it's a tried and tested solution," Alyx said. She was right too. Lara decided to leave it for now.

"Lots to think about," Vincent said. He looked worried. That, Lara could easily understand.

The walk was longer and harder than Lara had expected. But she eventually figured out why. They were ever so slowly ascending. It was so slight; it was hard to notice at first. But once she figured it out she looked back and it was obvious.

"What is it?" Alrion said. He looked back too, with a puzzled look.

"We're ascending. Slowly but definitely getting higher up."

"There's a reason the north gets cold. The height is a major factor," Alyx said.

"We may need to better equip ourselves," Vincent said.

"There'll be other towns, or villages. The further we go the less built up it is. As the land gets harsher, the settlements grow smaller," Alyx said. She emphasised the word harsher when she spoke.

"Speaking of harsher, this is getting tougher by the minute and I think we're all fading. Any ideas on where to stop?" Vincent said. Alyx slowed then stopped completely. She surveyed the area. There were large rocks around, with mostly rough shrubs.

"There's a good selection of rocks over there, should provide enough shelter in case it rains," she said, pointing with her right arm. Lara's gaze followed and she saw a large cluster of rocks. The biggest ones on an incline, casting a shadow in the afternoon sun.

"Works for me, let's head over," Vincent said. He looked like he had an extra spring in his step and led the way over.

"I don't know where he gets the energy," Alrion said. He just shook his head slowly.

"It's all in your mind. You should know all about that," Vincent said.

"Well, I've been a bit preoccupied," Alrion said. For the briefest instant Lara saw a look of pain and exhaustion sweep over Alrion's face. But he hid it quickly.

It's taking a toll on him, she thought. Hopefully this journey would not drag on too long. But if the frequent battles, travel, and the Blight communication were wearing Alrion down, he was going to struggle even more if the terrain became any more demanding. Which she assumed it would.

I need to change the mood, she thought. Lara bounded ahead, pretending she had hidden reserves of energy.

"Last one there has to cook!" she shouted. Alrion came alive, and increased his pace. Alyx maintained her speed, and was the last one to arrive.

"I think letting Alyx come last may not have been the most strategic move," Alrion said with a laugh as he watched her join them.

Alyx said nothing, busying herself with building a fire. Once it was going she disappeared into the twilight, and returned with two rabbits. She prepped them, put them on the fire and used some wet leaves to create additional smoke. Lara was sceptical, but also intrigued by what she was seeing.

"Finished," Alyx announced. She handed out portions of smoked rabbit on sticks to the others and settled back near the fire. Lara bit into the meat hesitantly. But it wasn't burned, and it wasn't raw. A wonderfully subtle smoky flavour permeated the meat and she was surprised that her mouth was filling with saliva.

"Wow, this is amazing!" Alrion said, between mouthfuls. Vincent was too busy eating to add anything.

"It's surprisingly tasty," Lara said. Alyx nodded.

"When you've lived the life I have, you get plenty of practise cooking out in the wilderness. A few small things make these kinds of meals more palatable," Alyx explained. She took another bite and Lara was just impressed that Alyx had bothered to learn how to do that.

"If the food is not palatable, it's harder to eat. And often you don't know when your next meal will be so you must be prepared," Alyx said. Lara just laughed. The rest of them gave her odd looks.

"What? I thought that maybe Alyx was some sort of closet gourmet, living on the land. But then she just killed it all by being so practical," Lara said. Alrion laughed too, almost choking on his food. Lara gave him a smile.

After they had eaten Alyx rose, and walked over to Alrion.

"You did well today, but now is not the time to rest. Get up, you need to train," she said, grabbing Alrion's hand. He looked shocked, but let her help him up.

"You too," she said to Vincent. He rose slowly, a curious look on his face.

"You two will spar and I will stop you as appropriate to demonstrate a point," she said in a matter of fact way.

"I really hadn't expected this, but fine. I'll do my best," Alrion said.

"She's probably just teaching you a lesson for doubting her cooking," Lara said, poking some fun at him. Alrion gave her a quick smile before readying his sword. It had been an intense day, and she felt like she had let everyone down. But these few moments of lightness and humour at the end of the day had helped.

As much as Alyx grated on her, she could appreciate the woman and her contribution to the team. They really did feel like a team already. And that was going to be important for what was to come. It was so easy to forget in a light moment what was going on. But Alrion and Alyx were infected, and time was marching on. Far too quickly for Lara's liking.

10

RENEWED FOCUS

Alrion awoke from a dreamless sleep. He felt groggy and sore and stiff. But relieved. He hadn't been tormented overnight. It took him a moment to remember exactly where he was and what the plan was.

"You look a bit out of it," Lara said.

"I think I am. Which is great considering everything. That training session at the end of the day was way too much, but it meant that I slept well," Alrion said. He looked over at where Alyx was standing. She noticed his gaze.

"As expected. I don't know if you were too tired, but your progress seems to be slowing," Alyx said. There was no criticism in her voice, just fact. But Alrion felt it sting.

"Hey, I'm still learning," he said indignantly. His anger started to flare up, but he forced it back down with some effort.

"Just stating the facts. You need to be aware of your condition. Maybe the Blight is affecting you," Alyx said. She turned away and walked over to talk to Vincent.

"She could be right. You need to be mindful of this," Lara said. She looked worried.

"I think it's more the extreme schedule we're on. No time for rest, constantly harried by the Blight. Then weapons training on top of that. It's too much. I'm not even complaining, just saying how it is," Alrion said. He actually thought that Alyx could be on to something. He had noticed several situations where his balance was off, or his strength was not what he expected. But he wanted to set Lara at ease, and judging by her reaction he had done just enough.

"That's true, but keep an eye on it. You can't push this hard forever, not with the infection ticking along. You've been lucky so far, but luck can only get you so far," she said. Her eyes lingered on him for a moment longer, then she turned to go join Alyx and Vincent.

Alrion rose, dusted himself off and joined the others.

"We need to keep walking. From here on we'll start getting into the lower mountains. That means fewer places to stop, less shelter, and terrible paths. But there is another village we can rest at not too far away," Alyx said.

"Definitely looking forward to the rest part," Alrion said.

"You shouldn't get his hopes up like that," Lara said.

"No, it's quite protected. You can't get large numbers through there due to the paths. I'm not familiar with the terrain much further north, so it may be our last chance to just take a break before we make the final push."

"Then let's get there as soon as possible. We can't rest properly like this," Vincent said, gesturing at the rocky surroundings. Alyx nodded and started out. Alrion let them get ahead, and followed at the rear.

He started to think back to the previous encounters and his reactions. And he began to see a pattern, as much as he didn't want to. But the more he mulled it over, the more he was convinced.

All the attacks so far, they're my fault. Even if they're tracking us, I always seem to lose it before they launch their assault. There has to be something about that. Maybe I am making things easy for them?

He felt a lurching in the pit of his stomach at the realisation. The Blight was affecting him, he was sure of it. And the mental noise and communication didn't help. But he wasn't in control of himself.

How much is that my lack of discipline, and how much is it due to the infection?

It was easy to just explain it all away. But he looked back at his journey so far. Anger had been there all along.

My first attempts at drawing my Spark were fuelled by anger. How much have I been relying on it?

Alrion felt like the wind had been taken out of him. All this time, his anger had been simmering away. It was his outlet every time he felt weak, or embarrassed, or wronged. And it had felt like it had served him well at the time. Like he had been using it to his advantage. But maybe that wasn't the case.

It's been festering and I've been nurturing it. And now I'm paying the price, he thought. It rang so true that he felt despondent. How would he make a change now? When he was so far gone to this infection?

He noticed Lara looking at him and forced a smile.

"Just lost in my thoughts," he said.

"They're not tormenting you again are they?" she said. A concerned frown was on her face again.

"No, just my own thoughts. You shouldn't worry so much, it doesn't look so good on you," Alrion said. He saw anger and annoyance flash over her face, but it was quickly replaced with a smile.

"Well, you shouldn't cause me so much reason to worry then!" Lara turned away and seemed to focus on the path ahead. Alrion chuckled to himself.

Still terrible with the ladies.

But he quickly moved on to thinking about other things. And the increasing difficulty of their trek gave him something to focus on.

A few bunches of red berries were cause enough to stop for lunch, Alrion's stomach rumbling despite the number that he shoved into his mouth.

"While we are paused, I wanted to consider how we would be keeping safe today. These paths are getting narrower, and there's less space either side," Vincent said.

"We will probably need to sleep out. I'm not sure how long it will take us. But it's a risk; the terrain around here is so exposed. It's even hard to take shelter from the elements, let alone a hostile force," Alyx said.

"Do we have any idea how they are tracking us? If we could confuse that, it would buy some safety," Lara said. Vincent shook his head and Alyx had a blank look.

"We aren't exactly hiding our trail, but we're not creating one either. It could be any number of ways," she said. Alrion sighed. He didn't really want to share his recent revelation, but knew he had to. It could be crucial to their survival.

"I have an idea, well, a guess," Alrion said. "It's related to me."

"In what way?" Lara said quickly.

"I think they have a way to determine my location because I'm infected. But I get the feeling it's not incredibly accurate."

"Then how are they always so close? And setting ambushes?" Alyx said.

"I've noticed a pattern. Around each of the major attacks, I've had an outburst. Generally, anger. And the attacks have been very soon after. It's like they just needed a final confirmation before beginning." He saw some thoughtful looks, and nodding.

"Are you sure about that? You don't necessarily need to assume it's your fault," Lara said.

"That sounds like a decent theory to me. Especially since you've managed to catch some of their communication. It's you they are after," Alyx said. She stood from the rock she was leaning on and started pacing.

"We must treat it as true, until we have a better idea. Then we can take steps to help minimise our chances of being discovered. It may not make any difference though, given our location. If they've tracked us this far, it will be easy to find us," Vincent said.

"Agreed. But if they're relying on Alrion to be a beacon as means of coordination as well, we can deny them that. You mentioned monks before, didn't they help you with this?" Alyx said.

"The trial I completed, and the monk I travelled with did help me refine my Will. And the ability to focus it. But this seems different. It's not just my emotions. I mean, yes I have responsibility but it's not the same now I'm infected," Alrion said.

"In what way?" Vincent said. He approached Alrion slowly.

"I can't believe I'm actually saying this. But I feel like I'm getting clumsier somehow. That things are a little bit harder to do, or not guaranteed to happen like I expect. Maybe I'm just imagining it all," Alrion said. He felt silly for even mentioning it, but it had started to weigh on him. And he didn't know what to think.

"That's not as crazy as you may think. The Blight doesn't just attack you at one point. It takes over your whole body," Alyx said.

"How much do you know about this?" Alrion said.

"Quite a bit. I've never experienced it myself, well until now. But I've seen many turn, and I've watched some do it slowly like we are now. I made it my business to know how they tick, because it was crucial to my revenge. I had to understand how they worked, so I could ensure that I would not fail. I only had one chance," Alyx said. There was no passion in her voice, only cold fact.

"How can you detach yourself like that? Those are quite intense experiences I can imagine."

"It's a technique you should try and learn. Maybe you can keep these creatures away by not giving them any help."

"How would I learn?"

"I'll teach you what I can. It's all about separating the fuel of the emotion from the emotion itself. You can deal with the emotion rationally, but harness the fire from it any way you like."

"That sounds interesting. You must be an expert," Alrion said. The more he spoke to Alyx, the more impressed he was. She had discarded everything unnecessary to her purpose, and in the process constantly refined what she was to perfection. He had gone through no such process. He'd just been fumbling along, taking the information he could get his hands on, and trusting his instincts and the people around him. But this was too important to leave to chance.

"I am too much an expert. Let's leave it at that," Alyx said. Alrion wanted to know more, but he respected her wishes.

Maybe she can't go back?

It was sad, if true. But then, it looked like she had made peace with that choice a long time ago.

"I have a suggestion," Alyx said. She stopped walking and turned around. She had a defiant pose to her.

"Let's hear it," Vincent said.

"Up ahead I can see we have a bit more room. I suggest that we give Alrion a quick sparring session. He can improve his technique a little, and also work on getting some of this anger out. It may improve our chances for the next attack," Alyx said. She looked at them all in turn and waited for a response.

"It's worth a try I think. It may buy us more time later," Vincent said. He looked over at Lara.

"I can keep a look out and advise of anything approaching. It should be easy to spot travellers on this road."

"I'm game. We need to try something. Either I'm giving them our location or contributing nothing in these fights. This works for both," Alrion said. He was willing to try anything. And he thought that just maybe he could stay a step ahead of the infection if he kept trying to hone his skills. It was worth a shot.

Alyx pointed out the area she had mentioned. It was a rough circle of dirt to the left of the path. There were steep drops all around it.

"You may want to avoid the edges," Lara said, peering down.

"Vincent you're up again. I need to observe the fight without participating," Alyx said. Vincent nodded and drew his sword. Alrion did the same. For some reason, it felt different this time. Like a lot more was riding on it than just a normal sparring match.

Here we go.

"Alrion, go on the attack. Use the sequences we worked on," Alyx said. Alrion stepped forward, thinking of how to begin. He started the first one he had learnt, the rolling barrel. However, instead of just flowing into the next, he repeated it. This time with more speed and intensity. The change caught Vincent by surprise, but he easily defended it all.

"It's too easy for him. Are you feeling frustrated yet?" Alyx said.

Alrion did in fact feel a bit frustrated. Normally he would ignore it, but he let it rise up.

"Imagine that the frustration you feel is actually fuel. It's making your muscles burn with feverish intensity. You can move even faster," Alyx said. Alrion listened carefully and tried to follow. He tried to recognise the emotion within him, and locate the intensity of the frustration. Channel it like he had done before.

He almost channelled it into his Spark, which came naturally. It was how he had originally increased his power. But he caught himself and instead did as Alyx had instructed. He imagined that it enhanced his muscles. The heat of the frustration working his muscles harder and faster. He could feel the intensity of the heat rising from them. He pushed more and more, upping the speed.

His arms moved almost automatically, seamlessly flowing into another sequence, interrupting it halfway to change into the rolling wave. With a bang their swords collided, Vincent stepping forward to halt the assault. Alrion looked up and saw sweat dripping down his father's brow. Alrion stepped back, letting go of all the tension. He felt wiped out.

"Much better. Don't you agree Vincent?" Alyx said.

"Definite improvement. I was almost overwhelmed by that slight change in intensity. It's a very powerful tool if you can harness it correctly," Vincent said. His breathing was deep as he recovered.

"And how do you feel now?" Alyx said to Alrion. He pondered that for a moment before replying.

"Better. Emptier, if that makes sense. Ready to go collapse somewhere."

"Not just yet, we have a way to go. Take a few minutes to recover, and when Lara returns we will be on our way again," Alyx said. She walked down the road to look for Lara. Alrion sheathed his sword and slump down next to a large rock. It dug into him a little but he ignored it. He needed to rest.

"ALRION." Wraith's voice thundered within his head.

And here we go, Alrion thought. But he kept his composure and prepared to listen as carefully as possible.

11

TRACKING

C eles slowed and finally dismounted. Everything hurt. She had travelled hard, but never like this. She looked over at Tarren and he looked like he could keep going. It had already been days of constant travel. Avoiding settlements and eating and drinking minimally.

"I don't know how you do it," she said.

"You don't want to know. I'd rather not," he said. Celes found a softer patch of ground near a tree and sat down. She should have stretched her legs more, but it felt nice to be sitting and not in motion.

"We're finally in a secluded place. I will rest also," Tarren said. He started to remove the bulky cloak he had been wearing.

This will be interesting.

She watched carefully, curiosity with a bit of fear mixed in. She would finally see him for what he was.

Tarren's face was relatively normal, although he had some black markings on his neck and forehead. He was skinny and wore all black clothing. From what she could see from his arms, they were covered in intricate tattoos. His pants were only knee length; his legs displayed the same pattern of tattoos.

"Interesting tattoos," she said. Tarren glanced at them and looked back at her.

"Part of the process. As far as I understand they were made with a liquid form of the Blight. The application and the design are crucial. It was an incredibly painful process."

"I can imagine. You seem quite hardy, and can travel incredibly fast for long periods. Apart from the tracking capability, what else can you do?"

"I don't want to spill all my secrets just yet." Tarren found a place to sit opposite Celes. He did look weary now that she could see him properly.

"I need an idea of what you can do. Otherwise how do we work together? What if we get attacked?"

"That's fair. I will add, that I can also meld into the shadows. Only useful at night, but it makes me just about invisible."

"That's very handy. Are there any limitations? Things I need to consider?"

"I can't hide in direct light. But where it casts a shadow I can obscure, to make myself harder to target."

"Thank you. I hope that nothing happens, but this is useful information. Since I know how you can be effective, we can play to that."

"How about you?"

"I'm good at stealth and picking locks. I also have a few potions that can be used to create opportunities."

"You're basically a thief then?"

"More or less."

"You don't see many your age. They tend to die out," Tarren said. Celes laughed.

"I am retired for a while."

"To bring up your son. And now you're out helping him?"

"That's right. You're quite perceptive," Celes said. The Tracker before her clearly had his full mental faculties. She always wondered how much people were transformed by the Blight.

"You could say I'm lucky in that way, since I've retained my memories, identity and ability to think for myself. But, that's also quite unlucky."

"Because you know what you're part of?"

"Yes. And there's no opportunity for me in normal society. I am shunned, and rightfully so." Tarren let out a sigh.

"What did you do before all this?"

"I was a thief catcher." Tarren let a tiny smile loose. Celes laughed again.

"That's too perfect. You would track down people like me?"

"Yes. I was incredibly good at it too. I could put myself in the right mindset, and used my skill to follow the trail. Or in some cases get one step ahead of the thief."

"You would make an excellent thief now!"

"That is true. I hadn't really considered it. I think somehow that's been a good thing. They would find me regardless, and then I'd be stealing for them as well."

"There's no escape at all?"

"No. Especially not with people like me out there. We are attuned to the Blight. With enough preparation and the right stimulus, we can find and track anyone infected."

"Like Alrion. My son."

"Yes. I hate to say it, but I am more and more convinced that he is the target for another group of Trackers. And he's infected too. Is there a chance that he's travelling with an infected wizard?"

"Unlikely. I mean, it's possible but it doesn't sound right."

"Then let's work on the assumption that he is until we find out more."

"Speaking of which, you haven't really told me much about where we are heading. Just that it's north." Celes stood and started stretching her legs again. They felt so stiff.

"Still north. Do you know where he might be heading?" Tarren said.

"I really have no idea. The only information I had was him needing to get to the desert. He must have a new destination that he's working towards."

"There's not much in the north lands. Fewer people, more mountains and lots of cold. Although you don't get much Blight activity up there."

"Could be something to it. If he's infected, it has to be something that he can use to get cured. Otherwise they wouldn't be tracking him so closely, would they?"

"They could wait for the transformation to take place and then move in. It would be less effort, and easier to track. That's what I would do." Tarren looked away after the comment.

"Don't worry, I'm sure you've had to do things you aren't comfortable with. There's a reason it's called the Blight, and why we're working to put a stop to it."

"Thank you for your understanding. I fear I've been a monster for so long now, I sometimes find the line blurred."

"I understand. But tell me a story about your life before. It will make me feel more comfortable."

"I like to reminisce about those times. Very well, but we should not dally telling stories. Let's take a slower pace but still progress." Tarren stretched carefully, then retrieved the heavy coat. Celes imagined him sighing as he put it back on. His disguise, hiding his real form.

He so desperately wants to be past it. I think we can work with that.

She cringed at the thought of getting on the horse again so soon, but there was nothing else to it.

Alrion needs me.

Celes gingerly mounted the horse and pretended it wasn't instantly uncomfortable.

"Story time, let me think," Tarren said. His eyes got a faraway look, but he started walking. Celes kept pace with him.

"Long ago, I was working in Altarbright. Very busy place, always something valuable being traded or transported. Lots to do for a man like myself. I was never without a job, sometimes having several on the go at once."

"How long ago was this?"

"Probably ten years ago."

"And when were you ... transformed?"

"A year ago. Recently, in the grand scheme of things."

"Very recently. Not that it's a short amount of time," Celes said. She didn't want to belittle his condition. He was certainly worried enough about it and the effect on his mind already.

"On this one particular day I was offered a job that was quite unusual. There was a rare and prized sword coming from Valrytir via the ferry. I was to catch the thief who was planning to steal it."

"You had a tip beforehand?"

"Yes. I was brought aboard the ferry not long before it was due to land, and concealed myself in the cargo. From there I kept track of all who came and went."

"Did the thief succeed?"

"Not initially. In fact, I started to believe that it was a hoax. Nobody came to check on it. I heard the ferry dock and all the passengers disembark but not a soul came to retrieve the cargo. There were other things than the sword. Which made it so strange."

"Please continue," Celes said. She adjusted her position on the saddle and nudged the horse closer to Tarren. Once she was used to his raspy voice, he was a good storyteller.

"Eventually, I decided to leave my hiding place and go find out what had happened. It didn't take long. As soon as I reached the deck I knew."

"What was it?"

"The first sign that something was not right was the location. We were not at Altarbright. We were in some sort of giant cavern. The ferry had been hijacked and brought somewhere else. Some sort of smuggler's cave no doubt."

"That's one way to steal a sword," Celes said. She was impressed by how bold it was.

"Indeed. The only other problem was that I had been betrayed. As soon as I reached the deck I was surrounded and had to surrender all my weapons."

"You were set up?"

"No, I don't think so. Not on purpose. I think that whoever was behind the scheme knew I would be planted on the ferry and therefore changed their tactics to suit. But they didn't know where I would be so they waited for me to emerge. I felt quite foolish for falling into their trap."

"How were you to know? That's not something you would normally expect."

"In hindsight yes, it was not something you could anticipate. Not without a precedent but there I was, captured and humiliated." Tarren had obvious emotion in his voice, like the feelings were still fresh.

"How'd you get out of that one?"

"Like you, I'm no stranger to locks. They locked me in a cargo storage cage and I let myself out when it was convenient. I suspected the captain was involved, but didn't know with enough certainty to take action. So I hid and watched and waited. I finally spotted the perpetrator."

"Who was it?'

"The quartermaster at the docks in Altarbright. He must have gotten wind of the sword and decided to make a play for it. I never did find out if he had prior arrangements with the smugglers."

"Corruption, it's almost always the answer," Celes said. She was a little disappointed.

"I know, it's at the heart of many things. I know I had an uphill battle trying to pin the whole thing on the quartermaster. The man who hired me would never believe it. The whole incident was completely unbelievable. So, I did the only thing possible."

"You stole the sword?"

"Of course. I had already memorised the manifest and knew where the sword was destined to go. I stole it back and rowed my way out of the cave and back to Altarbright. After quite an adventure I delivered the sword as promised, and was paid by its new owner after relaying my tale."

"We're not that different after all," Celes said. She smiled at him and tried to get a reaction. He chuckled a little, the sound horrifying to her ears. But she smiled back all the same.

There's still humanity there. How many of those who are Tainted or similar have we been tarring with the same brush as Blighters? There's way more to this than anyone understands, she thought.

"Speaking of which, what was your biggest heist?" Tarren said.

"There's been a few, but one stands out. One that spanned the beginning and end of my career. The Pure Diamond."

"I know of it. Last I checked it wasn't stolen."

"It has been now. That single gem has been so central to my life; I almost can't believe it thinking back. It's what prompted me to change my approach from small-scale thefts."

"Something I always wondered. What turns people to thieving?"

"Haven't you caught enough to figure that one out?" Celes said. Tarren shook his head slowly.

"I heard many excuses, but never a reason."

"That's fair. I never thought too much about it. But it has something to do with upsetting the order of things. And anyone can do it. There's no requirement for being born into the right family, or having wealth or privilege. Just the hunger for more, and the will to make it so."

"That does seem to be a central thread. I think that hunger is a disease for many, and they keep going after bigger and bigger targets."

"It certainly is. My obsession with the Pure Diamond introduced me to my husband, it made us flee Brangtur when we failed, and it recently led me back there. But here's the funniest part."

"Yes?" Tarren stopped walking and looked at Celes.

"In the end, I was caught. I needed help to escape, and someone else took it for me. That's life, isn't it?"

"Nothing ever goes to plan," Tarren said. He seemed lost in his thoughts, so Celes stopped talking. After a time, with there still being no settlement in sight, she had to ask him about it.

"Will we ever pass through another town?"

"Yes, soon enough. From the little that I know of the north, we can't help but pass through Rolyntide. And from there, I fear there aren't many paths to take. Good in some ways and bad in others."

"Easier to track them."

"And harder to remain hidden," Tarren said.

"We can defend ourselves, that's an acceptable risk." Celes withdrew two of her knives in a flourish.

"I don't doubt that. But, if we really get their attention we will be in considerable danger." Tarren stopped suddenly.

"What is it?" Celes said. She could sense something was wrong.

"They're preparing an attack on the wizard. It's significant. Perhaps even an ambush."

"How far?"

"I'm not sure. Too far for us. I need to be careful," he said. Tarren slowly sunk to the ground and sat cross-legged. He looked to be concentrating intensely with his eyes closed.

"Only a small Tracker presence, but they're not going to engage. There's something else. Something dark. This is not a good sign. Does he have help?"

"He does. My husband and another thief."

"That may not be enough." Tarren went quiet again. Celes felt so powerless. Her son was in danger again, and she was too far away. She had to catch up. She could help. She was about to speak to Tarren again, but his eyes suddenly opened and he looked right at her.

"We have a problem. They've detected my snooping and they're suspicious. We should prepare ourselves for the possibility of an attack."

12

A SURPRISING FOE

Alrion braced himself for another communication. But he didn't dare respond.

"Giving me the silent treatment? That is fine. It was about time you wised up," Wraith said. Alrion looked at his father.

"Find them," he whispered. Vincent seemed to understand, and took off to look for Lara and Alyx.

"You've been very helpful, aiding my Trackers. And we're not far away. That's why I'm communicating with you now. I am sending you a special gift," Wraith said. Alrion decided to respond, but without emotion. He had to see what he could do.

"Always so thoughtful," Alrion said.

"So, he speaks. I thought that perhaps you had been rendered mute from fear. Have you been enjoying the Blighters?"

"I'm a little tired of them to be honest. So dull," Alrion said. He was trying to turn the tables, to wind up Wraith rather than be the one that got angry. It did help that he felt a little calmer after his training.

"I completely agree. But that was just the warm-up. I'm sending you a taste of what's to come. I won't be there myself, but just imagine me coming soon."

"You're all talk, Wraith. For all I know you're still stuck in that pit."

"That was a clever move. But we both know you're not powerful enough to do that anywhere else. And without your Spark you're powerless. Just admit it," Wraith said. The mocking tone in his voice would normally trigger Alrion. But he had just enough control to keep his reaction down.

"I know what you're trying to do and I'm not going to bite. I'm still here, and all your attacks have failed."

"Oh, have they? I beg to differ. But all in good time. Just remember that there's nowhere you can go. Nowhere you can hide. I will be there and claim you for myself. You belong to me; it's just a matter of time. Keep struggling if you like. It'll just make your eventual failure all the more enjoyable," Wraith roared. He did seem a little annoyed. Alrion took pleasure in that.

"Just more empty words, Wraith. I'll see you when I feel it necessary. Goodbye," Alrion said. He tried blocking out any further communication. He wasn't sure if it was working, or if Wraith had just stopped talking. Vincent soon returned with Alyx and Lara.

"What's going on?" Lara said.

"Wraith was communicating with me. It seems out of the ordinary, I get the feeling that it's difficult for him to do it."

"And what did he say?" Vincent said.

"He said that he's not far behind, and he's sent me a special gift. One that's not as dull as a horde of Blighters. Make of that what you will." Alrion shrugged his shoulders.

"I don't like the sound of that. Could be a Shade?" Lara said.

"I get the impression that it's something else. Something different."

"Either way he's told you that something is coming. We should prepare for that," Vincent said. He looked at Alyx.

"I can't suggest a location specifically, although I do think we should move to a narrower section. That way we can control how we are engaged, at least in terms of numbers," Alyx said.

"But he said it wasn't as dull as a horde of Blighters. What if we get boxed in?" Lara said. Nobody had a good answer for that.

"Let's just move further down and assess places to make a stand. Clearly, we shouldn't remain here," Vincent said. Alyx started taking off and Alrion hurried to catch up.

"Do you have any ideas?" Lara said to Alrion as they walked.

"Not really. I just know that it is different. He seemed excited. That's a bad sign. I tried to antagonise him a bit, to see how he reacted. But I don't think it made much of a difference. He was too pleased with himself."

"That definitely doesn't sound good. I'll make sure we have a good place to defend ourselves," Lara said. She ran ahead to confer with Alyx and scout ahead. Alrion kept walking, lost in his thoughts.

"Alrion, prepare yourself!" Vincent shouted. Alrion was startled, and drew his sword. The rest of his group were clustered together ahead, but he couldn't see what they were talking about. He stepped forward, the nerves giving him both pause and also a manic energy.

"What is this gift from Wraith?" Alrion wondered. He stood beside his father and looked ahead. Blocking the path was what looked like a Shade. But it was completely quiet and looked asleep with its head lowered.

"Stop the games, we see you!" Alrion shouted. He didn't know what game was being played, but the tension was uncomfortable. He needed to know what he was dealing with. The creature slowly raised its head and looked at them.

"I bring the gift of fire!" it said. Its voice was reminiscent of Wraith's, with an alien, harsh tone to it. The gift was a fireball, slowly increasing in speed and size as it hurtled towards them. Alrion's first reaction was to swat it away, but Lara tackled him to the ground. He felt the searing heat passing over him and curled up into a ball. It passed and exploded against a large rock behind them, showering sparks everywhere. As he regained his senses he realised that Lara was shielding him.

"I'm sorry," he said, as she quickly rolled off and stood. Alyx and Vincent also rose from where they had sheltered and stepped in front of Alrion.

"You can't stop them right now. You have to remember that," Lara said. Alrion propped himself up with the help of his sword and looked over at their enemy. It was laughing.

"To think that you almost stood there and took the blast. You're more idiotic than I was led to believe," it said.

"Who are you?" Alrion said.

"Call me Fury. I am a former wizard and the first disciple of Wraith. I will show you the power that you will soon have when you join us!" Fury started to run forward with incredible speed. It drew back its right arm, preparing a strike. Vincent stepped forward and swung his sword, aiming at Fury's arm. The creature continued forward with the strike, knocking Vincent back.

Vincent steadied himself, keeping his eyes on the Shade. Fury examined its arm.

"No damage. Your sword won't work on me," it said. It laughed, a terrifying screaming sound coming out.

"He must be shielding himself. The sword can still work, you may need to create an opening," Alrion said. He approached Alyx and handed over his sword. The diamond glowed bright blue.

"Take this. You can do more with it than me, and your weapon has no chance of doing anything against this kind of enemy," he said. Alyx didn't argue and accepted the weapon readily. She gave her short sword to Alrion.

"I will take the lead. Vincent and Lara, you shadow me and look for opportunities. But make sure one of you can always cover Alrion. That short sword won't do much."

"Agreed. I'll follow your lead," Vincent said. Alyx started immediately, hurling herself at the Shade. It raised his arm, blasting a wave of force at her. She shielded herself with the sword, but flew back several paces. Vincent attacked from another angle with the same level of ferocity. Fury turned its attention over to him, throwing another wave of force. Vincent defended himself the same way. Lara used the opportunity to start flanking the creature.

"Don't think you can sneak up on me!" Fury roared. It spun completely and let loose a spray of fire that swept along aimed at

Lara. She turned and ran, just fast enough to outpace the fire. Fury kept laughing as the flames licked just behind Lara's heels.

Alyx attacked again, a little bit faster than before. This time Vincent was beside her. Fury noticed them and stopped his attack, swinging around to take a swipe at Alyx. She slid down, maintaining her momentum, and slicing at the creature's legs. Fury quickly brought up his other arm and fired a blast of force at her, pushing her back and preventing her weapon from coming into contact.

"Got you!" Vincent shouted as his sword came down. Fury quickly grabbed the blade with his free hand, screaming in pain. The sword cut free of the creature's grasp, and Fury stumbled back. Vincent held his ground, watching the scene unfold.

Fury stared at its hand and clenched it. It composed itself then let out a furious cry.

"That stung. But nothing more than that I'm afraid. I'm just getting warmed up," it said.

"That means you can hurt it, you just need to create an opening," Alrion shouted. He wished he could help more, but he had no power to use. The best he could do was watch the creature and figure out its limitations. It was clearly the same sort of creation as Wraith himself. But even Wraith had used magic sparingly. There had to be a degree of difficulty or cost to using magic in that Shade-like form. So Alrion would watch and think. He would figure out a strategy for them to use to bring this thing down.

Lara returned to Alrion's side panting.

"That was close," she said.

"I could see that. I know it has limitations so the more we push it the better chance we have of finding a weakness. Just make sure you have enough speed to get away," he said without taking his eyes off Fury.

"I understand. See what you can figure out," Lara said. She paused for a moment, her eyes darting back and forth, before diving back into the fight.

Alyx was crouched down and watching Fury. The Shade Wizard just looked back.

"Maybe he's waiting," Vincent said quietly. He took up a position next to Alyx. Lara joined them moments later.

"I will press from the front, you two go for the flanks," Alyx said. The other two just nodded and waited.

"Come entertain me, you weaklings!" Fury shouted. It had stopped clutching its hand and was now observing them. Alyx crouched even lower and sprung forward with incredible speed. It was like she was trying to win a foot race, not enter a fight. She held the sword in front of her like a spear. Fury laughed and threw a wave of force at her. But it just seemed to wrap around her. She increased her speed, moving forward with a single-minded purpose.

Fury scrambled to counter. It brought both hands together and looked like it was concentrating intensely. Another blast of force exploded, knocking Alyx aside. Rather than go down, she rolled and continued forward like it had been nothing. Fury didn't try another spell, instead readying to strike out at her.

Interesting. It needs to concentrate properly to cast spells with anything more than just general targeting. And doesn't like to chain together too many at once. I think we can use that. He continued to watch the fight.

Vincent crossed over, approaching Fury from the opposite angle. The creature stepped aside to bring both Alyx and Vincent into its field of vision. Lara ran further, coming back in a wide arc and splitting the Shade Wizard's attention further. She threw some daggers at it. Fury glanced at them, then turned away. They bounced harmlessly off his body. The distraction however bought Alyx an extra second of approach and she changed her stance. Instead of looking to spear the creature, she instead sliced at its legs again.

However, this time Fury couldn't stop the strike. A wave of fire started to emanate from its hands. Alyx must have noticed but ignored it. She continued her swing. As she connected, a wave of fire enveloped her legs. Alyx continued the arc of the strike, slicing through then rolling to safety. She rolled around quickly, trying to put out the fire.

Lara dived in to help, moving Alyx around and extinguishing any other flames. Vincent moved to capitalise on the attack and slashed again at the creature. Fury moved just enough, and caught the attack on the shoulder. The Runesteel cut deep and Fury cried out in pain and anguish.

The simultaneous attack did the trick. They didn't even need me to point that out. I hope they can finish this, Alrion thought. He didn't like the look of what happened to Alyx. Even if she had escaped the worst, her mobility would be gone.

Fury grew quiet, and looked to be testing its limbs. Without warning, it lurched forward charging towards Alyx. She just lay there, her legs twitching. Lara crouched over her, with her Runesteel dagger at the ready.

"You'll pay for that! I won't even keep you for the Blight. DIE NOW!" the Shade Wizard cried out. His right hand was aflame and his nails were extended out like knives.

There's no way Lara can stop that. And Alyx can't stand. Alrion's blood boiled and he felt powerless. He scrambled within himself, trying to find a way to access his Spark without reaching through the dark mass of Blight. He even considered trying it anyway, knowing the consequences. But movement ahead caught his attention. It was his father.

Vincent had launched himself at Fury's back, his sword outstretched. By some miracle he seemed to reach the creature before it could hit Alyx. The Runesteel slid effortlessly through the Shade Wizard's chest all the way to the hilt. But Fury kept moving.

Lara held her ground and moved with lightning speed. She grasped Fury's outstretched hand just enough to divert it, and with her right hand she drove her Dagger into its heart.

"Die, you abomination!" she shouted. Fury halted. It lost its momentum and started to topple.

"Move it over!" Vincent called out. He started to guide Fury over to the side and Lara aided him. With a resounding crash the creature fell to the ground just to the side of Alyx. Its protective skin started to flake away and turn to dust. Alrion ran forward to join them. He couldn't believe how close that had been. And Alyx wasn't moving.

Before he could reach her side, Vincent and Lara were standing over the weapon master with concerned looks.

"How is she?" Alrion said.

"Badly burned on her legs, but otherwise alright it seems," Vincent said.

"I've had worse," Alyx said hoarsely. But she looked to be in incredible pain.

"You did well Lara, I wasn't able to do enough to stop it," Vincent said.

"Thanks, but it was a team effort. We only managed that because Alyx slowed it down. At great cost."

"Just doing my duty," Alyx said. Lara and Vincent returned their weapons and Alrion carefully unclasped Alyx's grip and sheathed his sword. He stepped over and looked at the body of Fury. The transformation had been reversed. Now it just looked like an ordinary man.

"This could be me. This is why I must succeed. Death should not be the only release from this curse," he said. He turned and walked a few paces away, a surge of emotions within him. Alyx had almost died, they had killed a wizard, and Alrion had felt powerless throughout the whole thing.

As much as it was about him finding a cure for himself, he realised that he had a greater responsibility. It wasn't only his own fate that was doomed if he failed, it was all those who were infected. That was a heavy weight on his shoulders.

13

SLOW PROGRESS

Alrion was staring off into space, obviously affected by the battle. Lara decided to focus on practical matters.

"Can you sit up?" she said. Alyx didn't respond so Lara knelt to help prop her up. Vincent dropped down beside her, and the two of them managed to lift Alyx and rest her against a nearby rock in a seated position.

"How's that?" Lara said. Alyx paused to gather her breath, then responded.

"A bit better. I'm not sure how well I can move," she said.

"Let us worry about that," Vincent said. He looked around the area.

"He was waiting for us. Do you think there's more ahead?" Lara said.

"No, Wraith would have been here himself if they were that prepared. I think we have a window of opportunity to create some distance. But it will be hard with Alyx's injury," Vincent said. Alrion approached suddenly.

"I can heal her. My power isn't gone, it's just a bit beyond my usual reach," he said.

"No!" Vincent shouted. He cleared his throat and continued.

"Sorry, but it's not negotiable. You do not use your gift while infected. I've been told too many horror stories."

"But ..."

"Not ever. We need to get to a Healer. We don't have any supplies to even treat her," Vincent said.

"I'm done, leave me here. My legs are burned and I'm infected. I don't want to be the reason your quest fails. I'm already a lost cause," Alyx said. There was silence.

"We should consider it. If they aren't after her, maybe we can send help back. We're in the middle of nowhere and will have difficulty moving forward otherwise. You can't afford to be caught," Lara said. She had had disagreements with Alyx, and disliked the often-critical nature of the weapon master. But she had come to respect her and didn't like the idea of leaving her behind. In this situation, though, it sounded like common sense. It was too risky otherwise.

"I can't leave her here. They will do worse to her if they find her, or if she's left alone she won't make it. Alyx is the reason we survived that fight. What happens next time? If I can't heal her, then we find someone who can," Alrion said. Lara was surprised by the amount of passion in his voice. It was hard to argue against him. She just didn't want to get caught again in a difficult situation. It would be worse next time with an injured companion.

"We can't lose the time debating this. Alrion, let's try and get Alyx up and assess," Vincent said. Alrion nodded and helped his father. They strained and hauled her up. They held her weight and slowly lowered her feet to the ground. Lara could see the pain on Alyx's face.

"How bad is it?" Vincent said. Alyx tried putting weight down on each foot, one at a time.

"Quite excruciating. If you're insistent on taking me, then I can deal with the pain. But all I can do is try and prevent my feet dragging. I can't walk properly. I'll just fall," Alyx said.

"We will make this right," Alrion said. He already looked tired. And who knew how much of his strength had already been sapped by the Blight.

"Give me your weapons," Lara said. She walked over and

unbuckled all three swords, strapped one to her back and let the other two hang from her hips. They were heavy and a bit unwieldy, but at least Vincent and Alrion didn't have the additional weight. They shifted their holds then moved forward slowly. With great concentration Alyx managed to coordinate her feet to match their rhythm.

"Looking good." Lara wanted to encourage them, but it was way too slow. She could have crawled quicker.

"I'll be slightly ahead to spot any potential dangers or good places for breaks. Shout out if you need anything," she said. She knew she couldn't keep the same pace as them. It would frustrate her no end. At least this way she could keep occupied and help point out or avoid any obstacles.

The path narrowed, with what looked like sharp drops on each side. Due to the way it wound she had trouble seeing what lay too far ahead. It was a mix of rocks, short-cropped grass, and lots of dirt. There was a chill to the air, which felt refreshing while you moved, but would set in deep if you were still.

Lara felt the urge to push further forward to see what lay behind each bend. But she had to restrain herself. Otherwise she would bound too far ahead and be unable to hear any cries for help. So, she reined herself in, albeit with difficulty.

Her stomach rumbled but she ignored it. There were more important things to focus on. The clouds seemed closer now, and there were some strange grey puffs rising in the distance. Lara stopped quickly and looked closer.

That's not clouds. Maybe smoke?

Fighting the urge to run ahead and investigate, she turned and rushed back to find the others.

They were seated in the middle of the path. There was nothing to rest on.

"Sorry, we couldn't make it anywhere more sensible. It's been a long day already," Vincent said.

"Don't apologise, I wish I could help more. Should I swap with one of you?" Lara said.

"No, it's fine. We are in a rhythm now, and it would be good to have you fresh. Anything ahead?"

"I think I've spotted some smoke in the distance. Which could mean some sort of settlement. Maybe a village?"

"It has to be. We should press on and see if we can get there before dark," Alyx said. She grimaced and looked away. Lara looked over at Alrion.

"Is she alright?" she mouthed to him. He shook his head slowly.

"You've rested enough surely, Alrion. Don't let your father's age slow you down," Lara said. She wanted to break the mood. Alrion at least laughed.

"You're right. This ground is too cold for my liking anyway. Up we get," Alrion said. With another great effort they lifted Alyx up and started moving.

"Pick up the pace a bit?" Lara said. Alrion nodded and Vincent complied. Alyx looked pained but went along with it.

"Not far now, just keep it up," Lara said. She had no idea how far it was; the terrain being deceptive, but she knew that if they stopped again, it might be the last stop for a while.

~

Lara pushed forward again.

"Just one more bend," she told herself. The sight and smell of the smoke had strengthened which meant they were getting closer. She had started to wonder if perhaps the village was under attack, but dismissed the thought. That was just pessimistic thinking. It was going to be a collection of hearth fires that they could be warmed by.

Lara rounded the corner and almost cheered. Ahead there was a large wooden gate, and behind it a small village. There were several pillars of smoke rising up from houses. Some big and some small. They were roughly constructed out of stones but looked like they had been there a long time.

Finally, a place to rest.

She felt guilty because she'd had an easy time of it comparatively and still felt tired. It had been a draining day.

"Time to pass on the good news." Lara raced back to find the others. They were still mobile, which was a relief.

"Don't stop now, there's a village just beyond us," she said. She saw Alrion's shoulders instantly perk up. The weight he must've felt had been lessened.

"You heard her, let's finish strong," Alrion said. With a visible effort he shifted his hold and held Alyx even higher. She was practically being carried now. Vincent did the same and they almost doubled their speed.

"That's more like it. Don't drop her!" Lara said. This time she kept pace with them, keeping an eye on their progress and helping them maintain the pace. As they returned to where she had spotted the village she watched for Alrion's reaction.

"I've never seen a more welcoming place," he said with a laugh. Lara hoped that the village would be as welcoming as they all wanted it to be. But with a small village in a remote location, you never could tell. They had to knock on that giant door and find out. Just a few hundred more agonising steps to go.

"You can do the honours," Vincent said when they finally reached the gate. The huge wooden doors hung on titanic steel hinges. The wood was weathered by the elements and had a metallic rectangular slot in the middle of the right door. Lara walked up and rapped loudly just below the slot.

"Hello! We have an emergency and need to enter!" Lara shouted. She waited for a response.

"Hello!" she shouted again. The metallic panel slid open but Lara couldn't see anything through it.

"We aren't expecting visitors," a man said. He must have been standing near the opening.

"We didn't know we had to send word. We need immediate attention for one of our party. We must get to your Healer as soon as possible," Lara said.

"I'm sorry I can't allow that. There's been too many strange happenings lately, the gates are closed. You can make your case tomorrow when the town magistrate is accepting submissions for entry," the man said. He didn't sound particularly sorry. More annoyed that he was being disturbed.

"We have someone in dire need of attention. Your Healer will vouch for us," Lara said. She was gambling a bit, but needed something. They couldn't afford to wait outside all night.

"If you know the Healer, then what's her name?" the man said. He sounded doubly annoyed now. At least Lara was getting somewhere.

"I haven't met this Healer, but we were sent ahead by another Healer. Freyda from Rolyntide."

"Prove it."

"Well, she gave us directions. Said we could find help here on our way. How else do you think we found you?" Lara said. She was grasping at straws now, but she had little choice. Something had to work.

"There's only one main path, you would have found us anyway. I need more than that. Otherwise you can sleep out under the stars," the man said. He sounded like he was looking forward to that being the conclusion of their business. Lara looked over at the group. Alyx was struggling with something.

"Take the amulet," she said weakly. Alrion and Vincent adjusted their stance, and Lara came in close. She unclasped the amulet and dangled it into the hole in the door.

"She gave us this to help us on our way. Show that to your Healer and she will insist we come inside," Lara said. The man roughly grabbed the amulet from her hands and she heard him walk off.

"I hope this works," Alrion said.

"I think there's a good chance," Vincent said. "Alyx has good instincts."

"Well, if it doesn't I'm sure I can climb over this wall. Plynth was much higher," Lara said, chuckling. She managed to get a smile out of Alrion.

Good, he's still alright, she thought. Alyx looked terrible though. It was like she had expended all her energy and willpower getting here, and now she had nothing left. Lara felt bad for the animosity between them.

Why does she rub me the wrong way so badly?

Before she could ponder further, footsteps approached. And another sound. Metal clanking, and bars being drawn back. The doors started to lurch open with a creaking roar. A simply dressed guard stood before them. He looked less armoured than the ones they had encountered elsewhere and was suitably unimpressed at having to open the doors.

"You can enter. Take the first right and enter the house with the vines crawling the walls. That's the Healer's residence," he said.

"What about our amulet?" Lara said.

"The Healer will return it if she believes you obtained it lawfully. Otherwise I'll be around to throw you out," the guard said. It sounded like he would enjoy that, even though it would require him to do something. Lara didn't want to push their luck.

"Sounds fair, sorry for the trouble," she said. The guard shook his head and walked off.

"That was quite restrained of you," Alrion said.

"Well, we can't mess around right now. I'll make up for it later," she said. Alrion shook his head at the thought and Lara bounded ahead.

"Just a bit further," Lara said, urging them on. The main road was paved with cobblestones which were uneven and worn down. The entry to the village had a few houses and buildings packed in close, but as they turned the corner the houses started to spread out more. The Healer's house was easily spotted, as there was nothing around it. It spanned two levels and was the only one with a mess of vines wrapped around it.

I'll have to ask about that, Lara thought. It seemed at odds with the surroundings. She went ahead, and rapped smartly on the red, wooden door. After a delay she was about to knock again when she thought she heard footsteps.

"Who is it?" a female voice said from within.

"It's the travellers who brought the amulet. We have a critical injury," Lara said. The door opened immediately and a young woman peered out. She looked only slightly older than Lara and had darker skin. She looked completely out of place with the local residents and the colder climate.

"I'm Lara. Older gentleman is Vincent, the other one is Alrion, and the sickly-looking woman is called Alyx."

"Beatrix. Please come in, I see she needs immediate attention. I have a special couch set up in the room next door," Beatrix said. The Healer walked off immediately. Lara waited for Alrion and Vincent to make a start, and she stepped back to close the door behind them.

So far so good. It felt good to finally be within some enclosed walls, and not stuck out in the cold wilderness.

I'm definitely a city girl.

Now they could get Alyx some help, and prepare for the next leg of their journey.

I just hope we make it in time. He has to make it, Lara thought as she joined the others.

14

POISON

Alyx felt an initial surge of relief as she lay down on the couch. She had been tense for hours, and it was the first time she could fully relax. The feeling was enough to temporarily overpower the extreme burning sensation in her legs.

"This is quite a serious burn, and strange in its application. What did this?" Beatrix said. She looked at them with concern.

"You wouldn't believe us if we told you," Lara said.

"Try me."

"It's from a wizard that was transformed into a Shade," Alrion said. Beatrix's eyes widened.

"That's not possible," she said.

"We've seen it twice now. It's plenty possible," Vincent added. Alyx just nodded, not adding any commentary. The pain was flaring up, so she clenched her teeth and tried to ignore it.

"Wizard fire is a bit different to normal fire. More intensity and it also attacks the nerves. Let me fetch something," Beatrix said. She disappeared into another room. Alrion came over and held Alyx's hand.

"You're almost there. She is going to help you. I had no idea that this was even worse than a normal burn," he said. Alyx nodded. But she realised he probably wanted a response so she swallowed hard and prepared to speak.

"It was the right decision. I can rest now," Alyx said. She closed her eyes. Another wave of pain assaulted her and she tried to compartmentalise her mind and shut out the feeling in her legs. She heard footsteps approaching and opened her eyes.

"This will help," Beatrix said. She was holding a clear jar with white contents.

"Remove the pants," Beatrix said. Alrion looked away in embarrassment and Vincent and Lara struggled to get Alyx's pants off. Before the intense pain Alyx had to laugh to herself at Alrion's response.

He forgets that I'm not a woman, I'm a weapon.

Although, it was nice for someone to think of her as something else. Lara and Vincent were rough, but efficient. Soon the cool air was a relief to Alyx's legs. She shuddered suddenly, as she felt an icy touch. She looked over and saw Beatrix applying the cream liberally.

"So. Cold," Alyx said. It was unbelievable, almost the exact extreme to what she had been feeling.

"It's necessary. Don't worry it will settle down soon," Beatrix said. She continued to apply the cream, and Alyx finally relaxed. The burning started to subside, and her legs started to feel numb.

"That should do the trick. It's lucky you got here when you did, the damage is not as bad as it could have been," Beatrix said. She pulled a light blanket over Alyx.

"How's that?" Beatrix said.

"Better," Alyx said. The feeling of relief was incredible. She had trained herself to ignore pain, and focus herself. But the effort was incredibly taxing, and she had had to fight through it to get here. But at last she could start to relax.

"Good. It will take time for your legs to heal enough to put weight on. Why don't you all go somewhere to stay for the night?"

"Shouldn't we stay here?" Alrion said.

"And where is here?" Lara said.

"This town? Highroad. There's nothing more you can do, and I don't need more people underfoot. I prefer a quiet home. Your friend will be quite safe," Beatrix said.

"We can't thank you enough. Why did you help us?" Alrion said.

"That amulet is very special. It would not have been handed over to you otherwise. Let's talk more tomorrow," Beatrix said. She walked off to the edge of the room pointing them back to the front door.

"We will return at first light," Alrion said.

"I'll have to wake you up for that to be true," Lara said. The group had a bit of a laugh then left. Alyx heard the door close and footsteps return.

"Just me. I'll bring you some water, then you should sleep. Your body needs that more than anything else right now," Beatrix said. Alyx nodded, it was too much effort to talk again. But the Healer seemed to understand that. Alyx closed her eyes, and the padding of returning footsteps alerted her.

"Here, drink slowly," Beatrix said. Alyx forced herself to drink slowly, even though she was incredibly parched. The water was cool and delicious. She felt like she noticed a slight aftertaste though.

"Sleep well. I'll be upstairs and I'll check on you later tonight," Beatrix said. Alyx was about to nod off, but forced out a few words.

"I am in your debt," she said.

"No, you are not. You have bigger problems than worrying about repaying me. Rest, and we can talk more tomorrow," Beatrix said. Alyx couldn't keep her eyes open any longer and fell into a deep sleep.

Alyx heard footsteps padding closer to her on the soft carpet.

Oh, it's Beatrix checking on me, she thought. She listened out for any words of comfort or reassurance but Beatrix was strangely silent.

That's odd.

She was too tired to worry about small details like that. She felt a metallic cup pressed up against her lips.

Beatrix could at least warn me.

Alyx started to sip on the contents when she caught a whiff of something. She lashed out her hand and grabbed Beatrix's arm. The fluid spilled everywhere and Alyx's eyes shot open.

"D ... Darkroot," Alyx stammered and looked at Beatrix in surprise. It was dark in the room and Beatrix was strangely silent. But struggling against the firm grip that Alyx had.

"You're. Not. Going. Anywhere," Alyx said, digging her nails in harder. As her eyes adjusted to the surroundings she saw that the dark shape before her didn't look like Beatrix.

"Who are you?" Alyx said. She started to feel her stomach churn. How much of the Darkroot had she drunk? Was this an assassin? The figure continued to struggle and started to change tactics. It reached over to drag Alyx off the couch. Alyx couldn't stop it, but tried to break her fall as well as possible. The figure started kicking her, using the leverage to break her grip. Arcs of pain shot through her arm, but she dismissed it. She had dealt with worse. And this was a matter of life and death.

"This is going to hurt," she told herself, and lashed out her legs. They were not responsive, given their stiffness and burns. But they did obey, and her assailant didn't notice them coming. She managed to trip over the assassin and roll over on top of it and pinned down one of its arms.

A sliver of light through the window illuminated its face. It looked like a man, probably Tainted. He had dark hair and black clothes. His face was snarling and she noticed some black marks on his face.

"Tainted? Who sent you?" she said.

"You know the answer to that. I won't let you take me," the Tainted said. He used his free hand to pull out a dagger and swung it at Alyx. She saw it coming, threw out her hand and stopped it just in time. She was staring at the point of the blade. They struggled, the Tainted trying to drive the dagger home and Alyx trying to drive it away. Her strength was not what it used to be, and she felt a thrumming and shuddering inside her.

Cursed Blight. Or Darkroot. Or both, she thought. The Tainted smiled a cruel grin, victory on his face.

"Not today," Alyx said. She brought her leg up and kneed the Tainted in the crotch. He cried out and Alyx used the distraction to force the dagger down into the Tainted's chest.

Panting, Alyx rolled off him. She turned her head to look over, and he appeared to be dying.

That's a shame, but I couldn't take the chance.

The effort had reignited the flaming pain in her legs, and her breathing was laboured.

"Beatrix!" Alyx shouted, then blacked out.

Alyx opened her eyes again. She tried to sit up, remembering what had happened. She was restrained and she looked around frantically. Beatrix was seated on a chair next to the couch.

"What's going on?" Alyx said.

"You mustn't move. That will help the Darkroot spread," Beatrix said.

"Do you have an antidote?"

"I'm making one. But it's not perfect, and time is against us. Hopefully you didn't consume too much."

"I noticed what it was immediately," Alyx said. She started coughing. Beatrix put a reassuring hand on her shoulder.

"You did well, I'm impressed that you survived that attack. What's going on here? I've never seen Tainted so aggressively pursuing someone already infected," Beatrix said. She gave Alyx a pointed look.

"We can explain later. But Alrion is the key. I don't matter, as long as he makes it," Alyx said.

"He doesn't seem to believe that, based on his behaviour before. What's so special about him?"

"That's his story to tell."

"Fair enough. You know what's going to happen to you, right?" Beatrix said.

"With the poison?"

"No, with the Blight. You don't have a lot of time. You need that amulet," Beatrix said. She pointed and Alyx realised that she was wearing it again.

"What can you tell me about it?"

"Nothing. It's a secret. Just keep it close. You're going to need all the help you can get. Have some rest. We can talk more in the morning. Unless you think there'll be another attack?"

"I doubt it. They seem to be more concerned with slowing us down."

"Very well. Sleep," Beatrix said. She placed a hand on Alyx's forehead, then walked away. Alyx watched her walk away then let herself drift off again.

Yet again I had a chance to die, but did not. What's my fate? Why am I still here? She thought as sleep took her.

~

"What's going on?" Alrion said. The concern in his voice was obvious. Alyx awoke and looked around. Everyone seemed to be back, and Alrion was talking to Beatrix.

"There was an attacker overnight. I have kept the body in the next room. She was poisoned with Darkroot, but I'm not sure how much. I've been working on an antidote, which I can administer soon," Beatrix said. She kept her cool in the face of Alrion's emotion.

"What does it do? The Darkroot?" he said.

"It kills," Alyx said. She could feel her temperature rising, and knew that the poison was doing something.

"Slowly, so we have time. You needn't worry I haven't seen any warning signs yet," Beatrix said. She left the room and Alrion rushed over to Alyx.

"I'm so sorry. Who did this?"

"Not sure, you should go look. He looked like a Tainted, from what I saw," Alyx said. She wanted to say more but started coughing.

"It's all my fault. Ever since you've been with us you've suffered," Alrion said.

"It's not on you, it's just the journey we are on. I signed up to this you know. Let the Healer do her work," Alyx said.

"You're wearing the amulet again," Lara said.

"Yes, Beatrix said it would help. But she wouldn't say more. Incredibly frustrating," Alyx said.

"I think there's a connection between them," Lara said.

"Perhaps. The amulet did seem to be important. Why don't you take a look at the attacker and see what you can find out?" Alyx said. She needed a break from all the attention, and was curious about the man. She'd never had anyone try and assassinate her in her sleep before. And she wondered why she had been targeted.

It must be because I'm already injured.

If that was the case, then the objective was definitely to slow them down.

Going to so much effort to capture us. It must mean a great deal, Alyx thought. But she was too tired to puzzle it out further. She heard noise from the other room.

"What is it?" she said as loudly as she could. Lara and Alrion rushed back.

"Are you sure?" Alrion said to Lara.

"No doubt about that. That's the Tainted one that escaped from the fight. The one that we thought was advising the leader."

"He's a sneaky one. Anything else unusual?" Alrion said.

"He had a strange mark on his hand."

"I'll go take a look," Vincent said. He had been sitting quietly in the corner and Alyx hadn't even noticed his presence. Beatrix entered swiftly, going directly to Alyx.

"Drink this quickly," she said. It was a white liquid in a small vial. Alyx sat up as much as possible and drank down the liquid. It was thick and milky but had no real flavour. She eased back down with a sigh.

"That's the antidote?" Alyx said.

"Close enough to one. It should purge all traces of the poison. But it will take a day or so for you to be considered safe," Beatrix said.

"I'm not comfortable with that," Alyx said.

"We can discuss it later. For now, you need to rest. I'm going to see what my father thinks about the attacker," Alrion said. He strode off into the next room.

"You know, I think they got more than they bargained for. They've thrown a monster at you, burned you, and tried to poison you. But you're still alive and kicking," Lara said.

"Still here."

"I'm glad that you are. But I'm beginning to think you can't be killed!" Lara said, a smile breaking out on her face. Alyx appreciated the attempt at humour, even though she was exhausted.

"If only to frustrate them, I will live on," Alyx said. She felt a coolness slowly washing over her. Hopefully the antidote was working. At least she felt a little better.

This better not be for nothing. I don't want to be healed just for the Blight to take me, Alyx thought. She looked over at Lara. A strange girl, but very skilled and very intelligent. She seemed familiar too. Alyx couldn't shake the thought.

I'll ask her about it later. For now, she had to sleep again. Her body needed to focus on its recovery.

15

THE TRACKER'S STAND

"**T**here's no doubt about it now," Tarren said. He slowed down and started walking slowly.

"You mean about them tracking you?" Celes said.

"Yes. Once they had reason to suspect me, there was not much I could do. They know I'm not on this assignment, and I'm operating on my own. They will attack soon."

"How do you know?"

"Because they are collectively blocking me. They don't want me to know they're coming."

"Do we need to make a stand?" Celes didn't like where this was going. First, Tarren had detected something dark going after Alrion. And now, they were under attack too.

"That would increase our chances of survival."

"Can we make it to Rolyntide? That's the next town, right?"

"I would not advise it. We would have to push hard to make it before we were attacked, and maybe we would not make it in time. And then we would be tired and in a poor position."

"That's a good point. I also wouldn't want to endanger innocents unnecessarily."

"They will not restrain themselves for anything. You must take that into account."

"So, let's find a place we can defend. Do you know this area at all?"

"Not well. We have to assume that we can't hide. And if we stop moving they will approach with caution. The only thing we have working for us, is that they don't know how many we are."

"Really? They won't expect you to be alone?"

"No. It would be very strange for me to act independently like this without some sort of other party involved."

"I would have thought if you knew what Alrion was up to, you would seek him out anyway."

"That is true, I am certainly dissatisfied enough to do so. But they will not think that. They are suspicious and in this case, they are right."

"Alright that's settled. Let's find a place where we have a fighting chance."

"Agreed. Let us travel a little slower and look for appropriate locations." Tarren walked at a normal pace and seemed preoccupied. Celes looked at their surroundings. They were travelling alongside a small forest. That had potential as a way to thin out any attackers.

"Do you think they will attack at night?"

"They prefer to. But they will know I can see them. We can't rule out an earlier strike."

"Now's the time, if there's anything else you can tell me. Are you armed?"

"I have only a dagger with me. However, I am quite strong, so I can use my body as well."

"Then we need to get them in close. And not get surrounded. The nearby woods are a good possibility."

"I had thought that too. Let's enter here," Tarren said. He pushed through some smaller shrubs and brushed a tree branch aside. He held it back, and Celes nudged the horse carefully and passed through as well. They ended up on a partial track that led deeper into the trees.

"Somewhere along here then."

"Yes. Keep your eyes open for a suitable location." Tarren swung his head from side to side slowly. Celes did something similar, analysing the surroundings for anything that would be useful.

I wish I was better outdoors. Vincent was always the woodsman among us.

But she would make do. Alrion was counting on her.

"This could do," Tarren said. He pointed out a side track. It was rough and mostly overgrown. But it was narrow with thick tree density either side.

"Let's try it." Celes followed closely behind. It felt closed in as they navigated down the track. Which was a good thing for what they needed. Although it gave her no comfort in the moment. The horse seemed uncomfortable as well. The track ended at a small clearing with a giant rock at the end.

"It's a dead end. At least we can't get attacked from behind," Celes said. She dismounted and tied up the horse.

"And there's a little extra room here, but not too much. We could avoid being overwhelmed with any luck." Tarren paced around the area, staring out into the surroundings. He removed his cloak and draped it over the horse.

Celes did an inventory of what she had on her. Two smoke vials, one poison and a vial of exploding powder. Not too bad.

"You any good at rigging traps?" Celes said.

"I know a little, from another time. Let me take a look," Tarren said. He set off down the track once more. He returned a bit later.

"Sorry, there's not enough to work with. I only have a dagger. We just need to wait."

"That's fine, it was worth a shot." Celes paced around the area. What would Vincent do? He'd probably find a way to rig some sort of log trap. But that was only a diversion really. It wouldn't take out any of the enemy.

"Now we wait," Celes said. She hated this part. But there was nothing else she could do. Tarren sat in the middle of the clearing, deep in concentration.

Hopefully he can give us some sort of warning.

Tarren stood quickly. He started to walk forward.

"What's going on?" Celes said. Tarren was unresponsive.

"Hey! Tarren!" Celes shouted. He kept walking. She ran over and slapped him hard on the face. He shook his head and turned to look at her. The expression on his face was strange. Almost inhuman. Like he wasn't present.

"Are they here? What are you doing?" Celes said. Tarren's eyes flickered and he seemed to see her once more.

"I was too deep, trying to find them. They were inside my mind. There's Trackers here. Probably more too. Thank you for shocking me back here. We have work to do." Tarren crouched down, looking down the track. Celes heard something approaching.

"Blighters," Tarren said without emotion. As the first two came through the track, they changed from single file to side by side as they reached the clearing. Tarren sped forward at incredible speed, taking out both Blighters with his dagger in a blur. They fell and he returned to Celes.

"They're just testing us and wasting time. Stay on guard." Tarren went back to a crouch and Celes nodded. She readied herself and thought about when to use her tools.

"Don't overanalyse, you'll know," she told herself. There was more rustling ahead and she noticed what looked like more Blighters. Many more.

"More time wasting," Tarren growled. As before he dashed in, taking down the Blighters quickly. He paused to wait for the next two to come through. But they parted and a blur of black sped between them. With a loud ringing the attack was parried by Tarren, but he suffered another strike on his leg. He retreated quickly.

Celes saw the attacker now. It was another Tracker. He seemed taller than Tarren, and his skin was completely black. She wasn't sure if it was more tattoos or some other effect.

"They're crafty, I'll give them that," Celes said. Tarren nodded but kept his attention on the other Tracker. The Tracker stepped back and four more Blighters ran into the clearing.

"They're yours," Tarren said. Celes didn't waste any time, she ran over to the closest one. She feigned an attack then struck out at the one next to it. The Blighter dropped quickly, letting out a cry as it did. The other three converged on Celes. She retreated a step, then kicked her leg out. Thud, thud, thud she connected hard with a few legs. Two Blighters went down, not seeing the attack. The third dived at Celes. She fell back throwing a dagger as she fell. The Blighter landed on her, twitched then became still. Her dagger had pierced its eye.

A bit of luck to start.

Celes pulled out the dagger and shoved the Blighter off. The other two were circling around, trying to flank her. Sparing a second, she glanced over at Tarren. He had two Trackers attacking him from different angles. He was in trouble.

They don't even care about me. It's about him.

Celes knew that she had to end this quickly so she could help him. She threw a smoke vial. It shattered and a large plume rose instantly. The smoke distracted and slowed the Blighters. She waited a moment for the smoke to spread, then went after one Blighter. Before it could realise she had snuck behind it. A quick strike to the neck and it went down.

The other Blighter was still noisy, and Celes had a good idea of where it was. She ran over and tried to be quiet. It worked well enough, that the Blighter wasn't aware of her presence until too late. It shouted something, but she launched herself at it with her knees, knocking the Blighter down then finishing it on the ground.

Panting, Celes stood and surveyed the scene. The smoke was starting to clear. Tarren seemed to be on his knees. Without thinking Celes threw the vial with the exploding powder. It shattered between the two Trackers, knocking them over. The sound of the explosion was almost deafening. But Celes didn't waste any time. She rushed to the nearest Tracker and aimed for its chest. Just as she landed on it, the Tracker grabbed her hands. It was preventing the knife from piercing its chest.

It's too strong.

The Tracker gave her an evil smile and started to overpower her. Suddenly it stopped all resistance and the dagger plunged into its chest. Celes looked up and saw that Tarren was there, holding the Tracker's head in his hands.

"Nice save," Celes said. Tarren didn't even acknowledge her, he was turning to view another threat. He fell to the ground, clutching his chest. Celes stood quickly and assessed. The other Tracker had taken the opportunity to stab Tarren.

This is our last chance.

Celes could see that the Tracker thought it had won. It looked to be mocking Tarren, as he struggled to remove the dagger. She crept up, trying to remain unseen. The Tracker spun quickly as she was upon it. But she had expected that. And unlike before she didn't go for the chest. She drove her dagger through its foot. The Tracker screamed out in pain. Celes kicked it down while it was distracted. Before it could stand Tarren was on it. He had removed the dagger and forced it into the Tracker's chest. It groaned, then went limp. Tarren staggered off. Celes ran after him.

"Are there more?" she said.

"No, that was it. More than you bargained for, right?"

"Yes. But we survived." Celes checked herself but had no injuries. Tarren looked to be in worse shape.

"You're still with me. You look pretty tough, we can work through this," she said. Tarren coughed and slumped to the floor. He was clutching his chest.

"Not. Good," he said, then coughed more. Celes grabbed her dagger and cut off a section of his cloak. She knelt and applied pressure to his chest wound.

"It's no use. It was deep enough. They know what they're doing."

"I've seen normal people survive worse. Don't be a baby," Celes said. She looked around for anything else she could use.

"You're good. I almost believe you. The problem is, that even if this doesn't kill me outright, I can't walk. I'm too weak and my leg is also injured." Tarren touched his leg with his hand and winced.

"We have the horse, it's fine," Celes said. She looked over and the horse was gone.

"What?" she said, confused.

"They're crafty. Always have a strategy. Even though they perished here, they achieved their objective. I'm as good as dead and you're crippled. You can never catch up now." Tarren's eyes closed.

"Hey, open those eyes. You can't die on me now. How am I going to keep tracking them?" Celes said. Tarren let off a raspy chuckle.

"I'm busy helping you. I need to concentrate." Tarren remained still. Celes kept pressure on the wound with her elbow and cut another long strip of cloak. She then tied it around his waist, keeping the cloth pressed hard against the wound.

"And now the leg," she said. It wasn't a deep cut, but it was right across the calf muscle. And it also went straight through the middle of his tattoos.

"I'll do what I can here," she muttered. Working quickly, she bound the wound as well as possible, to keep it together and limit the blood loss. Tarren moaned and tried to sit up.

"I feel a little under the weather," he said. He smiled. Celes knew that something was wrong.

"You're smiling. What's happening?"

"I have helped you. They're at, or near, a town called Highroad. You need to get there."

"Thank you. But I would prefer a guide."

"I'm sorry Celes, but your son Alrion is infected. There's no doubt." Tarren looked genuinely upset.

"He's got good help, and I'm sure he's got a plan. I just need your help to get there faster."

"It's no use. I don't have the energy to move. Or a way to get help. So, I'm going out my own way. I sent them a message."

"What do you mean?"

"I broadcast something that your son will definitely get. I told him that you are coming. The rest is up to you now." Tarren sighed and tried to lie down. Celes dragged him across the ground so that he could lean against the giant rock. He seemed more comfortable.

"That's better."

"You seem different. Are you really dying?" Celes felt terrible. She had convinced this tortured soul to help her, and now he was losing his life and his chance at a better one.

"Yes. It's very freeing. I don't have to worry anymore. I should have done this a long time ago."

"Done what?"

"Helped someone. That's my only regret. That I let my shame prevent me from being true to myself. But you have given me an opportunity to play a part. A part in creating the cure for the Blight. Your son will succeed."

"Thank you for saying that."

"I'm not just saying that. I have seen his mind. He struggles, but he has the fire to succeed. That makes me feel better."

"What can I do for you?" Celes said. She needed to do something. To recognise what had just happened. Tarren just smiled at her.

"Go find your son. He cannot succeed alone. I'm fine here. I can finally find peace. But you must go. It is a long way to travel on foot, and I can't let this be for nothing." Tarren waved Celes off and closed his eyes.

"Thank you, Tarren. I won't forget what you've done." Celes draped the cloak over him and turned to leave.

A noble spirit can survive within a cursed shell. There is hope for us all. Even you, my son. The infection is not the end. I'm coming Alrion, just keep fighting, she thought. She had a destination, and a path to follow. Nothing would keep her from her son.

16

THE HOUSE OF HEALING

Alrion pulled a chair over so he could sit near Alyx. She seemed peaceful but was starting to stir.

"She is doing well," Beatrix said.

"Good. We're going to be staying here with her until she can be safely moved," Alrion said. He gave Lara and his father a challenging look but they said nothing. He felt reassured by that and looked back at Alyx.

Another casualty of my quest.

Another reason he had to succeed. To make all this worthwhile. Alyx opened her eyes and looked around.

"I'm still here," she said.

"Yes, you are. We are too," Alrion said.

"How long has it been?"

"Not that long. It's only just after midday."

"I see. How long do I need to stay here?" Alyx said to Beatrix.

"It depends. It might be a few days, given your previous injuries and then the Darkroot. I certainly wouldn't encourage any strenuous activity then either."

"Days?" Lara blurted out. She seemed shocked.

"I hope you understand the seriousness of her injuries," Beatrix said.

"But we don't have days," Lara said. She looked over at Vincent and he shrugged.

"It's hard to say. This assassin and the Shade Wizard both came alone. It could be that Wraith and whomever he is with are still a way behind," he said.

"That's not an assassin. It's that Tracker, and he tried his hand at poisoning. Look at what we think he has done so far: tracked me, scattered our horses, escaped the battle, tracked us again, and poisoned Alyx," Alrion said.

"Let's assume that's correct. He's a special type of Tainted. Are you saying that's more reason for him to be working alone and in advance of other Tainted?" Lara said.

"Yes. It seems like a specialised set of skills, right? They wouldn't be able to keep up. Nor would he want them to if he needed to travel without being spotted," Alrion said.

"That does seem plausible. There's a lot of evidence to suggest a new type of Tainted. I've never heard of that before though," Vincent said.

"We never saw Shade Wizards before either. Now we've seen two!" Alrion said. He stood from the chair and paced around the room.

"Who is making these creatures?" Alyx said. Alrion stopped pacing and looked at her.

"That's the right question. Who could do that? Wraith can't do that, surely?" he said.

"I have no idea. This is way out of my experience," Lara said.

"You know, it could be one of those Generals of the Blight," Vincent said. He looked thoughtful. He walked over and sat on the far edge of Alyx's couch.

"When I encountered Rindale, many years ago, he did something unusual. He made this black tar come from his finger. And he said that he could control how the infection reacted to me. That's why he had me captured. He was able to control my conversion to Tainted," Vincent said.

"Didn't you say he was cleansed by your father's spell?" Alyx said.

"He had to have been. Maybe he's still around, maybe not. But if he could do that, maybe the others have special abilities too," Vincent said.

"What did the Skull King do that was special?" Lara said.

"He did seem to have particularly good control of Blighters and Tainted. But I think it was his extreme strength and resistance to damage. He was practically indestructible," Alyx said.

"How'd you kill him?" Lara said.

"With my family's sword. It was special," Alyx said. She stopped talking and offered no further details. After a pause, Vincent continued.

"Let's assume then that there's someone out there who can create new types of Tainted, and it's not Wraith. Maybe that same person is working with Wraith. Another Shade Wizard attacked us recently. Maybe Wraith needs to be involved though," he said.

"Which is why he can't catch up as easily? He's trying to create more like him at the same time?" Alrion said.

"It's just a theory," Vincent said. He stood and walked around the room.

"I must admit, this is a strange conversation to be witnessing," Beatrix said. Alrion felt embarrassed, he had forgotten that she was even there.

"I'm sorry, we were a bit carried away there. Given all your help, I feel like I should at least explain what we're doing. Especially since we may be placing you in danger too. Alyx, you can listen in, and hopefully you can fill in any gaps," Alrion said. Beatrix brought another chair in and joined them. Alrion looked around to ensure everyone was ready, and started from the beginning.

"That's quite a story. Thank you for sharing it with me," Beatrix said.

"Thank you for saving Alyx," Alrion said.

"Thank me when she's walking again. Although I suspect it won't be that long. There are still things that I cannot tell you, but I will say this. I don't think the Mystics can help you, not the way you think. But that should not prevent you from seeking them out."

"That's interesting," Alrion said. He stood and stretched his legs. It wasn't something that he wanted to hear. He was relying on the Mystics to cure him and Alyx. But at the same time Beatrix had not said the Mystics couldn't help him.

"Can you tell us about them?" Lara said.

"No, I cannot. I just know they exist."

"Still sounds like more stories," Alyx said.

"Stories that will save you," Alrion said.

"I don't think I have that much time. Neither do you. Be honest, Beatrix, how long until I could walk out of here and be well enough to ride a horse," Alyx said. Beatrix looked away, a concerned look on her face. She turned back to face Alyx.

"At least another day, if not more. I need to monitor your progress to give you more certainty. But definitely no sooner than that. You need time," she said. Beatrix had an apologetic look on her face.

"That's too long. Even if Wraith is delayed, and he's sending attackers ahead to slow us down, he can't be that far behind. We will be swamped. And we must be days away from the Mystics. It doesn't work," Alyx said.

"What are you suggesting?" Alrion said. He didn't like where this was going.

"I should stay here. Rest up, and slow them down when they arrive. You can go ahead, and get to the Mystics safely. It can be my final service to you." Alyx stared at Alrion. She looked a mixture of defiant but resigned to her fate. Alrion shook his head.

"I don't accept that. Not after everything we have done to get here."

"We've already been delayed getting to this point. Another day or two has to be too dangerous," Lara said. She sounded exasperated. Alrion looked to Vincent.

"We seem to be getting stuck on this again and again. Is there a point at which you would leave her behind?" he said to his son quietly. Alrion thought about it.

"No."

"You would risk everything we have done?" Vincent said.

"Yes. If I can't save her, why should I save myself?" Alrion said. He hated having to justify his actions over and over. He knew they weren't being callous, but he couldn't accept leaving her behind. He had failed Falric already. He wouldn't fail Alyx.

"We can't change your mind?" Lara said. She didn't look angry, just sad. Alrion didn't understand why.

"No, you can't. I admit, I'm a burden right now. I can't help you much with anything. Especially with these new types of attackers. But I've taken on this quest at the cost of everything else. And I have to feel like I am comfortable with every decision on the way. And I won't abandon anyone to save myself," he said. Alrion looked around at them, and waited for a response. He finally rested his gaze on Alyx. She noticed him looking at her.

"I won't bring it up again. Beatrix, how can we accelerate my healing?" Alyx said. The Healer grabbed a lock of hair and twirled it as she thought.

"I could make you a sleeping potion. That may make the difference. Your body can just focus on healing."

"Are there any dangers with that?" Alrion said.

"None, providing I get the dose right. I'll go work on it now," Beatrix said. She left the room immediately.

"So, what do we do now?" Lara said.

"We need to prepare our defences. And no more staying at the inn," Vincent said.

"Good point. We have to assume they know where we are. If that assassin was a Tracker and found us, it makes sense that he reported back with the location."

"We just don't know how far behind they are, and what's coming," Lara said.

"Is there a way we can reverse track them? Since they can track us?" Alyx said.

"That's a great idea," Lara said. She looked at Alrion for confirmation.

"Well, we aren't as concerned about hiding our location. Maybe there's a chance I can do something. From everything they have said, it sounds like the method of communication they use works both ways. But it is probably harder to broadcast than it is to receive," Alrion said. He rubbed his chin thoughtfully and pondered it further. He hadn't really considered trying to use the Blight communication to his advantage.

Wraith had been a big proponent of it, even when he was still Branthor. There was no reason Alrion couldn't try something. He sat down and concentrated. He let his mind go clear, and tried to amplify the various noises that he was so used to dampening. Slowly but surely, he could hear more come through. It seemed too garbled though.

Alrion strained harder, trying to accept and navigate through all the possible sources of communication. He remembered what he had stumbled upon before and decided to use it as focus. The word wizard.

It took a few minutes of concentration, but slowly he started to notice something. The noise started to drift away. Like it was being blocked. And he was soon listening to nothing at all.

What's going on?

He had done something, that much was clear. But he didn't know why focusing on the word wizard would have that effect. Either way, if he could keep up this type of concentration in an ongoing fashion, at least it would give him peace and quiet.

That would be worth it, he thought. And it would be a good way to practice exercising his Will. He had ignored it since his time at the temple, and that was probably a poor choice. He had so few tools at his disposal right now, but potentially Will was the strongest and least compromised.

I'll continue this approach no matter if there's results or not, he thought. Suddenly out of the silence he heard something.

Wizard. Location. Tonight.

Alrion was stunned. He regained his composure and focus and kept listening.

Four. Trackers. Party. Approved.

Alrion kept listening, trying to find out more. But there was nothing else. Before he broke the news to his companions, he tested ways to keep alert. He found that he could at a less intense level keep that kind of filter open in his mind. He might not get all, but he would get some much-deserved silence and hopefully catch other messages concerning him.

Alrion opened his eyes and looked around. Alyx was sound asleep. Lara and his father were watching him with curiosity.

"What's going on?" Lara said.

"I have news. I found a way to listen in on their communication. And it's as you suspected."

"What?" Lara said.

"There's a team of four Trackers coming tonight. We need to prepare," Alrion said. Lara looked shocked, and his father was similarly surprised. Alrion felt some of his old confidence coming back.

I've found a way to contribute again, he thought with great relief. Now he just had to figure out how to help in the coming attack.

17

A DIFFICULT CONVERSATION

Lara regained her composure quickly.

"That's disturbing to hear, but great that you found that out. We can prepare," she said.

"Alyx managed to take out one by herself, so we have a chance," Vincent said.

"Especially since we know they're coming. Do we know how the other one managed to get in?" Alrion said.

"Lara would be best placed to determine that. Why don't you two look into that, I'll find Beatrix and fill her in," Vincent said. Lara watched Vincent walk off and beckoned to Alrion.

"Let's start here. This is where Alyx was lying. The attacker approached here, and tried to poison her."

"And mostly succeeded. Then they had a confrontation," Alrion said, pointing to the carpet next to the couch.

"Exactly. So, what are the most direct ways into this room?" Lara said. She looked around. They weren't far from the front door, but she didn't expect that to be the place of entry. Someone would have likely heard that. But, it was only Alyx and Beatrix. It was worth investigating.

"Let's start with the front door and see if we can eliminate that as an entry point," Lara said. Alrion nodded and followed along. They walked swiftly to the front door and examined it.

"Looks solid," Alrion said, feeling the wood with his hands. Lara inspected the lock. It was a standard lock, and didn't look to have obvious signs of tampering.

"It's not a complex lock, but it looks normal. We will have to ask your father if he found any lock picking tools on the other attacker," Lara said.

"Good idea. You don't think there's another way to open this door quietly without damaging it?"

"Not unless they can turn their fingers into keys," Lara said with a laugh. Alrion gave her a confused look.

"I'm not suggesting that," she said.

"I don't know what is and isn't possible these days," he said. Lara could understand the sentiment.

"True, but let's assume not for the time being." Lara walked back the way they had come, and pointed out the staircase.

"The staircase is not far from the room where Alyx is staying. It could be an option."

"Doesn't Beatrix stay upstairs?" Alrion said.

"I believe so. That would only make sense if the Tracker was so focused on Alyx that it snuck past her and ignored her. It seems less likely, but not impossible." Lara personally wouldn't have risked that sort of approach herself. Not if there was a more direct way.

"Isn't that assuming the Tracker knew exactly where she was?" Alrion said.

"Yes, that's a fair point. But let's exhaust this floor first," Lara said. She pointed down the corridor and Alrion followed.

"There's two rooms here. Let's try the one on the left first," she said. Lara opened the door and stepped inside. It had a large window and was filled with shelves full of different jars. Some were full of coloured liquids, others were empty.

"There isn't much space here," Alrion said. He pointed at the large quantity of tables and boxes littered throughout the space.

"And the potential for a lot of noise if coming through here in the dark. But there is a window," Lara said. She carefully navigated the mess and stood under the window. It could be pushed open and there was no lock.

"It would be tricky, but you could open this from the outside," she said.

"So that's an option we need to consider," Alrion said.

"Yes. Let's try that other room," Lara said. She weaved back through the many tables and boxes and squeezed past Alrion to reach the corridor.

"Let's see what's in here," Lara said. She opened the door and stepped inside. The room was almost empty. She saw a small mattress in the corner and another large window. The only other thing of note was a cheap rickety table pushed against a wall.

"This has potential," Alrion said.

"I agree. Especially if this window is the same style," Lara said. She walked over and inspected it.

"Yes, it's the same. My guess is that the Tracker came in through this room."

"We'll have to ask Beatrix if this window was left open," Alrion said.

"And get her opinion on upstairs too. For now, let's return to Alyx." Lara led the way again. She found Vincent and Beatrix talking near Alyx's sleeping form.

"Here they are. I just briefed Beatrix on the attack," Vincent said.

"We think the spare room with the bed was the most likely place of entry for the Tracker that poisoned Alyx. Was the window open?" Lara said.

"Yes, it was. I couldn't remember if I had left it open or not. The room is rarely used so I often air it out. Sorry, I should have mentioned that," Beatrix said.

"That's fine, don't worry. This is your home, not a fortress. We are incredibly grateful for you extending your hospitality this far," Vincent said.

"On that point, I don't think we should reinforce the house. In fact, we should do the opposite. We should make the entries we wish to defend look inviting. And at the same time reduce the chances of collateral damage," Lara said. Vincent looked like he was thinking it over. She was pretty sure he would agree.

"Don't concern yourselves about the house. It's just a building. Your lives are more important, and we need to stop these creatures," Beatrix said.

"No, Lara is right. If we do anything to give them pause they will know we are prepared and may change their plans. This is the best course. We just need to confer on how best to proceed," Vincent said.

"What about Alyx? Should she stay asleep?" Alrion said. Lara hadn't thought of that, but it was a good point. They had to balance the rate of Alyx's recovery against what she could contribute to the fight.

"It may be too risky to let her sleep through, even though she's not going to be expected to participate," Lara said. She walked over and sat on the end of Alyx's couch. She looked across the room, seeing what entry points she could observe.

"Agreed. She needs to be alert so she can at least protect herself," Alrion said.

"Then let's wake her up next time, that makes sense. Beatrix?" Vincent said, looking at the Healer.

"In an hour or two the effects of the drink should be wearing off, that's the best time."

"Let's reconvene then," Vincent said.

"I'll sit in the spare room and see if I can figure out anything more about the attack," Alrion said. Lara watched him go and approached Vincent.

"What do you intend to do?" she said.

"Nothing too fancy, just set up a good defensive position. Although, I was thinking maybe we can get something for Alyx. Perhaps a crossbow. That could make the difference," he said.

"Great idea. She is supposed to be a weapon master after all. I'll focus on downstairs and what we can do to alter the conditions," Lara said. Vincent nodded and walked over to the front door. Lara left Alrion alone and busied herself making preparations for an attack.

Beatrix ran down the stairs sooner than Lara expected.

"What's wrong?" Lara said.

"There's a presence here already. I can sense it. In the spare room."

"Alrion is there." Lara felt her stomach lurch then ran towards the spare room. Beatrix was close behind. The door was closed, so Lara shoved it open and dashed inside. The room was the same, and the window was still closed. Alrion sat cross-legged in the middle of the room. He looked up in a daze.

"I don't get it," Lara said, looking at Beatrix.

"It's you. What are you doing?" Beatrix said to Alrion. She sounded horrified.

"I'm tuning into the Blight communication to try and get more details on their attack," Alrion said.

"Stop that immediately. It's way too dangerous!" Beatrix shouted. Alrion looked over at Lara, his face a picture of confusion.

"Do as she says. She ran all the way down here because she sensed Tainted. And it was you. Don't you think that's kind of scary?" Lara said. Alrion closed his eyes and the tension disappeared from his body. He slumped down.

"Seriously? My one way of helping out and now that's outlawed too?"

"You are hastening your infection. I don't know how to describe it, but it's like you're inviting it in. It's so much worse than before!" Beatrix said. She sounded distraught.

"Maybe we should just get it over with then," Alrion said. Lara ran over and slapped him as hard as she could.

"I think you have this covered, I'm going back upstairs," Beatrix said. She left quickly and once she was gone Lara closed the door.

"What were you thinking? Have you lost your mind?" Lara said.

"It was just a comment. I'm not serious, I'm just so sick of being afflicted and powerless," Alrion said. He was nursing his cheek with his hand.

"It's not just a comment. Saying that, and seeing what Beatrix said; it's clear that this is affecting you deeply. You've already admitted to bursts of anger, some coordination issues, and now this negative defeatist thinking. This is not you!" Lara said. The exasperation was hard to contain. Because he was amongst it he was not seeing it the same way as her.

"I'll think about it. At the least I'll stop occupying that headspace. It's probably true that immersing myself in their communication and thinking, is affecting my own thinking."

"It's doing more than that. You need to buy us time, not squander it. Especially since you insist on staying here with Alyx. You owe it to us all." Lara didn't know what to do with him. She wanted to give him sympathy and a comforting hug, but it didn't feel like what he needed.

"Look, it's hard. I'm just travelling along, hoping that we find these Mystics who can help. And I'm being hounded every step of the way, with new and difficult obstacles. And Wraith himself is on his way. I don't think I'm strong enough to escape again." Alrion's voice became much quieter. Lara knew she was finally getting to the heart of it.

"He defeated you at the peak of your power. And you are scared of facing him again when you don't even have that?"

"Of course. Wouldn't you be?"

"You're not getting another chance to face him alone. It will be different this time. You'll be different by the time you need to face him again."

"If you insist," Alrion said, grinning.

"I do insist. Now let's go see how Alyx is going," Lara said. She held out her hand and Alrion grasped it firmly, standing with her help. He staggered a bit, and she caught him in her arms.

"I knew you were falling for me," she said playfully. He turned a bit red and smiled at her. She chuckled and released him, walking out of the room. Alrion followed close behind.

They found Alyx awake with Beatrix offering another drink of some kind.

"Why am I up?" Alyx said.

"We've another attack coming tonight," Lara said, Alyx finished drinking and nodded.

"At least we know this time. What's coming?"

"Four Trackers. The same as the one that tried to poison you," Alrion said. He walked over and stood next to the couch.

"Sounds fun. I'd like to give them a piece of my mind. I am not impressed with the poisoning," Alyx said. She looked over her body, a perplexed look on her face.

"Any change?" Beatrix said.

"No, not really. Which I suppose is to be expected. But I want to be more active in this fight."

"I thought you might say that. I've a present for you," Vincent said from afar. He stepped into the room and held up a simple but effective crossbow.

"Hand it over," Alyx said. It was like a new energy had entered her. She sat up straight and started checking the weapon over immediately. The winding mechanism, the bolt placement, and strength of the structure.

"This will do fine. I hope there's something I can fire too," she said.

Vincent handed her a leather pouch full of simple bolts.

"You know how to use that right?" Alrion said.

"Of course. I told you I was a weapon master remember. It's not just an empty title. I trained in and mastered all weapons."

"Why not just focus on the sword?" Lara said.

"I had my reasons for needing a variety of weapons. But that aside, mastery of a weapon also helps understand how to counter it."

"Would you like to coat the bolts with something?" Beatrix said.

"No, it's probably better not to. Just in case there's friendly fire."

"Friendly fire? I thought you said you knew how to use that," Alrion said. He had taken a step back.

"Anything can happen in a fight, never forget that. Don't worry I'll be careful."

"Maybe I can defend a different room," Alrion said with a

chuckle. Lara shook her head. At least he was cracking jokes. He seemed a bit more like his old self. But the more she watched him; she could see something under the surface. He was definitely dealing with a lot. Alyx seemed to be handling the infection better, although she was not as far along.

"Time to finish our preparations, eat, and wait for dark," Vincent said. There were no arguments and Vincent walked them through the initial plan.

~

All was quiet. Lara peered out the window again. The moon was high in the sky, and lit the surroundings well.

Maybe they won't come.

She had taken up a position in the spare room that they thought the first Tracker had come through. When she wasn't peering out the window, she was hidden from view. Nobody entering would spot her.

With any luck I can take one down for free, she thought. But her nerves were starting to fray. She had been waiting for what seemed like hours. On edge. As her mind started wandering again she heard a light patter on the ground. She looked around and saw nothing. She had purposefully left the door ajar and almost closed. It started to open slowly by itself.

No way. It's invisible?

There was no time to second-guess. She threw a dagger at what she thought was where the back of the Tracker had to be. It embedded into nothing, and she heard a cry of pain. The dagger was quickly dislodged, but not without some blood spilling.

Got you!

But she needed to alert the others.

"They're here. At least one is invisible!" Lara shouted. There was no more benefit to be gained by pretending they were caught unaware. If all four were invisible it would be hard to contend with them. Lara dashed out of the room trying to track the one she had injured.

Lara saw a few drops of blood in the corridor near the other spare room. She crept over and fully opened the door. The moonlight spilled into the middle of the room, illuminating one of the few places to stand in the mess. She could see the outline of the figure.

It's not perfect. Light still shows it.

The Tracker didn't seem to be fully aware of her presence, or it was preoccupied with the wound.

No time for games. Just end it and move on.

Lara placed one foot in front of the other. Desperately looking for any signs that the Tracker was aware. She imagined that it was trying to patch up the wound. Once she had closed the gap Lara dropped all pretence at stealth. She loudly crossed the remaining distance. The silhouette of the Tracker changed shape, suddenly readying itself. But Lara was upon it too quickly. Before it could do much, she had her Runesteel dagger plunged into what she thought was its chest. They both fell, Lara looking for signs of life.

Whatever effect had been hiding the Tracker was slowly reverting. It looked like a normal man. She had indeed pierced its chest, but it wasn't dead. Lara debated what to do next, but her thoughts were interrupted. She heard a scream from the other room. Lara retrieved her dagger and ran to investigate.

18

FURTHER NORTH

A lrion noticed the shape too late. As he drew his sword he felt strong hands around his throat.

I don't believe it, was his only thought. He was too surprised to think properly, and his air was steadily running out. The strength started to drain from him.

"Turn around!" Alyx shouted. Alrion understood what she meant. He dropped his sword and threw his weight around in a desperate attempt to turn. He wasn't sure it was enough but heard the crossbow bolt fire with a distinctive sound and thud into whoever was holding him. The grip relaxed and Alrion shoved it off. As he peered into the darkness to determine what it was he felt a stabbing pain in his leg.

"Argh!" Alrion screamed, the pain taking him by surprise. He scrambled around for his sword and plunged it into the shape. It stopped moving and he stumbled back trying to see how he had been wounded. He heard Lara shouting out.

"Too late for that warning," he muttered to himself. If she had found one, that meant there were two more lurking somewhere.

"Lights!" Alyx shouted. Vincent handed her his single torch.

"I'll get more," he said, and ran upstairs.

"Stay close to me, we've got a chance if we can spot them," Alyx said. Alrion shuffled closer. He could still feel something in this leg but didn't want to lose focus investigating it too much.

"Here take this," Alyx said, handing Alrion the torch. "I need my hands free. You can still swing with your other arm."

"Sure," Alrion said. He felt comforted by the heat of the torch, and swung it slowly back and forth to illuminate the room. The small hearth in the corner had long since burnt out, and only some smouldering coals remained.

We weren't prepared for this.

There had been ample light available to deal with normal attackers. They had even hoped the dimness would work in their favour, since they were ready and waiting. But it had done the opposite. Alrion spotted a blur of something out of the corner of his eye and lashed out with the sword. Nothing connected. He slowly approached the area, swinging the torch rhythmically.

I just need something to work with.

The pain ran up his leg but he ignored it. He was more concerned about not getting choked again.

"Behind you!" Alyx shouted. Alrion whirled as quickly as he could, leading with his sword and following up with the torch. He hit nothing, but did notice some movement as a shape tried to slip past him. He frantically lashed out with the torch, hoping to catch something. The flames showed the figure briefly, but weren't enough to set it alight.

Alrion tried to reorient himself so he could attack it properly, but it was too fast. A sudden noise startled him and he heard a crossbow bolt impacting the Tracker. It fell to the ground and Alrion rushed in with his torch. He watched carefully, using his torch to see better.

"It's cloaked in shadow," Alrion said. He couldn't believe it. The Tracker struggled, and looked to be reaching for something. Alrion was about to finish it with his sword but hesitated.

Maybe we can learn something.

He watched the Tracker to make sure it couldn't move significantly, then turned his attention to the stairs. His father was running down with two torches.

"There!" Alrion shouted, pointing with his torch. There was another shape creeping by the stairs, looking to pounce on Vincent. As Vincent whirled to face the threat, Lara was already there. She stabbed the Tracker with her dagger then quickly knelt to finish the job. Alrion rushed over, as fast as his leg would allow.

"Is it over?" he said.

"Lara?" Vincent said.

"That should be all four. Let's check," she said. They returned to Alyx. The one that had stabbed Alrion was still motionless on the ground.

"And one more over here," Alrion said. But as he approached something looked wrong.

"Hang on, I'm sure it was here," Alrion said. He waved the torch over, inspecting the ground. There was a crossbow bolt on the ground, it's end soaked in blood. Alrion picked up the bolt and turned it around in his hand.

"It still lives," Lara said. Alyx cursed.

"You should have finished it," Alyx said.

"I thought we could get information. It was originally a person, right?" Alrion said. He thought his instincts were right, but was starting to doubt himself.

"It was worth a try. And yes, nothing we have learned suggests that they still aren't infecting people to create these new variants of Tainted. Don't worry about it," Vincent said.

"You're injured!" Lara said, looking at Alrion.

"Yes, one of them stabbed me in the leg." Alrion sat down on a chair and properly examined his leg. The dagger was halfway up his calf muscle, and was well embedded.

"You were walking around with this?" Lara said.

"I didn't see any other choice," Alrion said.

"Oh no, I'm just impressed."

"If we're sure it's safe, I'll go fetch Beatrix. We need to treat that wound immediately. Anything else she needs to know about?" Vincent said.

"Not me," Lara said.

"Nothing here, well nothing new," Alyx said. Vincent nodded and disappeared up the stairs again.

"That crossbow sure came in handy," Alrion said.

"I knew it would. I wish we had known about their strange invisibility beforehand. I never noticed on the original attacker," Alyx said.

"Maybe because you were asleep he never activated it. It's quite unusual, it was like they were cloaked in shadows," Alrion said.

"That sounds appropriate when you think about it. But I'm amazed that it's even possible," Lara said. She brought over another chair and sat next to Alrion. When Vincent and Beatrix arrived, she moved the chair back to make space.

"Good, you're seated. This is going to hurt," Beatrix said. She had a bag of supplies, which she placed, on the floor near Alrion. She knelt and inspected the wound.

"Drink this," Beatrix said. She handed Alrion a small flask and he took a swig. It burned his throat and he started coughing.

"What is that?"

"My own concoction. It'll take the edge off."

"The edge off what?" Alrion said. He received an answer immediately. A wrenching pain went through his leg, and for an instant he couldn't handle it. The pain subsided and he opened his eyes, not realising he had closed them. Beatrix had removed the dagger and placed a cloth over the wound. She handed the dagger to Vincent who looked it over.

"Look at this," he said to Lara. She peered over his shoulder and examined it.

"Is there something on the tip? Is it poisoned?" she said.

"I don't think so. I've seen something like it before."

"What is it?"

"If I'm right, it's a liquid form of the Blight," Vincent said. That got Alrion's attention.

"What? You can get infected from a dagger?" Alrion couldn't believe it.

"I believe so. I've only seen it once. That was how they infected me. I think only the generals can do it. This doesn't bode well,"

Vincent said. He looked worried. Alrion could understand why. Wraith was bad enough, but to have one of those generals of the Blight involved too was terrible news.

"Seems to go with the whole idea that they're making these Trackers, right?" Alrion said. Vincent nodded.

"But why would they try and infect me again?"

"It could be that they wish to speed up the process. I wonder if it's working?" Vincent said. He looked over the dagger more.

"Is there any way of telling how much was on it?" Lara said.

"I don't think so."

"I'm just about done here," Beatrix said. She set aside her ointments and wrapped the bandage around Alrion's leg a little tighter.

"How's that feel now?"

"Much better," Alrion said. It was more of a dull pain now. He didn't want to test walking on it again just yet though.

"They've really worked you two over. Injured and infected," Lara said.

"It must be because we're the biggest threat," Alrion said, trying to keep things light. He got a small smile out of Lara and his father. Alyx didn't seem impressed.

"We need to rotate a sentry overnight in case they attack again," she said.

"I'll do it. You can all rest," Vincent said.

"No, its fine. Let me take a turn," Lara said. Vincent thought for a moment then responded.

"I'll wake you then. Thanks again for your help, Beatrix. And apologies for what we've done to your home."

"I wish I could say it's not your fault. But at least you're polite about it. Just make sure you deal with those bodies. This is my house!" Beatrix said.

"I'll take care of it. See you in the morning," Vincent said. Beatrix nodded and walked back upstairs.

"Everyone else get some sleep. You're fine with the spare room with the bed?" Vincent said to Lara.

"Not a problem."

"Good. Let's hope we can make a move sometime tomorrow," Vincent said. Alrion used some cushions to make himself comfortable on the floor. He wasn't sure if it was his imagination or not, but he was sure he could feel something new happening in his leg.

It's probably nothing, just sleep, he thought. Thankfully, sleep was not far away.

~

Alrion awoke to a ray of sunlight warming his face. He sat up quickly, unsure of the time. Looking around, he noticed that Alyx was still sleeping. The morning sun made the events of the previous night seem like a dream.

It really is a new day, he thought with relief. He stretched out and tested his leg. It felt a bit better but was definitely still sore. He didn't think walking would be a problem, but it might become an issue if they had a long trek ahead. Which he assumed they would.

"Maybe there are horses in town," he wondered. He rose slowly, and tested his weight on his injured leg. It stung, but wasn't too bad. He just had to take care. With measured steps he crossed the room and over to the spare room where Lara would be sleeping.

He opened the door slowly and looked inside. Lara was still asleep. He crept back without waking her.

I thought she was on watch?

Maybe something else had happened. He wandered into the spare room and peered inside. There were some signs of the night's activities, but nothing else new. He didn't want to venture upstairs, especially if Beatrix was still asleep, so he slowly returned to the living room and sat in a chair near Alyx.

She looked peaceful. Her strength was not so obvious when she slept. She almost looked normal.

What's normal these days?

It seemed like she'd had a hard life. He'd always thought of the stories of heroes, and their adventures and what their lives must have been like. He was sure that if he had heard a story like Alyx's it would have been glorified. And yes, she was an amazing fighter and incredibly skilled. She was a true survivor. But it didn't seem like that life had given her joy. And she'd had a hard time since joining them as well. He didn't like the thought of that.

We've just made her life worse, at the time that she had finally earned some rest.

There had to be a way to make that right again. He heard the front door open, so Alrion eased himself up and walked over to investigate. It was his father coming in.

"Good morning. How's the leg going?" he said.

"Could be worse. Not going to do well on a long hike though. Although I think Alyx is in the same situation. Any chance of horses here?"

"I've been looking into that this morning. There are some in town, but they won't part with them easily. I'm hoping that Beatrix can convince them."

"Why is that?"

"Healers seem to have some authority, or at least they seem to be a voice that is listened to. I suppose it's because they provide a lot of safety and assistance. These are dangerous parts. If there was no Healer in town, where would the people turn?" Vincent pointed back at the living room and they walked back there. They saw Beatrix hovering over Alyx.

"Everything alright?" Alrion said.

"She seems stable. I do wish we didn't have the adventures from last night, but at least she avoided additional injuries."

"Do you think there's any chance we can leave today?" Vincent said. He pulled up another chair and sat down. He looked weary. Alrion wondered if he had slept at all. He was starting to think that his father had never woken Lara.

"It all depends on Alyx. But you may have to. I hate to say this, but I think you're risking everyone's lives by staying here."

"That's completely fair. I think we need to risk it today. But to do that, we'll need horses," Vincent said to Beatrix.

"And they're not something anybody will part with lightly."

"Exactly. Do you think you could have a word?" Vincent said. Beatrix stopped to think.

"Yes. I know exactly who you are talking about. And he owes me a favour. But I won't badger him too much, I'll let him know it's for everyone's benefit."

"That would be a big help to us. And we'd also be out of your hair. No more late-night visitors," Vincent said with a smile.

"Yes, I'm afraid I'm not interested in any more of those. I'll need some time to prepare, and then I'll go see what I can organise for you. Some gold will help smooth things over."

"Take this," Vincent said. He withdrew a small sack and handed it to Beatrix. She didn't even bother opening it.

"That will do. I'll return soon with good news."

"I hope so. We really need it," Vincent said.

"Thank you, Beatrix," Alrion said. Beatrix acknowledged him and hurried upstairs.

"Do you really think she will succeed?" Alrion said.

"Absolutely. They're all better off with us gone. She can't get us out without horses. One way or another we will be off later today."

"Good. I don't want to put anyone else in danger," Alrion said. He had already endangered too many people, and been responsible for too much pain and suffering. He had to lead Wraith away from innocent people. He just needed enough time to find a cure so he could settle things once and for all. He was sick of being sick. Wraith was going to pay.

19

THE DIVISIVE MESSAGE

Vincent paced around the room. He didn't like waiting around when he could be preparing something. Alrion and Alyx were resting, and Lara looked as restless as he felt. But his hands were tied until Beatrix returned with news. He couldn't start until he knew what she had managed to bargain for.

She will definitely get horses. It's just how many.

He heard footsteps approach the front door and walked quickly across. Lara must have noticed and followed along.

Beatrix opened the door and stepped inside, making an effort to lock the door properly.

"Ahh, you're here," she said when she noticed Vincent.

"Just waiting for the good news," he said.

"I wasn't so sure, and I even struggled at the beginning of that conversation. But the more I described, the more he came around. The gold was not as big a lure as you may think. We're in quite a remote place here."

"I know, but it never hurts. When someone does come here to trade, it sure does help make the most of it," Vincent said.

"True. I've managed to secure three horses with saddlebags. You just need to go pick them up when you are ready to leave."

"Fantastic! That's plenty, we can figure that out. It might even make sense for Alyx to ride with someone anyway. She may not be strong enough to ride alone."

"That's a good idea," Lara said.

"I need some information on the terrain ahead. What will we be riding into?"

"The trails become thinner and harder to navigate. The weather will be increasingly cold until you reach the snow. You need to be prepared for that."

"Our destination is in the snow?" Vincent said. Beatrix paused before answering.

"My assumption is yes. We are well acquainted with the lands closer to home."

"You're still being evasive," Lara said.

"I cannot say more. Follow the paths, and then the amulet will show you the way."

"That's what the other Healer told us."

"I know. So, you will need lots of food supplies, as game to hunt, and foraging are slim pickings as you track north. Also, cold weather gear."

"Makes sense," Vincent said. He started making a mental checklist of the things he needed to procure.

"Why are they in such a remote location?" Lara said.

"You'll have to ask them," Beatrix said.

"They certainly don't like attention," Vincent said. He looked at Beatrix for any reaction and saw none.

"Well, thank you again for your assistance. Would it be unsafe to leave this afternoon?" Vincent said. Beatrix looked away, clearly concentrating on something else.

"I don't travel north that frequently. I believe there will be places to camp overnight, and you shouldn't be in the worst of the cold by then. I also believe that you can't leave any earlier. It's too risky, considering the injuries you have to contend with."

"And if we are gone by nightfall, then hopefully those following us will realise and leave you all alone," Lara said.

"That would be ideal. But don't think that I am making the recommendation based on that alone. Considering your need to move forward, the opportunities for staying somewhere overnight and the risk to the village, it's the best approach."

"I agree. Lara, are you interested in helping me prepare?" Vincent said.

"Why not? Nothing to do here now."

"Good. Let's go directly."

"You'll find a trading store at the edge of town. They should have everything you need," Beatrix said.

"Great, we will be back soon," Vincent said. He opened the front door, and held it open for Lara. After she stepped through he followed behind, hearing the door lock behind him.

"She doesn't feel safe," Lara said.

"Can you blame her?"

"No, it's quite a fair response. I don't feel safe."

"We'll be fine."

"You do seem to just take all this in your stride," Lara said. She slowed down and Vincent drew alongside her.

"I've had many interesting life experiences. Plus, my father was an exceptional wizard. It wasn't your usual upbringing."

"It sounds like Alrion had quite the opposite. Was that on purpose?"

"Definitely. I wanted him to have the routine, a home of his own. A place to return to. Even if he never feels the need later in life."

"I think you've done that. But don't you think he needed to be introduced to the world? Considering the legacy of your family?" Lara said. Vincent stopped walking. He was surprised to hear her go down this line of discussion. But she seemed to have his son's best interests at heart.

"Part of me was hoping he wouldn't need that. So instead I focused on an upbringing that would be a good foundation for whatever he wanted to do. He's learning about the world now, isn't he?" Vincent said.

"He sure is. He sure is," Lara said. Vincent let the comment go, not wishing to add more to that conversation. He sensed that Lara didn't want to talk about her past, since she never brought it up. He'd have to ask Alrion about it one time. Maybe she had opened up to him.

"I'd say that's the place over there," he said, pointing into the distance. There was a well-built stone building with a peaked wooden roof. Large double doors dominated the front porch, although there were some leather goods piled outside as well.

"I'm really curious what they have here," Lara said.

"It's a remote community. They probably have everything," Vincent said. He stepped up onto the porch, the wooden boards creaking as he put his weight down. He quickly glanced at the goods outside, and determined that they weren't for sale. They were more weathered and not saleable.

At least I hope they're not representative of what's inside.

He pushed on one of the great doors and it gave way easily, offering up some warmth from inside. Vincent entered eagerly, keen to escape the cold.

It's only going to get worse as we push further north, he thought. He waited for Lara to enter then closed the door. Looking around he saw a wide array of various goods. But what immediately drew his attention was the crackling fire at one end of the room. A withered old man sat there, reading a book in a comfortable cushioned chair.

"I think we will find what we need," Lara said. Vincent agreed. There were racks of coats and jackets, boots, and even ropes and saddles.

"Looks like you've got everything for an expedition," Vincent said as he approached the fire.

"Can't be too prepared in these conditions. Nor can you let someone go out there unprepared. That's akin to murder," the old man said without looking up. He carefully pulled a red ribbon to save his place in the book and put it down.

"Haven't seen you around these parts? Are you the visitors causing so much commotion?"

"We must be. I'm Vincent, it's a pleasure to meet you."

"Weyland. And the lovely lady is?"

"Lara. Nice to meet you. Great place you have here."

"Thank you. It has taken many years to build it up, but it has proven useful time and time again. I needed something to do when I was unable to keep exploring."

"Have you ventured far north?" Vincent said.

"Aye. It's a hard road if that's what you're thinking. Where are you going?"

"We're looking for the Mystics." Vincent carefully watched Weyland's reaction. The old man raised an eyebrow.

"People do from time to time. Some return, others do not. I gave up trying to dissuade folk a while back."

"Have you met them?" Lara said. Weyland was deep in thought.

"I believe one saved me, when I was younger and more foolish. There was no way I could have survived otherwise. I never did find where they live though. Very private and secretive bunch."

"But you know they exist?"

"Of course. You come to understand that some things exist without having to see them yourself. There's too many stories, too many coincidences and occurrences to believe otherwise."

"Thanks for the information," Lara said.

"You'll need cold weather gear. And lots of food and water. Fire-starting gear as well."

"What about this?" Lara pulled something off the wall. It was a long leather whip.

"That's a quality whip, but I wouldn't recommend it unless you were proficient with wielding one. From the way you are holding it, I would assume you are not," Weyland said.

"It's for a friend." Lara winked and Weyland nodded.

"Maybe you can recommend a full detail? Assume we have nothing. Well, we have three horses," Vincent said.

"I bet I know which three they are too," Weyland said, winking. "How many travelling?"

"Four."

"Alright, I'll write you a list but you can go pick it out. It's too cold for me away from the fire," Weyland said with a grin.

"Not a problem," Vincent said. Weyland hauled himself up and trotted over to a nearby desk. He wrote up a list of items and handed it to Vincent before taking his place back by the fire.

"Looks fine. How much?" Vincent said.

"No charge. But I have a request."

"Name it."

"I want you to bring something back. That will be payment enough."

"Something?"

"Anything."

"That we can do. I'll go assemble everything," Vincent said.

"Call out if you need help, I'll be here," Weyland said. Vincent nodded and walked off.

~

Within an hour, he and Lara had arranged a neat pile next to the door. They had clothing, a few tools, and some dried food.

"Next, we need the horses," Vincent said.

"Right. Lead the way," Lara said.

"We'll be back with the horses!" Vincent shouted. Weyland waved and returned to his book. Vincent opened the door, waited for Lara to leave, and followed close behind.

"Just up here," Vincent said. He pointed to a set of buildings at the end of the road. As they approached a man stepped out.

"Ho there! Here for the horses?" he said.

"Yes."

"They're ready to go. Come with me," the man said. He led them into the stables. Three horses were ready and saddled up. Two were brown and one was black. Vincent walked past, patting each one.

"You didn't waste any time," he said.

"I was informed that time was of the essence."

"Absolutely. Thank you for your help. Let's go Lara," Vincent said. He mounted the horse and looked around.

"Don't worry, here's a lead. They're used to working together," the man said. Vincent accepted the lead and nudged his horse forward. The other brown one followed closely. Lara wasn't far behind on the black horse.

Vincent took his time, navigating back to the street and taking care on the road. The horses seemed calm, which was reassuring. They would all be tested soon enough. They tied the horses up outside the store, and methodically packed as much as possible. Vincent donned his cold weather gear and stepped back to check it all.

"Looks good, you wear it well," Lara said.

"Thanks. I'm curious to know how much mobility we get with this."

"Enough. It would be harder without it if the cold gets much worse."

"Very true. Suit up and we can join the others," Vincent said. Lara threw on the extra layers, and helped Vincent pack the leftover gear. They took their time trotting down the street, not in a hurry. It was more important to build trust with the horses and not lose anything in the process.

Vincent tied up the horses outside Beatrix's house, and they knocked on the door.

"Who is it?"

"Vincent." The door opened promptly and Beatrix looked them over.

"You look ready. Come in."

"The real question is, are they ready?" Vincent said. He stepped inside and strode directly into the other room. He saw Alrion and Alyx seated together on the couch.

"Ready to ride?" Vincent said.

"Not sure really. But we can try," Alyx said.

"I should be fine," Alrion said. He reached out and touched his leg.

"Eat and prepare yourselves properly. You can leave anytime today that suits," Beatrix said.

"Especially the eat part. The food we are taking with us isn't exactly gourmet," Lara said. Alrion laughed.

"Sure, I'll stock up," he said, patting his belly.

Hours later they were on the horses and crossing the edge of town. A single path connected with the wilderness beyond. Vincent rode out front, Alrion and Alyx shared the black horse in the middle, and Lara rode the other brown horse bringing up the rear.

"Keep this formation, the path ahead looks narrow," Vincent said.

"Sure," Alrion said. Alyx was quiet.

"How's the ride for you two?"

"It's not too bad for me, just need to be careful with my leg. Alyx?" Alrion said.

"Not ideal, but it's manageable. It should get easier as we progress." Alyx reached down and pulled the whip out from the saddlebag. "What was the inspiration behind this?"

"I'm not sure, I just saw it and thought of you," Lara said.

"Lucky for you I am not just a weapon master in name. It won't be my preferred weapon, but you never know when you will need it. I think I'm fine to get started." Alyx looked back at Vincent.

"Good. I'll slowly increase the pace where possible. Everything fine back there Lara?"

"So far, so good," she said loudly and clearly, Vincent nodded and focused on the path ahead. He had chosen to ride up front to shield them from any obstacles or attacks. He wanted Lara's keen eyes watching the rear to see if they were being followed. They were approaching a rocky area, with the path seemingly carved between massive stones in places. The tight nature of the way forward made Vincent feel nervous. It was good that they could hold their own in tight quarters. However, he was concerned that they could easily be boxed in.

Just have to see how things go.

It was slow progress initially though. The path was strewn with smaller stones, which were enough to disrupt the horses. They had to pick a careful path through to not sustain any injuries.

At least this pace will help ease them into the ride, Vincent thought. He had no idea how far they had to travel, but he could tell it was a fair way. The fact that it was cold but not even close to snow was telling.

"Stop!" Lara yelled from behind. Vincent pulled up quickly and wheeled around. They hadn't left the village limits that long ago, and already there was trouble. It was too narrow to track all the way back past Alrion and Alyx, so he settled for coming closer.

"We have trouble. I spotted a Tracker skulking in the rocks. It must be the one that got away," Lara said.

"Is it still around?" Vincent said.

"No, it noticed me and took off. I think it just wanted to confirm our location."

"Not again! This is ridiculous we can't shake them," Alrion said. He was starting to get worked up. Vincent had to defuse the situation.

"Clearly they are resorting to more manual methods of tracking because you've been containing your anger. Well done," he said. Alrion looked up, a puzzled look on his face. Vincent looked over at Lara and caught her attention. He motioned towards Alrion with his head slightly.

"That's a good point. And I have to admit that there's only one path north. It wasn't going to be difficult to pick up the trail, as annoying as that is," Lara said.

"But that Tracker is only alive because of me. I didn't finish it off," Alrion said.

"Nothing wrong with that, son. This doesn't change our plan or our approach. We just need to be mindful that we will be followed every step of the way," Vincent said. He had hoped they were going to get a break, but it just wasn't going to happen. Suddenly Alrion clutched his head. Alyx did the same.

"What's happening?" Vincent said. He jumped off his horse and ran over. Alrion and Alyx were slumped over in the saddle. Vincent supported them both with his hands to make sure they didn't fall off.

What is this?

He had a terrible feeling. Alrion sat up again quickly, almost toppling off the horse. Vincent saw Alyx stirring and managed to switch focus to stabilising her.

"You're back with us?" Vincent said. He noticed Lara had joined him. She looked very concerned.

"I don't understand what happened exactly, but we just received a very clear message. It must have been from a Tracker." Alrion looked right at Vincent.

"What was it?"

"Celes is coming," Alrion said. Vincent was momentarily stunned. Then he started laughing.

"There's no stopping your mother is there?" he said.

"I guess not. I wonder where she is? And how did she even send that message?"

"If you think a Tracker sent it, there's your answer," Lara said.

"We can't rely on that. I need to go back and leave a message," Vincent said.

"We will wait for you," Alrion said.

"No, keep pushing. It's too risky otherwise. I'll catch up, and hopefully your mother will be not too far behind."

"I agree. Don't worry Alrion I still have this," Alyx said. She patted the crossbow hanging off the side of the saddle. "And at a pinch this lovely new gift you gave me." Alyx grabbed the whip now hanging off her belt.

"And I still have these," Lara said, twirling her daggers. Alrion sighed.

"Please hurry back," he said. He looked worried.

"Of course. You won't even know I'm gone," Vincent said. He put a hand on Alrion's shoulder and looked him in the eye.

Be safe.

Vincent carefully led the horse through and remounted once he was behind the rest. With one look back, he spurred the horse into action.

I have no idea what I'm riding into. But there's too much happening to not leave something for Celes. If she makes it this far, it will be very dangerous to continue, he thought. He admired his wife, and was constantly surprised by her. But this was a very dangerous situation to be wading into. Vincent pushed the horse to go even faster.

20

THE WAY FORWARD

Alrion watched his father ride away, fear dominating his thoughts. He hadn't realised how much he had depended on the reassurance and safety of his father's presence.

It must be because of my current condition.

It wasn't like his father was all-powerful or all-knowing. Although he did have a way of figuring things out and surviving no matter the odds.

"Let's pause when we get to a nice spot to stop. And then we will switch things up a bit," Lara said.

"Sure. Ready?" Alrion said to Alyx.

"Yes. Keep moving."

"As you command," Alrion said. He was trying to lighten the mood a bit by being flippant but his heart wasn't in it. Something about the recent communication had really thrown him. It wasn't just his father's departure.

How did it affect me so much?

The power of the Trackers was scary. The more he found out, the more elusive and surprising they were. But if his mother had discovered a way to use them, that was a bonus.

Alyx lay against his back, using him as support. He didn't think she was as good as she pretended. But he let it slide. They had to keep moving, and she was coming along. That was already decided.

His thoughts turned again to the infection within him. It seemed to be affecting his dreams more. Dark images and shapes. There was also a recurring scene. It was a plain and serviceable fireplace. A healthy and crackling fire burned brightly, sustained by thick chunky logs. But tendrils of darkness slowly crept in, looking to smother the fire. But instead of snuffing it out completely, the fire burned even fiercer. This time with a murky black flame.

He was under no illusions as to what the dream meant. Whether it was real or just his fear, it represented him being overcome and turned by the Blight. It showed his gift being turned into a tool of darkness. That was scarier than anything else. And he had now seen two examples of Shade Wizards. That is not what he wanted to be. He'd rather die than be a monster.

"Everything good up there?" Lara said. Alrion was shaken out of his thoughts. He looked around properly, realising that he hadn't even been paying attention to the surroundings. He was still on the path, but his pace had slowed considerably.

"Fine, just lost in my thoughts."

"Keep your eyes on the road, that's the priority," Lara said.

"On it," Alrion said. He wished it were that easy. His throat was throbbing, exactly where he imagined his black marks to be. He felt it with his hand, and touched the amulet he had been given at the academy.

He pulled it out from his clothing and looked at it again. It appeared unchanged, the pure white of the stone contrasting with the deep black of what was inside. The more he stared at it, the more he thought it was somehow throbbing in time with the marks on his neck.

Just your imagination.

It seemed funny though. In a way he and the amulet were the same. They both had a dark streak trying to spread. He stopped himself focusing on that and instead deliberately took in the landscape.

It was bleak and windswept. Very rocky with very little in the way of vegetation. There were some trees, but none accessible. The trees themselves seemed spindly and anaemic too, like they were on their last legs.

A bit like me.

It was hard to pinpoint but he just felt an overall sensation of unease. His infection was definitely progressing.

The path widened and they approached a broader section. Alrion slowed the horse to take a better look.

"We should pause here to take a break. There's even a few tufts of grass for the horses to nibble on," Lara said. Alrion led the horse over and dismounted carefully. He helped Alyx down then secured the horse to the lone tree nearby. Lara did the same. Alrion pulled his coat around tighter, then sat down with one of the saddlebags.

"Let's see what passes for food up here," he said. He retrieved some dried meat and some fruit and passed it around.

"Let's eat sparingly, we don't know how long we need it," Alyx said.

"Good idea. How are you feeling?" Alrion bit down on a strip of meat and it had way more flavour than he had expected. That was a relief.

"Worse. But we're making progress," she said.

"You mean in terms of getting closer to the Mystics?"

"Mainly." Alyx looked to have more to say, but ended up coughing. "Anyway, you have been neglecting your training."

"I wouldn't say that."

"Now. You and Lara. I want to see how you've progressed."

"I'm not sure we have time," Lara said.

"He won't last long enough for it to make an impact. Go get ready," Alyx said. Alrion looked over at Lara and she shrugged. He had to give Alyx the benefit of the doubt; she usually had some strategy behind whatever she asked for. Alrion stood with reluctance, and walked over to a clear space. He drew his sword and tried to ready himself. Lara stood nearby, drawing her Runesteel dagger and holding it at the ready.

"What's the plan?" Alrion said.

"Go through some forms. Lara will defend," Alyx said. Alrion looked at Lara and she nodded. He took a step forward and winced. He had forgotten about the injured leg. He pushed on, bringing his sword up into a whirling sequence. He started slow, letting his body warm up. Lara dodged and ducked mostly. However, as he was launching a big strike she timed a parry perfectly and threw him off balance. Before he could react, she kicked him in his good leg and he stumbled back.

"Good. You need to take this more seriously," Alyx said. Alrion felt annoyed. He was still injured and had been riding all morning. He didn't think it was fair to push him like this. Lara gave him an apologetic look but readied herself once more. Alrion spent a moment composing himself and launched into another attack. He decided that this time he would go straight to full intensity. They didn't have time, and he didn't have the energy for a long session.

He selected a flowing sequence that quickly alternated between low and high strikes. He hoped that he could use the extra reach to put Lara on the back foot. By intentionally keeping the first few strikes a little slower, he thought he could catch her off guard.

Lara dodged and lightly parried, keeping a defensive approach. Alrion saw his opportunity and pushed much harder. He really needed to move his feet, and struggled a little to keep the agility up. The pain in his leg flared up, which annoyed him. But he used the annoyance as fuel for his continued attack. Faster, harder he pushed. Lara became more active in her defence. She looked like she was finally being challenged.

There! Alrion thought. He swept low after forcing Lara to deflect a strike. Her position and posture were all wrong, and with only a short dagger she would struggle to parry it. As his sword swung she noticed the trajectory. Alrion knew it was too late. He turned his sword so that only the flat of the blade would make an impact.

Lara recovered into a crouch and launched herself. Just as Alrion's sword was meant to bowl her over she jumped over the blade and dived into Alrion. They tumbled down together, Alrion dropping his sword and losing all sense of what had happened. He looked up and saw Lara lying on him, her dagger at his throat.

"You're too slow. That's enough," Alyx said.

"Don't feel bad," Lara whispered, and winked at him. She lingered for a moment longer than necessary then rose. Alrion shook his head and collected himself.

"What do you think about that?" Alyx said. Alrion sat up and rested his palms on the cold ground.

"I can't beat Lara, that's for sure. My leg injury is also a problem."

"You had forgotten about it, hadn't you?"

"In the moment I did, yes."

"I know I saw that. Even when you pushed your hardest, you still weren't fast enough."

"I know," Alrion said. He didn't understand why she was labouring the point. He wiped the sweat off his brow. That had been a thorough workout, even though it was fast.

"You need to know your limitations. Even accounting for your injury, you're slowing down. You are no match for those Trackers, let alone a Shade Wizard."

"I get that. That's why you're here."

"You need to understand that you cannot fight them. You will struggle to run away from them. And you can't rely on me."

"Because of your injury?"

"Not just that. Take your right hand off the ground and hold up a few fingers," Alyx said. Alrion was puzzled but complied. He held up three fingers at waist height.

"I can't tell if that's three or four fingers," Alyx said after a pause.

"What?" Lara said.

"There's a darkness starting to cloud my vision. It's only a recent thing. But it is obscuring details right now."

"Wait a minute. The other night with the crossbow in the relatively dark room?" Alrion said.

"Yes, it was the same then. Don't worry they were big enough targets," Alyx said. Lara just laughed out loud.

"I'm sorry, but I just couldn't help myself seeing Alrion's face right then."

"This sounds really serious. I haven't encountered that side effect and I've been infected longer," Alrion said. Alyx paused and looked deep in thought.

"I think it is reacting differently, but I can't say for sure. From observing you, I think it is mostly making you appear sick and worn down. You seem clumsier and more sluggish. There seems to be a toll on your emotions as well. Steering them darker."

"And for you?"

"I feel like darkness is overtaking me. Look at the skin on my arm." Alyx rolled back the layers and showed her forearm. Alrion walked over and took a look. The skin was darker and slightly scaly.

"This reminds me of ..." Alrion started to say, but quickly stopped himself.

"Don't censor yourself, I am thinking the same thing. It is like a Shade. Perhaps that is my fate," Alyx said. Alrion didn't know what to say. It was one thing that Alyx was infected and carrying that around. And one thing that it was more rapidly affecting her. But it was another entirely that rather than be Tainted, or even a Blighter, that she might be on the path to becoming a Shade.

"I've never witnessed this transformation. I don't know what the trigger signs will be," Alyx said.

"You don't need to be so damned detached about it. This is terrible!" Alrion shouted.

"Sorry, but we need to consider the fact that in your current state I will be a danger to you both if I turn unexpectedly."

"It's much harder to contain a Shade without killing," Lara said softly.

"I've never seen it done. I don't expect you to do that. If I've turned, you must end my life. You must swear this to me," Alyx said. She stared at Alrion.

"I will not. Doing so would go against my very quest. If I can cure myself, I can cure you as well." Alrion kept his gaze level at Alyx. She looked at Lara.

"I will do what is necessary to defend us. But not before trying to restrain you," Lara said finally.

"That is sufficient. We should continue," Alyx said.

"Agreed. We need to reach our destination before anything else happens," Alrion said. He gathered his things and prepared the horse, before helping Alyx up.

"You take the lead again, I fear more from what's behind us than what is before," Lara said once she was mounted.

"Sure," Alrion said. He didn't disguise the weariness in his voice. Even nudging the horse forward was more effort than he wanted. That short stint of sparring had really shown how much weaker he was. They were going to struggle if they were attacked. And his father wasn't anywhere near.

Just keep moving forward.

There would be plenty of opportunity to fix things once they arrived. He rode for a time, focusing initially on the bleak landscape. Eventually though he decided to talk to Alyx.

"Why didn't you say anything earlier? About your condition?"

"It didn't seem worth mentioning, especially since I was burned and then poisoned. For a time there, I wondered if the Darkroot had somehow contributed. But I'm confident now that it's just the Blight, especially given how my arm is reacting."

"I'm not going to let you down," Alrion said. He clenched his jaw and urged the horse forward faster. The cold wind whipped up even faster, and it cut through all his clothing. His teeth chattered.

"We're really pushing north now," he muttered. "Is that snow in the distance?"

"Looks like it," Lara said.

"I'm the wrong person to ask," Alyx said. Her view was mostly blocked, and Alrion remembered the effect on her eyesight too.

"Just take our word for it. We can't be that far now. Explains the biting cold."

"Luckily, I have you to shield me," Alyx said. Alrion chuckled. At least he was good for something right now.

"Stop!" Alyx said, and Alrion tugged at the reins suddenly. The horse whimpered in complaint but stopped.

"What is it?"

"The amulet they gave me is reacting somehow. It's warm and glowing?" Alyx said. She removed it from her clothing and held it out. Alrion turned awkwardly to see it.

"Something is definitely happening there," he said. Lara slowly sidled up and took a look as well.

"I think that's the sign. What did she say? It would show the path?" Lara said.

"I think so. It wouldn't be the path we're on, would it?" Alrion said.

"No, that's too obvious. Every traveller would end up there. Hold my horse," Lara said. She handed the reins to Alrion and jumped down quickly. Alrion followed her with his gaze, and took in the surroundings. There was little to note, save that rock formations and small raised sections surrounded them. It didn't look like there was anything else. Lara walked over to the rocks and felt them with her hand. Holding both hands out she carefully progressed along, checking all the surfaces.

"You think there's a hidden path?" Alrion said.

"Yes. And that amulet is warning us about it," she said. "Oh, what do we have here?"

This could be the break we needed, Alrion thought.

21

HIDDEN BY SNOW

Alrion dismounted and paused to ensure Alyx was still stable on the horse. Then he walked over to see what Lara had found.

"This is quite clever," she said, standing back.

"What is it?"

"It's an optical illusion. It looks like the rock extends all the way, but there's actually a path here." Lara pointed but Alrion didn't get it. He stepped over to where she was standing.

"Oh, I see. Even from here I can't see the whole thing."

"Exactly! It's incredible."

"Do you think we can fit a horse through?" Alrion said. It was all well and good that they had found a secret path, but they would be in trouble if the horses couldn't get through.

"There's only one way to find out. I'll try it on foot," Lara said.

"What was it?" Alyx said when Alrion returned.

"It's definitely a path. You'll see it soon. But Lara is going first to make sure the horses can get through."

"Good. Isn't this a problem though? How will Vincent find it?" Alyx said. Alrion paused. That was a good question.

"We need to leave some sort of marker," he said. He thought hard about what to leave. It had to be something that his father would recognise. However, it also had to be something that would stay in place, and hopefully not be noticed by anyone else passing through.

"This is pretty important. I'm going to have to take a chance," Alrion said.

"What do you mean?"

"Well, I need to leave something valuable. The ring my father gave me. He said that it always protected him, and was of value. Even after Lara originally stole it, it still found its way back to me. I have to trust that he will find it and figure out the trick."

"As strange as that sounds, there could be something to it. It's magical, right?"

"Supposedly. Not that we know what it does."

"Do it. Just try and hide it a little though. I don't think it'll work if you leave it in the middle of the path," Alyx said.

"I agree. It's worth a try, Alrion. Now wish me luck," Lara said. She was leading her horse by the reins and she was in position.

"Good luck," Alrion said. He watched her intently. As she stepped forward she disappeared from view.

"Wow, that's pretty good," Alyx said.

"You saw that?"

"I may have reduced vision, but I'm not blind."

"True. Well, here comes the test. Let's see how the horse goes," Alrion said. The horse did seem resistant, but started to step forward. It also began to disappear until it was completely hidden from view.

"I'd say that's a success. Let me place this ring, then I'll do the same as Lara." Alrion walked over to where the secret path could be seen. He looked around at the ground, trying to find a good place to leave the ring. He spotted a cavity in one of the rocks lying around. It was shallow, but was deep enough to protect the ring. He placed it inside and stepped back.

The angle of the cavity did protect it from a casual glance. But if you looked closer it caught your attention.

That's as good as it's going to get.

He returned to his horse and began to lead it over.

"Here we go," he said.

"I'm ready," Alyx said. Alrion stepped forward carefully. He expected to feel something, but nothing happened. He continued pushing forward until the path widened a little. Looking back the path looked normal. Like it was obviously there.

"Maybe it only works in one direction," he said. Alyx turned and looked herself.

"Must do. You'd never think it, looking from here."

"And there's Lara," Alrion said, pointing. She was a bit further ahead, sitting on her horse and watching them. Alrion continued, on foot, deciding not to mount until he reached Lara. There was probably a reason she had stopped there.

"What did you think?"

"Very impressive. How's the amulet going?" Alrion said.

"It seems to have quietened down. How odd," Alyx said.

"They can explain it to us when we get there. Let's get a move on," Lara said.

"Sure." Alrion carefully jumped up onto the horse once more, and sidled up to Lara.

"Since we're on the path, I'll take the lead from now on. If we're lucky we'll lose them completely. Otherwise we should at least buy ourselves a head start."

"We could use some luck, there's been a terrible lack of it," Alrion said.

"Just make your own," Alyx said. Lara laughed and took off at a faster pace. Alrion didn't try to match it, but did try and increase his speed.

The winds were harsher in terms of both speed and chill. Alrion could see his breath, and soon there was evidence of snow. Not a lot, but enough to show that they would encounter it soon.

"What an inhospitable place. Who would live here?" Alyx said.

"It's just my luck you know? The last place I had to travel to was in the middle of the desert."

"Sounds like the people you need don't want to be found."

"Couldn't agree more. But I found the monks, and I'll find the Mystics."

"You will. I must say I am impressed, Alrion. You do yourself a disservice sometimes. How many can say they have done as much as you in such a short time and with no experience of the world at large?" Alyx said. Alrion was surprised. He hadn't expected a compliment from her. It was even more valuable, since she always seemed so driven and practical.

"Thank you. It doesn't hurt to be reminded of that sometimes. It helps me forget about the failures along the way."

"Failures are just lessons with harsher consequences."

"Interesting words," Alrion said. It sounded like something Certan would have said. He wondered what the monk would think of Alyx. Surely, they had a lot in common.

Lara had stopped ahead, so Alrion increased his speed a little to catch up.

"How's it going back there?" she said.

"Nothing much to report. How about you?"

"Weather is deteriorating. We should have a short food break and then push on. But stay closer together this time."

"Sure, sounds like a plan." Alrion dismounted and started rummaging through the saddlebag.

"Let me down, I need to stretch my legs," Alyx said. Alrion readied himself to help her down, but Alyx slid off the opposite side of the horse. She landed hard on the ground with a thud. Alrion and Lara ran over to investigate.

"What happened?" Alrion said. He helped Alyx back into a seated position on the path. She looked dazed.

"I was foolish. I thought I could get down unassisted, but I just made things worse."

"Any injuries?" Lara said.

"I think I landed on the burnt leg," Alyx said. She reached down with her hand and grimaced with pain.

"Do we have anything for pain?" Alrion said to Lara. She paused to consider before replying.

"I have something. But that's only a secondary effect. The main thing it does is dull whoever drinks it from many things. It's too potent though, there's no way she could stay on a horse if she had it."

"That's no good. Let's at least eat and figure out what to do." Alrion fetched some more dried meat and fruit, and some water. They all sat on the cold ground next to Alyx.

"Sure beats sitting on a horse, although it's definitely colder," Alrion said. He received a small chuckle from Lara and the smallest hint of amusement from Alyx.

"Good to see you acting like your old self," Lara said.

"I think I've crossed over to the other side. Things are actually so dire, I can't help but act like this."

"It still helps. Mindset is very important," Alyx said.

"The monks believe that too. Do you think you can sit on the horse?" Alrion said.

"Probably, although it may be uncomfortable."

"Good. We can keep on moving then."

"I can wait here though. Vincent can take me and you can go ahead," Alyx said. Alrion was about to speak but Lara piped up first.

"Absolutely not. We all made a decision, so the matter is closed. You can't even suggest it yourself. If I have to strap you to my back and ride like that you'll still be coming," Lara said. Alrion was surprised by the intensity in her eyes. He felt reassured by that.

"Glad I didn't have to say that. I just want to add that we sure aren't turning our back so close to our goal."

"Very well. I know what you said before. I just felt I had to offer it just in case. I cannot become a burden. Well, I believe I am, but you won't accept it as that. I will endure," Alyx said.

"Good, glad to see that you've accepted you can't change our minds. Now, with that in mind let's get going again." Alrion rose quickly, the activity waking his legs up again. It was definitely not a good idea to stop for too long in the cold. Especially if snow was ahead. Lara helped him get both himself and Alyx back on the horse and secured. Once they were satisfied that Alyx would not fall off, they set off once more.

The cold increased, and they came across the first snowfalls. At first, it was just a light dusting that didn't persist on the ground. But as they pushed on further it became heavier, and the ground itself became more blanketed. Alrion started to shiver through his layers, and wished he could use a fire spell. That would fix everything. But he accepted that he could not and pushed on.

The path started to become covered in snow, and the horses slowed down considerably. They were also slowly but surely ascending.

"This is so slow," Alrion said.

"At least we're not on foot." Lara grinned at him.

"You're right. I should be careful what I complain about."

"At least you can walk. If we were on foot, you'd be carrying me too," Alyx said.

"You've both made your point." Alrion looked around, trying to see if there were any significant landmarks. A thick blanket of white was starting to cover everything and it was hard to see into the distance.

"At least we're masked by the conditions," he said.

"Don't be so sure about that," Lara said, looking around. She looked spooked by something. "Tracker!"

Alrion wheeled the horse around quickly, looking for the danger. He couldn't see the Tracker, but didn't wait for confirmation. He quickly jumped down and drew his sword. Once he was confident he had a few more seconds to prepare, he handed the crossbow to Alyx. She accepted it quickly without words.

"Here!" Lara shouted. Alrion heard the clang of steel and ran over to help. He saw Lara defending herself from a barrage of strikes. The Tracker was wielding a short sword and pushing her backwards. Lara stumbled back a few steps and readied herself for another assault. But the Tracker used the opportunity to run. It was heading straight for Alrion.

Here we go.

He tensed himself, preparing for the fight. As the Tracker

approached Alrion stepped forward and launched into a sword formation. The Tracker quickly parried two strikes and kept moving.

Alyx!

The Tracker was trying to finish the job. He turned quickly and chased the Tracker. It was almost upon Alyx. She fired the crossbow, but it only caught the Tracker in the shoulder. It slowed for a few moments before getting back into the assault. Alrion pushed forward with more urgency, using the Tracker's delay to close the gap. He swung out with his sword trying to knock it down, or at least cause it to slow down.

The Tracker didn't turn to face the attack, and didn't properly account for the strike. Alrion's sword sliced into the Tracker's leg and it toppled over. Before it could stand again Alyx had another crossbow bolt fired. It caught the Tracker in the chest.

"Not this time," Alrion said. He didn't hesitate and drove his sword through the Tracker's chest. It shuddered once then went still.

"I think that's it," Alyx said. Lara was with them within seconds.

"Is it over?" Lara said. She slowed and stood next to Alrion.

"Yes. It is done," Alrion said. He looked over the Tracker in more detail. In the daylight it looked more like a normal man. There were only subtle details betraying its transformation. Some black marks around the eyes, some strange tattoos on its arms, and the jet-black clothing.

"Why did you kill it this time?" Lara said.

"I couldn't let it get away again. It wouldn't stop otherwise."

"I didn't expect you to do that," Lara said. Alrion looked over at Alyx.

"Likewise. That was a surprise."

"Do you disagree with my decision?" Alrion said. He felt uncomfortable now. Had he gone too far?

"No. It was a sensible one. Just not one I thought you would make," Alyx said. Alrion looked back at Lara. He thought he saw a look of sadness quickly pass over her face. But she replaced it so quickly he wasn't sure.

"I'll check it for anything that might help us. Then we should get moving once more."

"Sure," Alrion said. He walked away a few paces, kicking the snow with his feet. He had a strange conflict within. He felt sickened that he'd had to essentially finish off a wounded and defenceless enemy. But the last time he had shown restraint the same creature had escaped and kept hounding them.

· *I don't know what to do. Do I feel bad because I didn't even hesitate?* he thought. What weighed on him the most was the concern that maybe it was the infection within changing his thinking as well as his body. A thought so terrifying that he pushed it away immediately.

"I think you'll want to see this," Lara said. Alrion walked back quickly. She held a book in her hand. He snatched it quickly to confirm what it was. He opened the notebook and saw that it was exactly what he had guessed. It was the magical notebook that he had been carrying with him since the academy.

"They stole this," he said. Leafing through the messages. He didn't think any of the messages would give away too much. They were all so vague and related to his goals. But he noticed a new message.

The Mystics are not the solution. They are only the next step.

"There's a new message. Take a look," Alrion said. Lara read the message and handed it back.

"Well, they know about the Mystics now."

"They must. Also, I'm a bit worried. Does this mean they are not the solution to my infection? I don't think I, or for that matter Alyx, have enough time if that's not the case."

"I hope not. We can't read too much into it. What do you think, Alyx?"

"You cannot spend time speculating. It is good we have the notebook back, correct?"

"Yes."

"Then accept that as a good thing and let's keep moving. Do not waste the opportunity that this Tracker has given us."

"Can't argue with that. Let's go Alrion," Lara said.

"On my way," Alrion said. He mounted up and tried not to think of the Tracker lying on the snowy path. He took the lead, pushing forward as fast as he could. The message in the notebook had given him even more reason to be quick. He had to prepare himself for the fact that maybe the Mystics could not cure him. It was not an easy thought. But he tried to accept it as he pushed ahead.

"Looks like we won't have to wait long for an answer," Alrion shouted. He slowed and pulled up. Ahead he saw what looked like a settlement. The buildings were hard to make out in the conditions, but it was definitely a place. Their destination.

"Is that it?" Lara said.

"It has to be. We should hurry before we get snowed in."

"Lead the way."

"Happy to. Alyx, we'll be there soon. And one way or another they'll be able to help," Alrion said. Alyx didn't respond, which made Alrion even more worried.

You have to help us, he thought and spurred the horse on again.

22

FAST FOLLOWER

Weariness threatened to topple Celes over. She had pushed as hard as possible. But she had been on her feet the entire time. There were no horses in Rolyntide, although she did manage to confirm with the residents that Alrion had passed through there.

The trek since then had been hard and long. Her feet were screaming out, and her shins were riddled with sharp pains. But as she rounded the bend she saw the gates in the distance.

That has to be Highroad.

The gates were closed but that didn't bother her. There was always a way inside. But first you had to get there. Now she finally was.

The final approach was agonising. It was like her body had decided that since she was close to rest, it would let out all the complaining it had been keeping inside. She persevered and leaned against the giant wooden doors.

At least the weather keeps you cool.

After taking a minute, she banged on the door twice. The metal grate on the door slid open and a male voice spoke.

"State your business."

"I'm following some friends of mine that came here. I am hoping to meet them."

"What are their names?"

"Alrion and Vincent."

"They're not residents here." The grate started to close.

"I know. I know. They're travellers. Truth be told they're my son and my husband. I must find them!" Celes was desperate. She didn't have the energy to find another way into this town.

"What's your name?"

"Celes." She decided to be honest and not use a fake name.

"Fine. The Healer mentioned you." The metal grate closed swiftly and the great doors began to open. Celes saw a surly guard standing within.

"Come with me," he said.

"Thank you." Celes followed close, despite her aches and pains. Another guard began closing the gates. It looked like a small town.

Reminds me of home. But a bit more suspicious, she thought. The guard stopped abruptly outside a house.

"In here. Healer is called Beatrix and is expecting you."

"Thank you. I am in your debt," Celes said. The guard's face softened a bit.

"Well, it's fine. Just don't cause any trouble." He walked off quickly and Celes knocked on the door.

A woman opened the door slowly and cautiously.

"Who is it?" she said.

"Beatrix, isn't it? My name is Celes. I hear you are expecting me?"

"Yes, I am. Please come in." Beatrix opened the door the rest of the way and smiled. Celes rushed inside and Beatrix closed the door behind them.

"I take it you've come a long way. I can see the resemblance, by the way."

"Thank you. Yes, it's been a long slog. It would have been a lot easier back in the day. But here we are. You must be aware I'm following my family."

"Yes, I am. Vincent left a message with me to expect you."

"Great. Because the information I have only led me this far. I have no idea where they are heading and for what purpose. But first, is Alrion infected?"

"Yes, he is," Beatrix said. Celes cursed inwardly. She knew it had to be true, but hearing it confirmed was something else.

"How bad is it?"

"Well, he's infected. But he seemed well enough. For some reason it seems to be progressing slowly. There's a good chance for him, if what he believes is true."

"And that is?"

"A group called the Mystics can help cure him. They are based further north. He is pushing to reach them. Not just for his own sake, but for one of the women travelling with him."

"Lara?"

"No, not her. She's fine. Alyx."

"I don't know her," Celes said. There was obviously a lot she had missed.

"They filled me in on a lot of the story. Come in the next room and sit. I'll make some tea and we can talk over everything."

"That's a lovely idea, but I don't know if I have time." Celes felt exhausted, but knowing that she had a link to where Alrion had gone, was like she was being pulled north immediately. Beatrix looked Celes up and down.

"You're in no condition to travel immediately, and you need to know what you're walking into."

"How far ahead are they?"

"A few days. And they have horses. Resting a little won't make any difference."

"Fine, I guess I can stay a little while," Celes said. Beatrix smiled quickly and led her into the next room.

I can sit for a short while. It might be nice, Celes thought.

∽

"That brings us to now," Beatrix said. Celes had been quiet, choosing not to interrupt too much. She just absorbed the story.

"I was attacked by two Trackers on my way here, I know how dangerous they can be."

"Why were they after you? Because you were following them?"

"No, it was the man with me. He was one of the original Trackers and was helping me. They noticed and went after him. I was just someone with him. He fought them off, but he received a mortal injury."

"I'm sorry to hear that. There's been so much life lost."

"There really has. I feel like everything is changing under us. Maybe I've been living in peace and quiet for too long. But Shade Wizards and Trackers? It was never like this."

"Things are definitely changing very rapidly. I think the Blight is coming to a head. It's no coincidence that as your son succeeds in his quest, that the enemy starts to reveal its true colours."

"How was Alrion? How was he really?" Celes needed to know. Beatrix paused and thought before she answered.

"He's had trouble dealing with the infection. Especially the loss of his magic. But he seems to be coping. But I fear it's the kind of coping that can't be maintained forever. If he keeps going like this he may snap." Beatrix looked like she was ready to say more, but she stopped.

"Thank you for being candid. Well, they're surviving. That's all I can ask. Next question. What was the message for me?"

"There wasn't much to it. Mostly Vincent wanted to ensure that you were let inside and I told you everything I knew. One thing he did mention in particular was that you should just keep pushing north; there is only really one main trail. He would find a way to alert you to the path when a deviation was required."

"That's suitably vague. I bet he doesn't know what the path looks like or how he will mark it," Celes said. She chuckled to herself. Same old Vincent.

"I do fear they are figuring things out as they go."

"Understandably. Since I'm here, do you mind if I stay a little longer?" Celes was not used to just inviting herself to stay. But she was so tired, and Beatrix had hosted her family already.

"No problem at all. I just hope you don't get attacked like they were."

"Oh no, I'm not anything for them to worry about. It's been very quiet since I've been travelling alone. Too quiet in fact. It's so nice to have company, even if for only a short time." Celes relaxed back into the couch. She could fall asleep so easily. But she couldn't. Not just yet.

"I can see you're about to crash out. Let's get some food into you and sort out a proper bed." Beatrix had an amused glint to her eye.

"I think you're right," Celes said. She could use some rest. It had been such a hard slog to get this far.

Celes opened her eyes and turned over. Vincent was still not there.

This better not be the new normal.

She sat up and took in a deep breath. She felt better and refreshed. Not perfect, but much better. She stood and looked out the single window. It was definitely morning, but not too late.

I can't lose any more time.

Leaving the room, she found Beatrix seated in the lounge and before her, a tray of breakfast. The smell tantalised Celes, causing her mouth to water.

"That smells amazing!"

"It's not much. But please enjoy," Beatrix said. Celes sat down and started eating.

"I can't thank you enough for what you have done for me. I promise I will find a way to repay you." Celes resumed eating. She needed to eat slower but couldn't restrain herself.

"Not required. I believe in what you are all doing. The Blight has taken so many lives, caused so much pain. I want a world without it. This small assistance is nothing compared to what we may all gain."

"While you're feeling generous, I need something else." Celes paused to drink some juice.

"I'm sorry we cannot spare any more horses." Beatrix looked apologetic.

"Oh well, I had to ask."

"But I do insist that you take some cold weather gear. You'll encounter snow further up and you aren't equipped for it."

"You're absolutely right. I do have a question though. You're a Healer, what brought you here? It's a very remote town." Celes was genuinely curious. It made sense to have a Healer here. But what would entice one to stay?

"That's a long story. Suffice to say, I once made a trip to visit the Mystics. They helped me, so I decided I would make my home here and help those who would also make the trip. Along with the rest of the town of course."

"Oh, now that's interesting. What else can you tell me about them?"

"Nothing. You must see for yourself. I can only confirm that if you persist you will find them." Beatrix looked apologetic.

"Sure. Don't worry, I'm not upset. How could I be when you've already been so helpful?"

"I'm glad. Please take your time and ready yourself. I went to the liberty of getting you some equipment early this morning. I'll bring it now," Beatrix said. She quickly left the room.

This was the break I needed. There's no horse, but I've got a second wind. I can make it now, Celes thought. When Beatrix returned she was laden with clothing and bags. Celes looked through and selected an appropriate coat, scarf, and boots. She also packed a bag to get her through the final leg of the journey.

"I think this is goodbye. I'll return soon with the rest of them. We all owe you our thanks."

"Good luck and good speed to your travels. I look forward to hearing of your adventures. Follow the path outside and you'll reach the way north." Beatrix waved and Celes left. She heard the door locking behind her.

On my way again. This time I'll finally catch up with them.

She still lamented the lack of a horse. But there was no use worrying about it. They'd given her everything else.

The walk through the town was quick, and soon she was on the trail. It didn't take long for the weather to deteriorate, and the cold chill to start piercing through her layers of clothing. The track was slowly ascending the whole time, which made things harder without seeming like it should be.

Just accept that you're climbing the whole time, she thought. She just needed to put one foot in front of the other for a while.

How will I know when to look for Vincent's marker?

Whatever he left had to be something subtle; otherwise someone else would take it. She thought over the information she had already. The Mystics were far north. Beatrix had visited them and told her that there would be snow. That was a good indicator at least. Until there were decent amounts of snowfall she just had to keep going.

"But snow may also obscure the marker. This won't be easy," Celes realised. But that was fine. She had a destination and was on the path. Alrion and Vincent were up there somewhere. Hopefully already with the Mystics.

Alrion, I'm still coming.

She hoped that he would be all right. The infection had to hold out a bit longer. Together they could figure something out. Their family had been apart for so much of this quest. Surely, they were better off together.

23

THE MYSTICAL DESTINATION

The settlement started to take the shape of buildings. And as they approached the buildings took on real forms. They were large domes of some material that Alrion couldn't figure out.

"This has to be it. Look at those buildings," he said.

"I think you're right. There can't be anything else all the way out here. And those structures certainly look different," Lara said.

"Let's speed up, we're so close."

"Hold up there. The snow is getting deeper, and the wind is picking up. Let's not stumble at the finish line." Lara gave him a serious look so Alrion took note. It wasn't just his desire to get Alyx and himself to what he hoped was safety. He was genuinely excited about discovering this place. What an incredible find. A group of magic users hidden from the world, their very existence a secret. He could learn so much.

He suddenly realised something he had lost since being infected. His sense of wonder had all but dried up. Sucked away by the vile infection coursing through him. He had been so preoccupied with it; he couldn't see beyond it. But even at the first sight of the Mystic's home, hope was rekindled. It was so reassuring.

"I have a good feeling about this," he said.

"Me too," Lara said. She nudged ahead, and Alrion let her lead.

The snow was falling and visibility was poor. They were initially shocked when they saw a figure standing in the snow before them.

"Welcome," a female voice said. Lara stopped and Alrion slowed down, stopping beside her. The woman was wearing thick blue robes with a hood. It was hard to make out any other features.

"Hello. We have come a long way to find you. We need your help," Alrion said.

"You can tell us everything inside. Follow me," the woman said. She walked effortlessly through the snow like it wasn't there at all. Alrion started to wonder what this place would really look like. He looked for gates, but saw none.

"Are there no gates here?" he said.

"No. Why would we need any? Only those who are truly determined come here."

"Fair enough." Alrion didn't understand, but it was a very remote location and hard to get to. Maybe they didn't need gates.

There was a clearly marked path now that they were entering the settlement. It consisted of carefully laid stones. The horses' hooves reached the stone through the varying layers of snow and the loud clop sound initially surprised Alrion. He looked around and saw the dome-shaped buildings in more detail. They were also built from carefully arranged stone, which he had never seen before. Each only had a single entrance. None of them seemed to have windows. He didn't want to question it though. It seemed better to just follow along quietly.

"Where are you taking us?" Alrion said.

"To a place where you can rest and recover."

"We need urgent attention first. Two of us are infected."

"You will be able to rest here. The Blight infection will struggle here, and take longer to complete," the woman said without even breaking stride. Alrion pulled up his horse instantly.

"I don't need time, I need a cure."

"We don't cure the Blight here."

"I don't accept that. I need to meet with your leader." Alrion remained still, not moving any further along. The woman finally stopped walking and turned to regard them.

"I don't think you will get what you want," she said.

"That's my problem, not yours." He was not going to be shuffled off somewhere to rest and wait for the infection to do its work. No, he was going to tackle this. There had to be a reason he had dreamed of the Mystics, and travelled so far to find them. He needed answers, not a bed. The woman continued to stare at him. Her gaze shifted over to Lara then back to him.

"Very well, as you wish. This way," she said. The woman left the path and they cut through the snow to another path. Alrion didn't notice anybody else walking around.

Must be the poor weather.

He doubted that the place was deserted. Before them rose a much larger structure. It was one giant dome with two others either side of it. Each structure had its own door, the main one with two giant wooden doors. The woman walked up and threw them open with only the slightest touch.

"Something is definitely going on here," he said to Lara.

"Agreed. But I'm going to keep quiet and observe. You take the lead, you're doing well."

"Thanks. This can't be for nothing." Alrion checked on Alyx and she seemed to be asleep. He dismounted and looked at how he was going to get Alyx down safely. Two women appeared next to him.

"We will take her to a bed. Don't worry she won't be far," one woman said. Alrion looked over to Lara and she nodded.

"Thanks," he said. He watched them carefully take Alyx away and Alrion walked into the giant dome with purpose. He wasn't going to be turned away.

It was surprisingly warm inside. There was a large fire in the centre of the room. The edges of the room were littered with torches on the walls, and lots of padded seats. Some had women sitting in them, but many of them were empty. At the end of the room, on a raised section was a crystal throne. On it sat an older woman, and before her was a small fountain filled with water.

The woman who had been leading them continued, and they followed her through the room. Alrion felt the eyes of the women on him, but he tried to ignore it. It was a disconcerting feeling though, like they were looking through him. Once they reached the foot of the throne, the young woman who had led them pushed back her hood and moved up the steps to take a position next to the older woman. Their leader presumably.

She looked old, yet still strong. She didn't carry the same frailty he normally attributed to old women. She was dressed in similar robes to the rest, but had more jewellery. There was a fire in her eyes, and something about them was familiar.

This is the woman from my dream!

Alrion realised it wasn't just a vision, it was a memory. His grandfather had known this woman, known of her powers.

"So, you have finally come to Wyr's Peak. Cutting it fine, aren't we?"

"My name is Alrion. This is Lara. And you are?"

"Jovana. I would ask you what brings you here, but I know the answer already. Therefore, I have a different question for you. Where is your father?" Jovana stared directly at Alrion. It made him a little uncomfortable. And the comment about his father threw him completely.

"He's on his way, he was delayed. That doesn't matter. I'm here and I need your help."

"That's a pity. I wonder if he did that intentionally. Come back when your father is here." Jovana turned her attention to the pool of water in the fountain before her. Alrion waited, and she said nothing further and didn't even look in his direction. He looked at Lara and she shrugged.

"I don't think you understand why I am here." Alrion was about to say more but he was cut off.

"Why are you still talking? You're dismissed. Come back when your father is here." Jovana waved him away and returned to staring into the water. Alrion didn't understand. He needed her help. His father being here was irrelevant. Any important information could be relayed later.

"You won't even let me explain my situation," he said. Jovana looked at him once more, this time giving him an icy stare that caused him to shiver.

"You are Alrion, son of Andar and grandson of Granthion. You, and one of your companions are infected. You believe that by coming here you can be cured. You have been informed that the Blight infection will travel slower here, yet you still push for this cure. We can help you, but at the proper time. Go wait and rest, and when your father is here I will see you again. Until then we have nothing to discuss and I won't even acknowledge you speaking. That is all." Jovana finished speaking and stared into the water once more. The woman standing next to her had a grin on her face.

Alrion was stunned. He hadn't expected this. First the strange refusal to help, then the way in which the woman had known all about what they were doing. He just shook his head. He looked at Lara and she seemed as confused as he was. The young woman walked down the steps and joined them.

"My name is Marla. I'm sorry about that, but I tried to warn you. She's very particular about things. Don't worry. You will get the help you need. But come with me now." Marla gestured towards the exit. Alrion appreciated the kindness after the stern talking to they had just received.

"This is not what I was expecting," he said.

"Good, then everything is as it should be," Marla said.

"You know more than you're telling us," Lara said.

"Yes, I do. But you have nothing to fear. All will make sense soon." Marla reached the exit doors, and held them open for Alrion and Lara. They stepped through and Marla continued to lead them back the way they had come.

"We're just supposed to wait around until my father arrives. What's so important about that?"

"You will see. And are you suggesting that you aren't exhausted and hungry?"

"No," Alrion said stubbornly.

"Then you need the rest anyway and you will be better prepared for when your father does arrive. Doesn't that make sense?"

"That part does. I'm sorry, but you can't understand what we've gone through to get here. And to be treated like that, it's difficult."

"Jovana is our eldest, and our leader. She is the wisest of us all, and very particular about things. But she is always right. You will see," Marla said with a smile. Alrion just shook his head again. Lara smiled.

"You are just used to getting your own way. This is a nice change," she said with a laugh.

"At least you're seeing the humour in this."

"Have you lived here your entire life?" Lara said.

"Yes. I have travelled extensively, but this has always been my home."

"Is it always this cold?" Lara pulled her coat around her tighter.

"Usually. It does vary by season, but it's always cold here. You get used to it. Here's your room," Marla said. She stopped in front of a smaller dome. She didn't walk inside. Alrion walked up to the door and pushed it open. It was a lot heavier than he'd expected, given how easily Marla had been opening them.

There's a lot of surprises here, he thought. Inside was a small fireplace at the rear and four beds. Alyx occupied one. They were low to the ground without any frames. In the middle of the room was a round table laden with food. Mostly fruit, but some bread and meat were also there.

"This looks comfortable," Lara said as she entered.

"Yes, it does. Perhaps we can rest a little," Alrion said.

"You can find me in the great hall if you need anything. But I wouldn't bother our elder until your father arrives. Don't worry, there is plenty of time," Marla said from the entry.

"But it's not just the infection. There are some who are chasing us. They may find this place."

"It is unlikely, since we are protected here. But if that is the case we will know before they arrive. You have time. Rest." Marla left and once the door closed fully the room felt much warmer and comforting.

"You know, we don't get a lot of opportunities like this. Let's just take advantage of it," Lara said. Alrion just sat down on one of the beds and started picking at the food. He was much hungrier than he had realised.

"We made it," Lara said when she had finished eating.

"We did. And Alyx too." Alrion looked over at her again. She seemed to be sleeping peacefully.

"Don't worry, everything will work out. They're mysterious and cryptic, just like everyone said they would be. And they're still helping us."

"I know. I'm grateful. But I can't rest properly until this infection is behind us. And my responsibility to Alyx. I can't move on with my quest otherwise."

"I know. But we have time now. Rest."

"I'll try," Alrion said. He was incredibly tired, and the food had done the job. But he had trouble relaxing. There was still so much to do, so much resting on his shoulders. But sleep came faster than he realised it would.

24

FAMILY REUNITED

Vincent slowed the horse down. He had been riding hard for a long time and he felt like the terrain was changing significantly. And he worried that he may have missed the path.

He had expected it to be obvious, as few would bother to travel this far. In his mind the amulet that Freyda had handed them was more of a token to make them feel more comfortable. But more and more he suspected that it was more than that. That there was something else that he was missing.

The path travelled up and up, and he didn't feel like it was the right direction. It seemed to be meandering into more rocky cliffs than a real destination. So, he turned the horse around and retraced his steps.

He worked his back to another narrow pass and paused. There was something different about this area. He remembered it from when he rode through initially, but he was too preoccupied with his speed to pay it any attention. But now, once again, he had a feeling that something was off. But he couldn't put his finger on it.

Vincent dismounted and tied the horse to a large stone nearby. If there was something here he had to take care and look properly. His feet crunched on the ground as he walked around, looking for some signs of an alternate path. Something was nagging at him, but he couldn't spot anything of note. As he turned something did finally catch his eye. A glint that didn't belong. He turned back and crouched down, carefully examining the area. There had been some snowfall recently, but he spotted the glint again. In a recess of a rock he spotted something. He reached in and plucked it out.

"My father's ring," he said quietly in astonishment. It had been placed there deliberately, a sign for him to follow.

"Well done Alrion. I feel bad that I almost missed it, but you did well to signpost the way." Vincent cleaned off the snow and put it back where he found it.

With any luck my wife will find it too, he thought. It was worth a shot. He had no better way of alerting her, and if need be they could always retrieve the ring. He stood and examined the rock wall from another angle, and saw something odd. He placed his hand on the stone and it passed right through.

An actual hidden path. Now this is certainly mysterious. They give the wizards some competition!

After experimenting with the effect briefly, he strode back to his horse and quickly untied it. Leading it behind him, he ventured through what he thought was the new pass.

It was unnerving but soon he and the horse had passed through completely. Looking back, it was like there was no wall at all.

"Very clever. But now I need to make up for lost time." He mounted the horse swiftly and nudged a little too enthusiastically. The horse bolted forward, and Vincent scrambled to hang on.

That's the way, he thought with a chuckle. Although with the weather ahead, he expected he would need to slow down considerably.

The ride moved ahead without anything of interest, although he did spot a black hand sticking out of the snow. After investigating he realised it was a dead Tracker, and that they had managed to account for the last one that was closely tailing them.

"I should have been here," he said as he remounted the horse. But he couldn't have continued without leaving a message for Celes. She was incredibly resourceful, but needed to be updated. It was dangerous country and she would most likely be alone. He had no choice but to make arrangements.

The first view of the buildings should have filled him with wonder, but instead it just focused his thinking.

"I'm not far now. Hopefully I make it in time." He tried to spur the horse faster, but the snow was falling thicker and caused plenty of trouble. Light was fading too, so he had to balance the need for speed and the danger of rushing along in treacherous conditions and low visibility.

Finally, he saw a figure standing before him. He slowed the horse to a slow walk and approached carefully. The figure was in a robe and was waiting.

"Hello there!" Vincent shouted as he closed in. He wanted to know if the figure was friendly or another attacker.

"Welcome, Andar," the female voice said. Vincent was initially shocked but hid it quickly. He had to assume they knew all about him. It was just a shock hearing his original name used again. He would have to get used to it, since he doubted they would call him Vincent.

"My son has arrived already?" he said after he dismounted.

"Yes, he is resting. Did you want to meet the elder now or wait until morning?" The woman gave him an odd look. He knew she was waiting to see how he would respond. He knew what he should do.

"Has she met him already?"

"Yes, he insisted. She sent him away until you arrived."

"Then I'll wait. Let's do everything at once," Vincent said. In a way she had given him an out by mentioning how Alrion had been sent away. But he could guess as to why.

"I didn't get your name."

"Marla."

"Nice to meet you."

"And you too. I'll take you to where they are staying." Marla strode off confidently and Vincent rushed to keep up. Two women came to take the horse, and he handed over the reins. He looked around now at the domed buildings, marvelling at how they had been built.

Not by any means I know of.

Perhaps they were a clue as to the abilities of the Mystics. The cold was sharp and biting, and he looked forward to getting inside. It had been a long and hard ride to get here. Marla stopped in front of one of the domes and threw the doors open. She gestured inside.

Vincent entered quickly, and saw Lara jump to her feet.

"You still have great instincts. But it's just me," Vincent said. Lara ran over and hugged him.

"That's a welcome. Everything alright?"

"It's fine. Just happy to see a familiar face. And Alrion was turned away because of you."

"I heard. I also spotted the fourth Tracker on the way here. Sorry you had to deal with that."

"We survived. Alyx too." Lara looked down at her. The weapon master was sleeping soundly.

"Good. I suppose I should take a rest too."

"We will summon you in the morning," Marla said, and closed the doors.

"They sure do love their mystery and ceremony here," Vincent said.

"They do. I hope they can help. We found the missing notebook and there was another message?"

"What was it?" Vincent walked over and sat on the last bed.

"The Mystics are not the solution, just a step."

"Hmm how did Alrion take it?"

"He seemed fine generally. But a bit worried." Lara looked over at him sleeping, then sat on her bed.

"Anything worth mentioning for you?"

"No. I rode back and asked Beatrix to pass on a message to my wife and explain what we're up to. Then I came straight here."

"And you found the clue?" Lara chuckled.

"I did. Well, after I rode past it once. It was a clever idea. I left it for Celes, hopefully she finds it too."

"I'm sure she will. I hope whatever happens here, it happens quickly. Alyx's infection is quite progressed."

"That is a worry. But we're here now; there will be what we need. Looking back, I can't imagine this trip without her. She's been instrumental in our survival."

"I know. Well, you probably need to rest. All will be revealed tomorrow."

"It most certainly will," Vincent said. He doused a nearby light and prepared for sleep. He was nervous about what would happen tomorrow. He had no idea how it would go. But one thing was for certain. It would not go well for him.

Vincent awoke first. It was to be expected but still he was glad. He had time to prepare himself before Alrion woke. Lara woke next, but they didn't talk much. They waited for Alrion. When he did eventually wake he sat bolt upright.

"Where are we?" he said, looking around.

"The Mystics, remember?" Lara said. Alrion nodded, but he had already spotted his father.

"Dad! You made it."

"Of course I did. And I appreciated you leaving that ring. I had underestimated the difficulty in finding that path, and I had already missed it once. How are you feeling?"

"Not amazing, but good enough. Now that you're here we can go get some answers from the Mystics."

"Of course. Marla did mention something about summoning us, but I'm sure we can initiate something," Vincent said with a wink.

"Absolutely. I didn't trek to the end of the world to wait around for a summons." Alrion rose quickly and walked around the room. He spotted some food and started to eat. Vincent chuckled to himself and joined his son.

They all ate quickly, and prepared to leave.

"We'll be back soon with a cure, Alyx. Keep resting," Alrion said. Alyx made no response.

"She'll be fine, just needs to recover a bit more," Lara said.

"They will take good care of her. Let's go get those answers you're after," Vincent said. He felt a clenching in the pit of his stomach. But he couldn't avoid it any longer. He had to face up to it.

They walked slowly through the settlement. There were still very few people moving around. Those that were continued going about their business, completely ignoring the travellers.

"Here we are," Alrion said. They stood before the giant hall. Vincent whistled.

"Looks spectacular. I should have expected it. I'll do the honours," Vincent said. He opened the giant doors and walked inside. The room was almost full. The sides were packed with seated women in robes. A large fire burned in the centre of the room and at the very end sat an older woman in a throne, with what looked like Marla at her side.

"That's the elder, Jovana," Alrion whispered to his father.

"Thanks," Vincent said. *And here we go*, he thought. He walked through the room with fake confidence, his footsteps echoing through the eerie quiet. Alrion and Lara followed close behind, remaining quiet. As they approached the throne the older woman waved her hand and Vincent stopped. He saw her disapproving gaze and felt the full force.

"Only now, at your most desperate, have you come to me. My son," Jovana said.

"I'm sorry. You seemed more of a memory than a person I could actually visit," Vincent said. His voice was stronger than he expected. Alrion pulled him aside.

"She called you her son. She's your mother?"

"Yes, she is. My father took me away when I was very young."

"You knew this the whole time? And you said nothing?" Alrion looked angry and confused. Vincent sighed.

"I see your son is surprised also. Rightfully so. You kept this from him too?" Jovana said.

"Until recently he even hid the fact that Granthion was my grandfather," Alrion said. Jovana shook her head.

"You have disrespected and neglected your family. For what?" Jovana looked through Vincent. He didn't have a good answer.

"It was easier that way. You may not know, but I left my father. I forged my own path."

"Of course I know, you're my son. And what good did that do you? You're here with the same problem that he was faced with."

"The Blight."

"Exactly. It was his obsession, and eventually his undoing. Your sticking your head in the sand for over two decades didn't help at all did it?"

"At least my son had a normal upbringing!" Vincent felt like he was right in what he had done. Even if he had insulted his family in the process.

"A normal upbringing? He's the grandson of the greatest wizard and Mystic that ever lived. Why should he have a normal upbringing?"

"Because I never had one." The room went quiet.

"Well, because of your decision you have missed a lot. Did you know that you had a twin sister?" Jovana said. Vincent was floored.

"No," he managed to say, his voice cracking. He looked around the room.

"She's not with us anymore. She passed giving birth to her daughter, Marla." Jovana reached out and held Marla's hand. Vincent looked at her more closely. He could see a resemblance. It made sense now.

"I'm sorry, I have done you all a disservice. But it was not out of malice."

"Of course not. You're just a foolish boy. I knew that you would be in trouble with your father, but that was how it had to be. So here we are. Much too late you have arrived on my doorstep asking for help. You should have done so sooner, and all of this could have been avoided!"

"What do you mean?" Alrion said.

"You really should know better. Had you come to me earlier, you could have been trained properly."

"Trained in what?"

"The power of Soul. Our power. It runs through your veins, because you are my grandson. My son has it also, not that he ever thought to use it." Jovana had a defiant smile on her face. Vincent felt his blood run cold. He had never considered that. He always assumed that his parentage was just a fact, that it had no repercussions.

"That's not possible. Only women are Mystics," he said.

"Generally, yes. But there are exceptions. And a wizard can make a big difference."

"I am a wizard and a Mystic?" Alrion said.

"Yes. And as a Mystic, if you had come to train with us, you would already be immune to the Blight." Joana's look was half-amusement, half-concern. Alrion looked incredulous.

"I don't believe it."

"Why do you think the infection has moved so slowly?" Marla said. Alrion just stared at his hands.

This is not quite what I expected, Vincent thought. He was as blindsided as Alrion. Perhaps things could have been different. If he had embraced his family, really thought about what the benefits could be to Alrion, he could have avoided so much. He felt sick. His own selfishness in doing what he thought was right had cost them so dearly.

"You are not beyond help. You can both be trained. We should not waste time," Jovana said.

"How will training help me now? I'm so far gone. Can't you just heal me?" Alrion sounded defeated and overwhelmed.

"I can't heal you. Why do you think we never cured the Blight? Because that is not how our power works. I have done the impossible many times in my life, but that is one thing that cannot be done with Soul power alone."

"So what hope is there for me then?"

"Learn the power. Unlike your Spark, it cannot be tainted by the Blight. Unlock your full potential and you will cure yourself!" Jovana looked triumphant. Alrion looked up at her, a hopeful look on his face. But he needed encouragement.

"Alrion, we will do this together. We will set things right. Correct the course that we are on. You can cure yourself, then you can learn how to cure Alyx. He can do that right?"

"Your father found a way, and he had no Soul power. I'm sure Alrion will discover the secret. That's the whole point of your quest, isn't it?"

"Yes," Alrion said.

"And I will learn too. So that I can't be infected. Then I can protect you." Vincent was resolute. He would not fail his family again.

25

A NEW POWER

"**M**arla will start your training. Immediately," Jovana said. She waved them away and returned to staring into the bowl of water before her. Marla descended the steps smiling.

"There's a lot for you to learn, cousin," Marla said. Alrion blinked. Of course.

"Sure. Sorry I had no idea we were related. I had no idea of a lot of things," Alrion said. He felt completely blindsided. He had travelled all this way, not knowing the real reason. And his father had gone with him, all the while saying nothing. He couldn't believe that, after all that had happened, he still hadn't revealed this. He looked at his father as they walked through the hall. The women on chairs had been silent the entire time. Just watching proceedings.

"Mum was so angry at you when you revealed who your father was. This is just the next level," Alrion said. Vincent winced in pain.

"You're right. I'm in serious trouble when she arrives."

"Jovana would say you deserve it."

"I would agree." Vincent paused and opened the giant doors. Lara walked through first. Alrion watched her go. She had been quiet the whole time. He rushed past his father to catch up to her.

"Dad we will discuss this again later. Lara, what are you thinking?"

"I'm still trying to grasp everything. You're not just a wizard, but also a male Mystic? It's a lot to take in. They can't cure Alyx?"

"I guess not."

"What the eldest said is true. But, we can help her. We are Healers after all," Marla said. She overtook them and started to lead the way.

"Before we start, we need to see her. To explain what is going on." Alrion needed Alyx to understand the situation. He had promised to cure her, but he hadn't expected to be the one to do it himself. She had to understand that it was his top priority.

"Very well, we will stop there first. But this is not a fast process. Even though you are descended from the eldest, it will be very difficult for you. Perhaps even more so with your ... infection." Marla looked at Alrion's neck as she spoke, and he shied away. He was very self-conscious of the marks. They showed how far his infection had come. But it sounded like he could do something about it. The Soul power could keep the infection away, or even overpower it. That was something he desperately needed. The sooner he could be rid of it, the sooner he could access his Spark.

"Don't be alarmed, we already have some Mystics visiting your friend," Marla said. They had reached their dome, and Marla opened the door. She waited outside and ushered them in.

Alyx was sitting up and alert. There were two Mystics beside her, their hands glowing with a bright white light.

"What are they doing? The elder told me you can't cure the Blight," Alrion said.

"The Blight is repelled by the power of Soul, so by using it in an appropriate way it can help slow the process," Marla said. The two Mystics remained quiet.

"I think it's helping," Alyx said.

"How are you feeling?" Alrion said. He moved a little closer.

"Mostly the same, but I have a bit more energy. The final part of the journey was a bit hazy, but I see we made it. What's the plan now?"

"It's a long story, but essentially my father and I seem to possess the same power as the Mystics. The eldest, Jovana, is my grandmother."

"That seems like quite a revelation. Your father said nothing before today?"

"No." Alrion looked at his father. Vincent didn't say anything.

"Very well. How does that help us?"

"If I train in this power, I can cure myself. And then I suppose figure out how to cure others. They weren't particularly clear on that."

"That's because it's your part of the equation. Soul power will be required, but we can't cleanse the Blight in others with it. As a wizard you have that capability," Marla said patiently.

"I see. Well, there seems to be a lot more to this, but it seems clear that they should be able to hold off my infection long enough for you to cure yourself. Then you are both more effective at fighting the Blight, and you can figure out how to cure me."

"That's it."

"A better position than we were in a day ago. You'd best get started though," Alyx said. She pointed at the door.

"As you wish. Good to see you're doing relatively well. Take care," Alrion said. Vincent said his goodbyes too and they left the dome.

"Soon you're going to have to explain things more. I'm not quite satisfied," Alrion said to his father.

"That's reasonable. But there's not much else I can say. Try to imagine that you don't remember your mother, and I described her as living in a faraway place and never talked about her. Would you feel compelled to seek her out?"

"Yes. I would need to know."

"Then we are different in that respect. Let's talk about it more later." Vincent looked away, clearly uncomfortable. Alrion wanted to say more, but decided to leave it. They had something else more important to do.

The snow crunched under their boots as they made their way to another dome. This one initially looked like it was completely covered in snow. But once Alrion was closer, he saw that it was made from a lighter colour of stone.

"This one looks different," he said.

"Yes, this is the Pool of Reflection. It is instrumental to our training." Marla stopped in front of the building, next to the main door.

"That's interesting. Any connection to the Pool of Knowledge?"

"I don't think so. Come inside," Marla said. She opened the door and ushered them in.

Inside the lighting was dim, but Alrion could see the pool immediately. It was large and still, began in the centre of the room and took up half the space inside. The most interesting aspect though was the light glow that shone off the surface of the water.

"This is incredible," Lara said. She stepped forward carefully.

"Is the water the only source of light in here?" Alrion said. He couldn't spot any torches or windows anywhere.

"Yes. Below the ground is what we call the Great Source. It is a large well of water that is infused with Soul power," Marla said. She walked forward and sat cross-legged before the pool.

"Was that done by the Mystics?" Alrion said.

"No, it has always been that way. We believe that is why our home is here."

"Is that what the elder peers into as well?" Lara said.

"You are quite perceptive. Yes, every day water is drawn from here and taken there. The elder uses it for various purposes."

"Such as?" Alrion said.

"She can see a great many things in the reflection."

"Is that how she would have watched me?" Vincent said. He still looked uncomfortable.

"I suppose so. Nobody else knows how to do that, it's a skill only the elder possesses."

"Why do you call her the elder, and not grandmother? Or something similar?"

"She is the eldest first, and my grandmother second."

"Can this water give us power?" Alrion said.

"No, the water is a focus and an aid. Nobody can give you Soul power. It is within you. Much like your Spark."

"You said we could train it?"

"Yes, that's what we are here for. I will begin by explaining some of the basic concepts. Then your friend will need to return to the visitor residence. She cannot participate in the training."

"But ..."

"Don't worry, I have other things to attend to. Let's hear the overview," Lara said. Marla swivelled around so she faced them.

"I hinted at this earlier, but in many ways Soul power is the complete opposite to Spark. You use it to manipulate the world outside, but struggle to manipulate yourself."

"That's right. I learned a healing spell, and I was told that it was next to useless on myself. I needed another wizard to heal me."

"Exactly. Soul power is used to manipulate yourself, and cannot be used on others. That is why we cannot cure people of the Blight."

"There has to be exceptions though. When I was almost dead at the Pool of Knowledge, I managed to heal myself enough to not die. The wizard who attacked me couldn't believe it."

"Your Spark did not do that."

"Then what did?"

"In your time of need, you must have tapped into your Soul power. Even a trickle would have been enough to make the difference."

"I never considered that." Alrion went quiet, he was thinking over what it meant. He didn't think there were any other situations where he may have used it.

"If Soul power only affects you, how come you can heal others?" Lara said.

"Excellent question. There are two aspects to the healing. The first is that by having mastery over our own bodies, we can better diagnose and cure others."

"That makes sense. Mostly," Lara said.

"The other aspect is that we can enhance our bodies with Soul power, perhaps even to the point of saturation. Then the effect spills out and can affect others. That is what you witnessed with your friend Alyx."

"Wouldn't that be a lot less effective?" Alrion said.

"Of course. But with the proper training you can overcome that. There are also other tricks where you can help convince the body to better heal itself. We've been doing this for a long time."

"And doing it in a subtle way. Were those Healers we encountered on the way Mystics?" Vincent said.

"In this area, yes all the Healers are Mystics. Some return here regularly, others only come once to master their gift and never return."

"And they never said anything. It was all vague and supportive, but not specific," Lara said.

"Of course. Our order survives on its secrecy. Many years ago, some of us acted openly. But they were cursed as witches and hunted ruthlessly. We learned our lesson, and hide in plain sight. There is a good reason why we also learn the art of herbs and other treatments."

"She's got an answer for everything," Lara said.

"They're not answers, they're explanations. This is what we do, and why."

"Anything else I need to know?" Lara said.

"Yes. Soul power regenerates slowly over time. There are only a few ways to speed it up, and they are not particularly effective either."

"Well, I wouldn't need to use it that much, would I?" Alrion said.

"To overcome your infection, you would need to draw upon perhaps the entire amount. That is significant. I also assume curing anyone else of the Blight, should you figure out the method, would also be very taxing. You could probably only do one person at a time."

"That's worth considering," Lara said.

"Yes, although it's not that strange. I have limits to my Spark too and I have to rest to recover."

"Good. You will just need time to become accustomed to your Soul power and its reserves. Now, I believe that is enough of the introductory statements. Lara, you will need to leave now." Marla gestured to the door and Lara nodded.

"I'll keep Alyx company. You better learn fast, we need more options for when Wraith eventually knocks on the door."

"I'll do my best," Alrion said.

"Do better!" Lara said, and left. Marla waited until the door had fully closed then turned her attention back to Vincent and Alrion.

"Any other questions before we proceed?"

"How long will this take?" Alrion said.

"It will take a lifetime to master, as with anything. However, the eldest believes that since you are her descendent, you should have a large capacity. Therefore, even if you lack the skill and finesse, within days you should be able to access enough to overturn your infection."

"Good that she thinks it is possible. If we didn't have terrible things bearing down on us I would jump for joy at that suggestion. To think that I may be rid of this curse that soon is incredible. But, it may be too long."

"It's a fantastic opportunity, don't overanalyse it just yet. Let her begin, and we will get a feel for how it is progressing," Vincent said. Alrion saw the value in that, and he gave his full attention to Marla.

"Good, now we can begin." Marla quickly spun around, facing the water once more. "Sit next to me and cross your legs as I am."

"Sure," Alrion said. He sat on her left, and Vincent sat on her right. Alrion found it uncomfortable sitting with his legs crossed but ignored it.

"Now, take your right hand and hold it out with your palm facing the water." Marla demonstrated and Alrion followed along. His hand was hovering above the glowing water. He looked over and saw his father doing the same.

"Good. Now focus your attention on your hand. Can you feel a warm tingling sensation?" Marla's face was calm and she looked over at Alrion. He concentrated but didn't feel anything yet.

"I can," Vincent said.

"Good, hold that feeling. Alrion try harder," Marla said. Alrion sighed and resumed his concentration. He tried to remember the exercise he had done with Certan, maintaining his will over the floating strip of wood. There had been effortlessness to it, once he'd figured it out. This would be the same kind of thing. He slowed everything down, isolating the feeling in his arm, then his hand. He felt a cool sensation, almost slimy. He had a good idea of what that was, but pushed it away. He searched harder for what Marla had described. Focusing on his hand, letting it tell him what it was feeling above all else. He started to feel it, faint at first, but getting stronger and stronger.

"I'm getting it," Alrion said, almost in a panic. He felt he could lose it at any moment.

"Excellent. The water helps as a focus, and an amplifier. That's why we train here. Now I need you to take that feeling, and trace it all the way back to your heart."

"Easier said than done." Alrion had struggled to even get that far. And now to go even further? But it was all he could do right now, so he set his mind to it. He latched onto that feeling, and nurtured it. He coaxed it back up his arm slowly. He suspected that actually the feeling was emanating from somewhere else, that he wasn't really working it up his arm. But the idea helped him continue, so he ran with it. Bit by bit, he felt the sensation travelling up his arm. Then it started to cross over to his chest, just under his collarbone.

His thoughts immediately turned to the black marks on his neck, the source of his infection. And like that, it was as if the slimy ooze of the Blight had overwhelmed him. The warm sensation was lost immediately, and Alrion slumped down in despair. He looked over at his father, sitting calmly.

"I have done it," Vincent said quietly. Marla nodded and looked over at Alrion.

"What happened?"

"It was working, but then something happened. I'm not sure if my focus was too close to where I was infected, or it was my thinking about it. But it was all lost in an instant. It was like the Blight overtook the feeling and my concentration."

"There's something to that. Partially in your mind, but partially interference. The infection coursing through you does not want you tapping into your Soul power. It fears it. You will have difficulty learning."

"Great, just want I needed to hear!" Alrion said. He felt defeated.

"The reward is worth it. Or are you going to give up on Alyx?" Vincent said. Alrion felt a surge of anger.

"Just because it's so easy for you! Of course I won't give up." Alrion knew his father was only trying to help. And holding onto the anger wouldn't be helpful. But at the same time, he couldn't seem to let go of it just yet.

26

FALTERING

Alrion lay back down, exhausted.

"You've earned a break," Marla said. Despite the cold, Alrion oozed sweat from the sheer concentration required. It was slow and frustrating progress. His father seemed to be having an easier time of it, which just made it all harder.

"Will it at some point get easier?" Alrion said.

"It will, when you cure yourself. Until then, I doubt there will be a significant change," Marla said. Alrion looked over at his father.

"You seem to be doing better."

"Only because I don't have the handicap you do. You're working harder than both of us," Vincent said. He gave Alrion a reassuring smile. It should have worked, but it just annoyed Alrion more.

"I just wish there was a way to know it was working."

"Of course it's working. You are finding a way to work through the exercises. What else do you need?" Marla said.

"Some sort of feedback that's more tangible than this feeling I'm chasing. Being a wizard is very different. You see something happening from the very beginning."

"Again, that's because your talent lies with manipulating the world. Soul power will be less tangible, because you are just affecting yourself. And you are at the same time learning to be more sensitive to your body. It's just how it is." Marla sounded like she was sick of repeating herself. Alrion figured that she had probably never trained anyone who was infected before.

There's a first time for everything, he thought.

"I do think Alrion has a good point though. When will we know that we've reached a breakthrough?"

"You'll know it when you feel it. It's like an explosion of warmth and light and envelops your entire body. You feel calm and at peace, a tranquillity that feels like it will never end."

"That would be obvious."

"Does that mean that I would be cured?" Alrion said.

"Yes. I don't see how the Blight would be able to survive such a transformation."

"That's good to know. I'll just have to keep working at it then."

"Good. Now that you've had a short rest, we should continue. Next we will be focusing on your head." Marla stood and gestured for Alrion and Vincent to do the same.

"This time you get to cheat a little bit. We're going to dunk our heads in the water." Marla looked at them both, awaiting their response.

"Wouldn't that contaminate it?" Vincent said.

"You think this water cares about whatever's on your skin?" Marla raised one eyebrow.

"I suppose not."

"What about me? Can't I taint it somehow?" Alrion was still concerned about his infection.

"Have you been paying attention? Your infection is internal, and there's enough Soul power infused in this water to drive the Blight away. No more excuses, just follow my lead." Marla stepped up to the water. She knelt carefully, then with a swift motion dunked her head in. It was over before they realised and she quickly swept her hair back to keep the water from running into her eyes.

"Alrion next," she said. Alrion joined her, and kneeled on her left side.

Let's see what this does.

He ducked his head into the water without thinking. It felt heavy, like it could pull him in. He struggled against it, pulling his head back and gasping for air. The water streamed down his face and he wiped it away.

"Why did you keep your head in the water?" Marla said. Alrion gave her a confused look. He noticed his father was hovering over them, concern on his face.

"I didn't keep it under. My head felt heavy, like the water was pulling me in. I had to force myself back up again."

"I've never heard of that before." Marla went very quiet.

"You were under for a good thirty seconds," Vincent said. Alrion felt sick.

"It didn't feel like that long. Wow, was the water trying to drown me. Can it do that?"

"Of course not. Never mind, it's done now. Vincent your turn now," she said. Alrion watched very closely. His father dunked his head in swiftly, and had it back out of the water instantaneously.

"That's what I expected," Marla said. Vincent swept the hair out of his face and looked at Alrion.

"We have to assume it was a weird reaction due to the Blight. Don't dwell on it too much. What do we do now?" Vincent said.

"Now we focus once more. This time we need to feel the energy within our core. Then we are going to run it up to our head. This will be tricky, but is a crucial step in both your training and preparation."

This is going to be difficult.

All the exercises that seemed to come close to his neck had either been sabotaged or a strain on him. It was no coincidence either, with that being where he had been infected.

Well, one way or another I need to get this to work. Here we go, he thought. He started to focus, capturing the feeling within his chest. The strange vibration and tingling. As he felt it he kept the sensation going. He made sure it was as strong as he could get it. Then he started to move it upwards.

It was slow to travel. He wasn't sure if that was because of the weight of it, or whether it was due to where he was moving it. But he pushed the thoughts away and kept his focus. He pushed more and more. Guiding that feeling along. It was half-pushing, half-coaxing. He couldn't describe it properly, just that it was a strange mix of actions to keep it moving along.

It began to approach his neck. There was no other way to reach his head; he had to push through it. As expected there was resistance. Like a wall, or a blockage that would not budge. He urged the feeling onwards, did everything he knew to keep it going. He tried to tear down that blockage, to will it away.

He tried and tried, and it seemed like he was slowly wearing it down. He could feel the energy within him gathering, getting ready to smash through and continue on the path he had set for it. Then suddenly he crashed. The feeling dissipated completely and he felt groggy.

Alrion was lying on the floor. He sat up slowly, and looked around. Something was wrong. He looked up at the ceiling and it was slowly oscillating. The room looked like it was threatening to spin around.

"That was not good. I feel dizzy," he said. It was scary. Like his senses were working against him.

"Your infection wound is on your neck, right?" Marla said. She was examining him closely.

"Yes, take a look."

"Hmm, this is obviously new territory for us all. It seems to be quite resistant. You may need to skip this exercise."

"Skip? What do you mean?"

"Let me explain. As I mentioned before, these exercises are a mix of training, but also preparation. You must learn how to feel the Soul power within, as well as move it around the body. But at the same time, we are unlocking your ability to use it."

"What do you mean by that?" Vincent said.

"There are multiple places in your body that are like gateways for Soul power. You need to activate those gateways to allow it to be easier to flow. It will not only amplify your total power, but also speed up the flow and transfer. The head is a very important connection to make, so that's why I asked you to dunk your head. Saturating it with water infused with Soul power helps overcome some blockages. But not all, it would seem." Marla stared at Alrion's neck. He felt really self-conscious and found himself adjusting his cloak to better hide it.

"That makes sense. But what does it mean for me?" Alrion said.

"You may need to come back to that exercise last. When the rest of your body is better prepared for the Soul power. Then you can overwhelm the Blight and cure yourself in one go."

"That's probably better than I had thought. I can just come back to it?"

"Yes. It will make the rest of your training harder, but you're already used to that right?" Marla smiled. Alrion shook his head and laughed. It was much louder and fuller than he had expected.

"Yes, nothing is ever easy. How much more are we expected to do today?"

"That's it. You should return and rest. I will brief the eldest and we will continue again tomorrow." Marla rose gracefully and tied up her wet hair.

"Should we dry this off?" Vincent said.

"No, it's better if you leave it."

"As you wish." Alrion stood and stretched a little. He felt quite stiff from all the sitting. He'd started to have a headache too.

That's the last thing I needed.

But he tried to stop the inner complaints. He followed Marla back to the entrance. She opened the door and pointed outside.

"I must remain here a bit longer before I report back. You can find your way back to your accommodation."

"Of course. Thank you for your assistance," Vincent said.

"You are welcome. You are family after all."

"So we are. Thank you and see you tomorrow," Alrion said. He followed his father out into the freezing cold. He had forgotten just how cold it was.

At first, he thought it was due to how well the building had been heated. However, he realised that it hadn't been well heated at all.

I wonder if that's a result of us training? I'll have to ask tomorrow.

They walked back to their room in silence. Alrion didn't feel like conversation, and his father seemed to understand that.

"Welcome back. How was everything?" Lara said as they entered the room. It felt a lot warmer inside.

"It was a difficult day. But we made good progress didn't we, Alrion?" Vincent said.

"I suppose so. The Blight is holding me back, but I'll find a way. I'm starving too!"

"Dig in, we can hear all about it later." Lara gestured to the food. Alrion looked over at Alyx and saw that she was asleep.

"Don't worry, she's fine. Sat up all day, but finally crashed," Lara said.

"Good." Alrion started with the food immediately. The more he ate, the more ravenous he felt.

It was deceptively hard. I hope I can do this in time, he thought. As he ate he glanced up periodically. It felt like Lara was watching him closely. But every time she appeared to be looking elsewhere.

Once Alrion finished, he shuffled over to his bed.

"Sorry, but I'm exhausted. It was a tough day, and I had a few setbacks. My dad can fill you in. But the good news is, when I do eventually have a breakthrough it will hopefully cure me of the Blight."

"Wow, that's amazing! It sounds worth the effort."

"It truly is. You rest son, I'll update Lara. You need to recover and get back to it tomorrow with your full focus."

"Thanks. Goodnight," Alrion said. He didn't even wait to hear what they said. He closed his eyes and sleep was waiting to pounce on him.

～

Alrion did not have a restful sleep. He kept dreaming of white orbs of light, travelling down dark hallways, being blocked by black walls. A part of him knew this was somehow related to his day, but it was only a dim awareness. Each time the orb was blocked, he felt his anger and frustration rising. Finally, there was a group of four lights all trying to go down a single corridor. But the black wall was steadfast, and oozed a black liquid. One by one it extinguished the lights. Alrion screamed in frustration.

"There you are!" Wraith said, his voice echoing and booming. Alrion found himself inside the dream corridor. He hadn't just been dreaming it, he had been present.

"What's going on?" he said.

"Oh, I was just hosting this little show for you. I see you enjoyed it!"

"These are my dreams. How can you do this?"

"With great difficulty I'm afraid. And a little outside help. But you left me no choice. You ran away to a secret place and started plotting your own cure. But now I have you."

"What do you mean? This is just a dream."

"Oh, that is true. But I know where you are. I have your location. It doesn't matter how many secret paths or tricks there are before getting to you. I know where you are, so I will find the way. You can't run any longer."

"I don't need to run. I'll face you. And I have help here." Alrion hoped Wraith fell for the bluff. He didn't feel confident in the slightest, but he had to try something.

"Your little band of Mystics? They don't scare me. In fact, I have one of them with me now. She's quite the interesting sort. We're poking and prodding her. Learning all about that special power." Wraith laughed, the sound rising in volume and echoing all around. Alrion blocked his ears trying to ignore it.

"You're lying!" Alrion said. The laughter died down.

"I'm really not. Her name is Freyda. And when I'm done with her, she won't be resistant to the Blight anymore," Wraith said. Alrion's spirit dropped. She had helped them. She had given them the amulet that had shown them the way. And Wraith had taken her and done who knows what. It was his fault.

"You've gone silent. You know I'm telling the truth. Good. It doesn't matter what you're up to over there. I know where you are, I know how to handle your Mystics, and I can create more Shade Wizards. You have no chance. So just sit tight and get ready to hand yourself over." Wraith shrieked one more terrifying laugh then went silent. Alrion looked around at the space around him. In the dream all the ways had become black and oozing. And they were closing in.

"You won't win. I'll never let you!" Alrion shouted. As the walls finally came into contact with him everything went bright white.

Alrion sat up quickly, gasping for air. He looked around the room in shock. He was in his bed. It was the visitor room. Nobody else seemed to be around.

That's odd.

He stood and paced around the room. There was food laid out. And the other beds were neatly made. He spotted a folded piece of paper on his father's bed. He opened it up and read the contents.

You look like you need the rest. Lara and Alyx have been summoned to see the eldest. I am starting the training early. Come join us when you are up.
    - Dad

Alrion folded the note and replaced it. He now had an explanation for where everyone was, which was good. The details of his dream were firmly etched in his mind There was no forgetting them. He immediately started thinking of Freya, and what Wraith might be doing. His appetite quickly disappeared.

"Try not to think about that. Eat, and come up with a plan," he told himself. Walking over to the food, Alrion sat and forced himself to eat. He felt his hunger reappear as he ate, even though he wasn't enjoying the food.

Wraith knows where I am. He has more Shade Wizards, he has captured Freyda and he will probably know all he needs to know before he gets here. All because of me.

No matter how he twisted it around, it all came back to him. He had failed to deal with Wraith. He had become infected. He had led everyone to the Mystics, and in doing so put them in Wraith's path.

What if they're not?

He could leave the settlement. Let Wraith track him somewhere else. The Mystics would be spared and he could surely continue the training they had started him on.

This might be better for everyone, he thought. He didn't want anyone else to suffer for him. He started to feel his anger rise again at the thought. His failings had put him in this position, and everyone else had suffered because of it. He had an opportunity now to set things right. He could draw Wraith away from them, and spare them. At least he would do something right It was a move he could actually make by himself.

"I have to do it. They'll understand. But I have to start now. Otherwise Wraith will be too close and won't divert himself." Alrion started packing his things. He packed some food that would last well, and thought about making his bed.

No, that's too obvious. I need to buy time.

Taking one last look around the room, he cemented his decision.

"No more being a burden. I'm finally doing something." He opened the door to leave, before he lost the will to follow it through.

"Where do you think you're going?" Lara said. She was standing right outside with Alyx. Alyx looked a lot better, and Alrion was surprised to see her on her feet. He was about to explain when he felt Lara shove him back inside.

"We need to talk. Before you do something stupid," she said.

27

MEETING OF THE MINDS

"**U**nbelievable!" Lara said as she entered the room. The shock on Alrion's face was worth it though. She had to capitalise on that.

"We were summoned by the eldest, Jovana. I was surprised quite frankly. She didn't seem to be the sort to want anything to do with us. But she said we needed to convince you not to leave."

"I thought she was mistaken, that you would never leave us. But here we are," Alyx said. She sat down on her bed.

"Sit!" Lara said, pointing at Alrion's bed. He sat down. That was good, he was listening. She had a chance.

"So, what was going through your mind? Why were you trying to sneak off?" Lara said.

"Why would you?" Alrion started to say.

"Don't bother with that. Jovana told us she saw it happening, and here we are. Do you think we're going to believe that you packed that bag to go train?" Lara stared at Alrion with all her fury, and he seemed to resign himself.

"You would agree if you'd been through what I did last night."

"Just talk to us. What happened?" Alyx said. Alrion sighed. He looked reluctant but he started to talk.

"The training was hard. And frustrating. The Blight is holding me back. I got angry a few times, and I think it tipped off Wraith."

"What do you mean?" Lara said.

"He was in my dreams last night. He told me he knows where I am, that the Mystics wouldn't stop him. And he's bringing more Shade Wizards."

"That's not great news, but we can stop them. Look, even Alyx is on her feet!"

"I'm happy about that, but that's not all. He has Freyda!"

"The Healer? That's not good," Lara said.

"And whatever he's up to, he knows she's a Mystic. He even said that he's figuring out how to bypass her resistance to the Blight!"

"He's bluffing," Lara said. She looked at Alyx.

"Of course he is. Don't take it all to heart," Alyx said.

"He's not. I can feel it. He's not just saying that, he believes it. If he can create Shade Wizards, and Trackers, or whatever else he's been up to, then he can with enough time turn a Mystic. I can't let them suffer for my mistakes."

"Oh, now we're getting somewhere. You're going off by yourself to protect everyone else?" Lara said. Now she was beginning to understand. It was still ridiculous, but made more sense.

"It's me he's after. How many more need to suffer? If I leave now, he won't even make it to this place. He will need to track me somewhere else."

"And how will you cure yourself?"

"If I can succeed with the Mystic training, I will be cured. They've shown me most of it, I just need to continue until I get a breakthrough. It's not ideal, but at least I'll be doing something to help them." Alrion looked desperate. Lara could see that Wraith had really rattled him.

"How are you going to heal me then? He'll track you down, and you'll be alone. You'll just get captured and infected again," Alyx said.

"Didn't you swear you would cure her? Going off by yourself is just irresponsible!" Lara said. Alrion looked down. He seemed to be weakening.

"I know it's a long shot. But I can't stay here knowing what's coming."

"You are progressing in your training, your father told us all about it. Yes, there have been some setbacks. It was never going to be easy. Not with your infection. But we can all work together to take down Wraith," Lara said.

"You will be able to cure yourself and then me a lot faster if you stay. Isn't that worth the risk? Doesn't that tip the odds in our favour? You and me full strength standing together?" Alyx said. Alrion looked up at her, a new look of hope on his face. He didn't seem as defeated.

"Isn't it better to gamble on us, than to gamble on yourself alone? We're stronger together, and the Mystics are your family. They won't desert you. I doubt they would let you leave. Just save everyone the time and hassle and stay." Lara could see him coming around. He just needed another push.

"You don't even need to think about our next move. Lara and I will figure out a plan of attack. You just need to focus on working with the Mystics. Focus on the training. That's what's most important!" Alyx said. Alrion sighed one more time and closed his eyes. He sat still for a long time.

"I can't fail again. Not to him," Alrion said quietly.

"You won't. We'll be beside you," Lara said.

"Fine. I'm sorry about all this, but it felt like the right move. Maybe Wraith did all that to make me do something stupid. Anyway, I'm too scattered right now. You're right. You figure out a plan, and I'll focus on my training. Once I'm cured, I can stand on an equal footing with you both." Alrion stood tall with a new determination in his eyes.

"That works for me. Alyx?" Lara said.

"Yes, that is a good plan. Good luck with your training."

"I better get to it. See you later," Alrion said. He walked to the door, opened it quickly and strode out of the building. Lara watched and waited. After he was gone for thirty seconds she went and collapsed on her bed.

"We did it. He bought it. You can rest now," she said. Alyx slumped down onto the bed. She looked completely exhausted.

"Did they say you would improve?" Lara said.

"No. They could only keep things at bay. And the more I exert myself, the weaker their techniques get. I'll have to be careful and only do what I must to show Alrion."

"Yes, please just be comfortable now. I have to say, I only half-believed Jovana. But she was completely right. Had we been any later we would have missed him!"

"That's the proof. I'm not sure what she can see in that water of hers, but it saved us right now. It would have been catastrophic if he left now."

"Exactly. He's not ready to be alone. But it's certainly alarming that Wraith knows about this place now, and has a way to deal with or even infect the Mystics. We need to go tell Jovana about that."

"Maybe she already knows," Alyx said. She used a pillow to prop herself up a little and face Lara.

"It's definitely possible. I'll go talk to her later just in case. So, we convinced Alrion to stay the course. It took some bluffing but we did it. Now we need to come up with a plan."

"It's not like I can do anything else like this," Alyx said. She closed her eyes and lay back. Her hair spilled out of the tie she usually used. Lara could see that underneath the facade and the dress, Alyx was actually beautiful. That reminded her of how Alrion kept looking at the weapon master. Maybe he saw it also.

"I want to ask you something, before we start," Lara said. Just even broaching the topic made her uncomfortable, but she would have no better opportunity.

"Yes of course."

"I've seen how Alrion looks at you," Lara said, watching Alyx's reaction.

"Oh," Alyx said, sitting up with some effort. "He's sweet, but it doesn't mean anything."

"I'm not so sure about that," Lara said. It had been worrying her, and she was convinced it was why for the longest time she was hostile with Alyx.

"No, truly. I'm not that experienced in these matters, but I am familiar with this situation. It is not an attraction, it is equal components admiration and responsibility."

"What do you mean?"

"He was overwhelmed by my skill with weapons and my fighting style. Only because he is just a recent student of the sword, and his recent circumstances have led him to be reliant on it. Secondly, he feels responsible for my infection. So, he places the burden upon himself, which extends to anything that happens to me. To be fair, I've had a rough time since we met." Alyx didn't show any emotion. Lara understood what was said, but still wasn't convinced.

"You have feelings for him, right?" Alyx said.

"Yes," Lara said, after a long pause. Alyx nodded.

"He feels the same."

"Has he told you?"

"No, but I am confident."

"There's no way to know for sure," Lara said. She felt troubled. From the very start there had been something about him. Even that first encounter where she stole from him. She never did that anymore, not to strangers on the street. But it was an opportunity to interact with him, in some way.

"When two people are so focused on something, they don't have the time to acknowledge any feelings. As you know, I have spent my life avenging my father's death."

"Yes. I still can't believe it."

"It gets easier with time. Too easy, in fact. It will be difficult to live a different life. Anyway, there was a time when I opened my eyes to another possibility."

"What happened?"

"It was my commanding officer when I trained at Valrytir. He was kind and strong and understanding. He treated me like a human, not like the weapon I had forged myself into. Much like Alrion treats me.

I did not say anything, and told myself that he felt nothing. So, we continued, like normal."

"What happened?"

"I volunteered for a scouting mission with him. He wanted to take another woman with us, a specialist archer. I convinced him otherwise, keen to have the opportunity to spend some time with him. But it was my great undoing." Alyx sighed and a tear rolled down her face.

"Why?"

"We sprung an enemy ambush meant for our main force. We retreated quickly, but there were too many. He saved my life, and we escaped. But he had been hit with two poisoned arrows. If we had taken the archer, it would have been a different story."

"He died?"

"Yes. I confessed to him before he passed, explaining my foolishness. He admitted to me he had feelings too, but thought that it was nothing as well. But in the vain hope he had let himself be talked out of taking the archer. We were both fools, but he paid the price." Alyx turned her head away and lay back down. Silence sat upon the room. Lara couldn't believe the story. She had treated Alyx like everyone else had. Assuming that she was just a soldier. But, of course, deep down she was like everyone else.

"I'm so sorry," Lara said.

"It was a long time ago. I keep it buried. I just wanted to say, the reason I shared the story was to show you that I only appreciate Alrion's attention and kindness for what it is. I seek nothing more. And as a warning for you. We come to dangerous times. If you both fail to acknowledge anything, you may make a fatal mistake. Like I did."

"I don't know what to say. But thank you."

"You are welcome. Now, perhaps some planning?"

"Yes, absolutely. I've actually been thinking for a while, there seems to be no way to defeat Wraith. But today, I had a revelation."

"What was it?"

"He's a monster in his current form. Almost indestructible and has a good selection of spells. He seems much more adept than the Shade Wizard we defeated."

"Yes, I believe the tactic we used may only create an opening for Wraith, and it would be hard to defeat him in a single strike."

"Exactly. But, what if Wraith wasn't a Shade Wizard? Then we could deal with him."

"True. But we can't change that."

"Maybe we can. What if Alrion cures him?" Lara said. It sounded crazy out loud. Healing their enemy. But it also took away his power.

"If it worked, then yes. He would be a normal wizard. We could work with that." Alyx was suddenly more alert.

"I know. But, Alrion hasn't even cured himself. Let alone someone else."

"Do you think Wraith would back off if Alrion was cured?"

"Maybe. I guess it would depend on the situation. He didn't back off at the temple with the monks."

"But that was before Alrion could cure the Blight." Alyx sat up again, energy in her features.

"Alrion curing himself could make Wraith reconsider coming here, because he's at danger of being cured. That might buy us the time we need." Lara thought there was something to that. But it didn't seem altogether right.

"There's something we are missing," Alyx said. Lara felt that too. But she couldn't put her finger on it.

"He would just wait and come back with more firepower. We would lose the advantage," Lara said.

"What advantage?"

"That we know that Alrion can learn to cure himself, and then cure others."

"True. But at least he wouldn't be able to track Alrion so easily," Alyx said. Lara nodded. That was definitely a benefit.

"That's right but he still had no trouble tracking us before Alrion was infected. I still think we need to play on this edge we have over Wraith." Lara stood and paced around. There had to be an angle they could exploit.

"I have it. But it's incredibly risky," Alyx said. Her voice sounded unsure, but her eyes shone.

"I can see that you've got something good. What is it?"

"What if Alrion only cures himself when Wraith is already here. Then Wraith has no chance to back off, then Alrion can cure him too. Then he becomes a normal wizard," Alyx said slowly. Lara thought through the suggestion. It was a good one. They could lay a trap for Wraith. They could finally go on the offensive.

"I love the idea, but it's definitely risky. We have to draw Wraith in, get Alrion to cure himself, and then have Alrion cure Wraith. There's a lot of things that could go wrong."

"There is." Alyx looked undisturbed though. She still seemed interested in the idea.

"The more I think about it, the more I think we have no other option. Alrion is sick of being chased by this monster. It's quite poetic to take its power away. I think we need to go to them with this." Lara felt like they had a unique chance. They had to try it.

"She seems like a tough one. I would get Alrion to buy into it first."

"You're right. I guess we wait until he returns this evening. Then we will know where we stand."

"Sounds good to me. I'll rest up as much as possible. You're going to need me in this fight."

"We really will," Lara said. She was concerned about the difficulty they would have laying a trap for Wraith. But she was excited by the possibility of turning the tables on him. It just felt right. They had to find a way to make it work.

28

THE STRENGTH OF SOUL

Alrion collapsed on the floor. Sweat dripped from every part of his body, and his head throbbed. His muscles ached and cried out.

"This is too hard," he groaned. He rolled onto his back and stared at the ceiling.

"You're so close. You just need to rest a little more and attack it again," Marla said. Alrion nodded weakly. He looked over at his father. He was sitting cross-legged and composed.

"Vincent, this is it. You've done the worst of it. If you can do this final ritual, you should open the door," Marla said. Vincent nodded.

"I'm ready."

"Good. What you need to do now is focus on your heart. That's the centre of everything, of your Soul power. You need to gather it then push it to all areas of your body at the same time. Every individual gate we unlocked. Touch them all at the same time. This will allow you to activate the power." Marla walked around and crouched in front of Vincent, watching him closely. Then she wandered off.

Alrion watched his father. There was an intense concentration in his face. But he seemed calm and collected. It was like he was almost resting. But his face showed the true effort of what he was doing.

Alrion felt bad that he was lagging behind. He had worked hard to conquer the other areas of his body. But the final test of accessing his head with the power had proved too difficult. He would need some sort of special approach to finish it.

Suddenly Vincent flashed bright white, and he let out a cry. He blinked and looked at his hands.

"Yes! You've done it! You have enhanced your vision with Soul power. You are looking at the channels of Soul power that you have been training and working on," Marla said. Vincent turned and looked at Alrion.

"Oh my," he said.

"What is it?" Alrion said.

"I can see the Blight within you," Vincent said. He closed his eyes and opened them again.

"Back to normal?" Marla said.

"Yes. Do you always use that?" he said.

"No, it's quite taxing and as you saw shows a lot of things you don't need to normally see."

"I can believe that. It's a bit overwhelming actually."

"Good, that means it was working properly. Once you have more mastery over it, you can switch it on and off as required."

"Very handy. There's a whole world I wasn't aware of. I know, I know, I could have found out a long time ago." Vincent chuckled and looked over at Alrion.

"I'm glad you made it. Didn't take as long as I thought. It means there's still hope for me," Alrion said.

"Due in no small part to your lineage. But I must admit you have applied yourselves well," Marla said.

"Thanks," Vincent said.

"I'm just glad that there's light at the end of the tunnel, so to speak." Alrion laughed, and his father joined in. Even Marla smiled.

"It's good that you haven't lost your sense of humour. You're so close now," Vincent said.

"Your father is right. You know what to focus on now. I think you will want to meditate for a while to help build up your reserves. It will probably take everything you have to break through your infection."

"I have a question," Vincent said. He stood and stretched his muscles.

"Yes?" Marla said.

"Am I ready now? Can I just start using my new power?"

"Yes and no." Marla paused before speaking again. "Yes, you have now unlocked proper use of your Soul power. However, you expended a lot in the act of unlocking it. I would caution against using it much at the moment, give it time to replenish."

"I can handle that. How does it regenerate?"

"Naturally over time. Your body rebuilds it automatically. You can also meditate, that would help speed up the process."

"Great. Take note Alrion, I'm sure you'll want to be up and running immediately so I hope you've been paying attention."

"Can't use it immediately. Wait or meditate to hurry it up," Alrion said. He kept his eyes closed and rested on the ground.

"You don't strike me as the patient type. There's one more lesson that I think will be doubly useful for you," Marla said. Alrion opened his eyes and looked back at her.

"And that is?"

"Meditation."

"I can't argue with that. Well, I could but I don't really have the energy. You've sold me on the benefits. I think I need a minute to rest though."

"It's actually better to start immediately. Sorry," Marla said.

"I don't think she's actually sorry," Alrion said to Vincent, pretending to whisper. His father laughed.

"I'll stick around for this one too. It should be quite useful."

"Well then, sit next to me. Much of this will be familiar, but don't skip any steps. There are shortcuts," Marla said. Alrion forced himself up and he trudged over. He was physically and mentally exhausted. And he felt more and more like the Blight had a hold over him. But this was his only way to move forward, so he just found a way.

❧

"I think you're doing quite well. But now's a good time to return to your friends and actually rest," Marla said. She stood quickly and gracefully. Alrion had more trouble.

"I think my legs fell asleep. Is that normal?"

"More normal than you may think. Don't worry."

"I was going to blame it on my more advanced age," Vincent said. He also looked a bit wobbly getting up. But Alrion didn't say anything.

"Alrion, take it easy tonight. You've done enough and forcing it won't help. Tomorrow is another day," Marla said.

"Do we have enough time?" Alrion said, looking at his father.

"We should do. This is important, don't rush it."

"Fine. I'll probably find it easy to rest, to be honest."

"Good. I'll see you back here, first thing tomorrow." Marla left the room with purpose, letting in a gust of freezing wind.

"Just in case you forgot what it's like out there. Better rug up again," Vincent said. They put on their discarded heavy layers and stepped out into the cold once more.

At first the cold was a welcome change. But soon, it wore thin and Alrion grew irritated and his muscles became stiff. At least it wasn't too far to walk. When they reached their room Alrion let his father open the door, and stumbled through it. He noticed Alyx and Lara deep in conversation. They abruptly stopped when they saw him.

"You've returned. What news do you have?" Lara said. Vincent nodded at Alrion.

"My father has unlocked the power of Soul. I am a bit further behind, due to my delightful infection."

"That's fantastic!" Alyx said.

"I'm glad how enthusiastic you are for my father, but it's not quite the outcome I wanted." Alrion was confused by her excitement.

"No, she means it's fantastic that you're not cured yet. We have a plan now," Lara said.

"I'm curious," Alrion said. He allowed himself to lie down on the bed and rest. But he remained alert.

"I came up with a way to defeat Wraith for good," Lara said.

"I'm all ears," Alrion said.

"You cure him of the Blight," Lara said. Alrion sat bolt upright. He immediately regretted it.

"What? Why would I do that?"

"Just think. He has few weaknesses, and is incredibly dangerous. But if you cured him, he would just be another wizard," Alyx said.

"And you defeated him before when he was just a wizard," Lara said. Alrion could see the logic there, but it didn't feel right.

"To be fair I got lucky back then. But you're right in that he was vulnerable. Something doesn't seem right though," Alrion said.

"I think it's a good plan. What's it got to do with Alrion not being cured yet?" Vincent said.

"Well, from what we know Wraith is quite bullish. But he's also cunning. He could have followed us faster I'm sure. But he's taken the time to slow us down. Why do you think that is?" Alyx said.

"Clearly his experiments with Shade Wizards, and now Mystics," Alrion said. He felt horrible just saying the words out loud.

"Why would he do that if he can just snatch you up quickly?" Alyx said.

"Because he knows I'll be infected eventually anyway. Or, at least he believes that," Alrion said.

"Yes, but he's also not prepared to fail again. Remember, even with the huge force he sent to the temple, you managed to clear the trial and escape," Lara said.

"Let's say I buy into your thinking that he's cautious and careful right now. What does that mean?" Alrion said.

"If you were Wraith, and you were tracking yourself via your infection. You would know if something were to happen, right?" Lara said.

"He'd probably know immediately that something was up," Alrion said.

"And he would quickly come to the conclusion that you are cured in that scenario. Correct?" Lara said. Alrion nodded. He looked over at his father who also nodded.

"What's the first thing you would do when healed?" Alyx said.

"Heal you of course."

"Which he will also detect," Lara said.

"He will figure out that I have healed myself, and one other."

"What position does that put him in? What power does he have over you in that situation?" Lara said. Alrion could see their point. If Wraith had any sort of consideration or caution, then he would stop his approach. He'd need to stack the odds in his favour again.

"He might back off and regroup. But it would get the Mystics out of the line of fire."

"For how long?" Alyx said. Alrion thought it over.

"Well, what's your proposal then? That I just not cure myself?"

"We propose that you wait until he arrives. Then heal yourself. He won't have time to prepare any counter-attacks, and then you can cure him. The tides will turn immediately. With their leader gone, the rest will either flee or be easy targets," Alyx said.

"There's just one problem with that," Alrion said. He sighed and sunk back into the bed.

"What is it?" Lara said.

"There's a delay. Alrion will expend all his Soul power cleansing himself. He needs to wait for it to replenish. It doesn't sound like a fast process," Vincent said.

"They said I can meditate, but I don't think that's going to cut it," Alrion said. He could see what they were getting at. But there was no way to make it work.

"But you don't know how long is required. You're just making assumptions," Lara said. She looked determined. Alrion just felt weary.

"You're right. We shouldn't eliminate it completely. As tiring as it sounds, I'm starting to warm to it. I can picture Wraith's face when I am healed. It will be a sight to see," Alrion said.

"We should consult with my mother. Alrion, I know you're tired. But this can't wait. We need to know if this strategy will work. Otherwise, we need to come up with something else," Vincent said. Alrion knew his father was right, but he didn't want to move. Summoning vast amounts of energy, he sat up once more, then stood. His left leg wavered a bit, but he stayed up.

"I swear the Blight is messing with me. I don't know how you're walking around, Alyx," he said. He took a few steps and felt his strength return. It wasn't much, but at least he was solid on his feet.

"Please be quick. Good luck," Lara said.

"Of course," Alrion said. He let his father open the door and he charged back into the freezing cold.

The walk over to the grand hall was agonising. Alrion just wanted to nestle into the snow and sleep. It looked positively inviting.

"Easy there," Vincent said. He gave Alrion a steadying hand.

"Sorry, that patch of snow there looks thick and soft," Alrion said, half-joking. His father chuckled.

"That particular patch does look especially warm and cosy," Vincent said.

"Sounds like you want it now. I saw it first!" Alrion said.

"Once you defeat Wraith, it's all yours," Vincent said. He paused before the great doors. "Are you ready?"

"Yes. I'll fall through if you don't open them soon." Alrion smiled and waited for his father to push back the doors. They stepped into the relative warmth and Alrion felt sleepy.

Stay with it, he thought and pinched himself. The room had emptied out once more. Only his grandmother sat at the far end of the room, peering once more into the water before her.

"Approach!" she said, her voice carrying across the empty space. Alrion walked steadily over, his father staying close and sneaking lots of worried glances.

"I won't fall over here, don't worry," Alrion whispered. But he wasn't as confident as he sounded, and it didn't look like his father bought the act. As they approached the giant throne, Alrion saw a chair had been placed before it.

"Sit, Alrion. I know you are tired," Jovana said. Alrion didn't think twice and rushed over. The comfort was initially overwhelming. He looked up at her suspiciously.

"Of course you're exhausted, you've been training all day. I can see that you have almost achieved your goal. You're very close to not disappointing me."

"Uh, thank you," Alrion said. He looked at his father.

"You are very kind. We thank you again for your understanding and help."

"You are family after all. Did you think anything else would happen?" Jovana said. There was silence.

"I see you have come to ask for help? Spit it out then," she said.

"Yes. We wanted to find out how long it would take Alrion to replenish his Soul power after curing himself. Enough to cure someone else," Vincent said.

"I've been thinking of this myself. To answer your question, several hours at least. Partially because it is his first time, and partially because he will need every fibre of his being infused with Soul power to even consider expelling the Blight from another being. No matter what wizard tricks he uses to do it," Jovana said. She gave Alrion a stern look, and he wilted. Hours were no good. Even speeding that up to an hour would be way too long.

"Thank you for your time. That tells us what we needed to know," Alrion said. He started to rise, but heard Jovana clearing her throat. He looked up at her, puzzled.

"I told you I was thinking about it already. Why haven't you asked what can be done to speed up the process?" she said.

"Well, even an hour is way too long. I just presumed," Alrion said but was cut off immediately.

"You presumed to know better than me? The greatest Mystic that has ever lived, and the one who built this place?" Jovana stood slowly, looking down on Alrion. He suddenly felt very small.

"Surely even meditation cannot make that much of a difference," Vincent said.

"Who said you could only use meditation?" Jovana said. Her voice had a dangerous edge to it. Alrion started to speak but his father silenced him with a touch.

"What else could be used?" Vincent said. Jovana started to smile.

"It seems that you can learn, eventually. You're looking at it," she said, pointing to the small stone water fountain before her.

"You've witnessed the pool in the training room. This source is purer and more potent. With the right focus and application, you could be recharged in minutes."

"How many minutes?" Alrion said.

"At best, between five to ten. Will that be fast enough?" Jovana said. Alrion looked at his father.

"There's a lot riding on it. It's up to everyone else. I think we need to let them make that decision," Alrion said.

"I think you're right," Vincent said.

"You're not going to consult me? You don't think my Mystics will be involved in holding that creature at bay while you ready yourself to cure it?" Jovana said. Alrion's jaw dropped. Vincent just laughed.

"I'm so sorry mother. Time and time again we keep underestimating you, even when you remind us. Of course, we need your blessing to even consider such a plan. To be honest, we wanted to consider it ourselves first, before even bringing it to you."

"I know that. It's your only choice, if you want to get on with your quest. That man will never stop until you take away his power."

"You'll help us?" Alrion said. Jovana looked down into the water for a long time.

"If your friends agree that it can be done, I will support you in whatever your plan requires," she said finally. There was a sadness to her face, which Alrion was surprised by. As soon as he thought to comment on it, it was gone.

"We have some planning to do. I'll advise you as soon as we have something," Vincent said.

"Go now. Time is shorter than you think," Jovana said, pointing to the door. Alrion didn't like the warning in her voice.

29

SACRED GROUND

"You must stay here, no matter what you hear," Vincent said. Alrion nodded. He was back in the grand hall. The night had passed so quickly that he felt like he had just blinked and come back.

"Wraith is close?" Alrion said.

"We believe so. Preparations are underway now. But forget about all that. You have an important job to do. Meditate and prepare, you need to be ready." Vincent held out his hand. Alrion looked at it oddly and shook it. His father's grip was strong. He saw something pass quickly over his father's eyes.

"What was that?" Alrion said.

"You're a man now, and I wanted to treat you as such. I believe in you, and I know that you can do this. We're all putting our trust in you."

"Thank you. I don't feel confident right now, but I'll pretend that I am. But I was more asking about your eyes." Alrion pointed. Vincent gave a small laugh.

"Here I am making some gesture and you're just noticing something else. I took a look at you through Soul-enhanced eyes."

"And?"

"You look a lot better. The infection is still a mess, but it seems to have mostly consolidated into the one area. It will be hard, but you will succeed. I know it."

"That's actually good to hear. You can't stay here encouraging me the whole time, I'm sure they're waiting for you."

"They are. See you soon," Vincent said. He gave a quick wave and marched out. Alrion turned to see Jovana watching him.

"Should I just sit down somewhere?"

"No. You need to practice with the source. Come up here." Jovana stood and stepped aside, making space for Alrion in front of the pool of water. He carefully walked up the steps, and stood beside her. He stared into the water. It seemed to have layers to it. The surface seemed crystal clear, but it became darker the deeper you looked.

"This is unusual. Why is the water like that?" he said.

"That's not the water, that's a feature of the fountain it sits within. It aids with seeing."

"Seeing?"

"I am all-knowing, but how do you think I am so well informed?"

"Because you can see things in the water?"

"I don't stare in here because I'm senile!" Jovana said. Alrion shrugged.

"I still don't know half of what's possible. How does the Soul power help you see things?"

"It's a special property of blending your own power with that of the Source. Imagine that the water becomes a mirror, showing you that which your eyes wish to see but cannot."

"You can see great distances?"

"Oh, and more. But we don't have the time to properly instruct you now. And in your current condition it would not work properly. For now, you need to acquaint yourself with the water." Jovana rolled the sleeves up on her robe and placed both hands above the water.

"You too," she said. Alrion did the same, placing his hands close to hers.

"Now, the first thing we will be repeating is the first exercise you were taught. Feel the sensation in your hand and run it back to your heart." She closed her eyes and concentrated.

Alrion closed his eyes, and tried to push away all his feelings. He couldn't worry about what was about to happen. He had to focus on the here and now. With some difficulty he managed to recreate the sensation in his hands and slowly moved it along his arm and to his heart. It seemed a bit easier than the first time.

"Good, you've been paying attention. Was that easier or harder?"

"Easier. Is it due to the water?"

"No, well an insignificant amount may be. It was easier because you have been training yourself and reinforcing those pathways. Now, try again, but have your hand touching the surface of the water ever so gently." Jovana demonstrated, placing one hand down carefully. She just touched the surface of the water with her hand. She closed her eyes and Alrion nodded. It was his turn.

He followed her example very carefully. The water felt cool, but at the same time had a warm tingle to it. But he didn't worry about that so much. He started to repeat the exercise, but found it very different. His hand felt like it was almost on fire, rather than the light tingling from before. Moving the feeling down his arm was different too. It felt like it was easier to get momentum, but harder to control. He gasped when it reached his heart.

"Good. Feels different, doesn't it?"

"Much stronger. Harder to control."

"Exactly. Now one final example. This time fully submerge your hand." Jovana demonstrated once more. She was less careful this time, just plunging her hand under the water. But she did only use her hand; her arm was out of the water. After she closed her eyes Alrion tried himself.

Even though he knew the water was cold, it felt hot. It was the strangest sensation. As he began the exercise once more he was so shocked he almost pulled his arm out immediately. His whole arm was aflame with the Soul power, and directing it was incredibly difficult. But he focused his mind and contained it. With great trouble and persistence, he managed to push it along into his heart. But he also felt a spark within his stomach. He fell back with the shock, pulling his arm out of the water completely.

Jovana grabbed his arm roughly, steadying him. She was a lot stronger than she looked. Alrion just stared at her in confusion.

"I must admit, you're better than I thought. But even the control you did exert was not enough. You activated two gateways at the same time!" Jovana nudged him back until he was seated in the chair. She stood in front, looking him over. He noticed the strange flash over her eyes too.

"This is good. You will be able to contain the power. So, tell me, what did you think about that?" Jovana stared at him intently, waiting for an answer. He closed his eyes and thought. It was too distracting watching her watch him.

"The more contact I have with the water, the more of the power I absorb. But it is a lot harder to control. I'll need to balance the control and the speed of absorption if I am to use it effectively," he said. He opened his eyes and saw a smile on her face.

"You're smarter than your father. That's a relief. I'd prefer it if you learned more on your own, since that's the most effective method. But I'll need to feed you a few more pointers."

"I'm ready."

"As you are probably figuring out, I'm going to ask you to repeat all your activation exercises. This will help reinforce your Soul power and give you practice with the source. When the time comes, you will flood yourself and direct it all at that infection. It will most likely be agonising, but you will defeat it." Jovana gestured for him to stand and she sat down.

"That sounds easier."

"It won't be. But it will be faster. To complete the activation, you must not use the water. It will complicate things."

"I understand."

"Good. Now, after you are cured, you will want to replenish yourself as fast as possible. Balance is the key. Directing a torrent of power will not be effective. Save that for when you are desperate. We will give you the time you need to do it properly." Jovana stopped talking and sat back in the chair. She seemed weary.

"I'm sorry for all the trouble I've caused," Alrion said. Jovana laughed. A loud cackling that rang all over the room.

"Don't be sorry, there was no other way for it to happen. It will be an honour to have you succeed in my presence. Now, go back there and continue your exercises. You need to be ready for when they come."

"I will be," Alrion said. Against all odds he had a plan and the means to succeed. He couldn't let anyone down now. For the first time in a long time, he felt like the Blight was being held back. He was in control. And he would make sure that was how things stayed.

Vincent left the hall quickly.

That went well. Alrion doesn't suspect just how close they are. Although surely my mother knows, he thought. He almost ran to the entrance of the Mystic settlement. Marla was standing out front but there was nobody else.

"Are we ready?" Vincent said.

"Yes. My Mystics are spreading out throughout the space. Lara will join us soon and can relay messages quickly."

"You don't have other ways?"

"We do, but it's important to keep things simple. We also don't know what the situation is with Freyda. I'd rather not risk giving too much away."

"That seems wise. Here's Lara now," Vincent said. The thief ran along the snow with ease. She pulled up quickly, then took a moment to catch her breath.

"The Mystics are in position. I just need to report in when the party starts."

"Good. Alrion is working with my mother. He will be ready."

"Do you think we will see a large number?" Marla said.

"No, I think it will be a more focused group. Shade Wizards, Wraith, and Freyda. Maybe some Trackers?" Vincent said.

"That would play to our strengths more. Provided we can be effective at negating the wizards," Marla said.

"Amplifying your speed will be key. I hope your combat training is still fresh," Vincent said.

"You'd be surprised. All of us require it frequently. We are targets, even though people don't know who we really are. Just being women is enough. We see to ourselves, and are often posted as Healers. To many we look like easy marks."

"Those that heal can also harm," Vincent said.

"Only when required. We will do what is required, don't you worry."

"I'm not, I'm just nervous with all the waiting," Vincent said.

"Oh, I love the suspense. And every moment we wait, Alrion gets more time. Maybe I'll take a nap," Lara said, laughing. Vincent appreciated the gesture, although he saw that the laughter was a bit forced. She was right though. As tense as it may be, waiting was for the best. He dug his feet in and tried to think of other things.

"They're here," Marla said softly. Vincent peered into the distance but couldn't see anything yet.

"Look properly," she said. He realised what she meant, and reached for his Soul power. He wondered if it would ever feel natural, but assumed it would in time. By channelling it into his eyes and focusing on the distance he could see the colours around much more vividly. The landscape was not as bleak and white as he had thought. What captured his attention however was the procession heading towards them. It was a long column, all heading in single file. He had trouble discerning what they were. All he could see were dark shapes.

"I can see them now, but not any details. Is that me, or are they just that far away?" he said.

"A bit of both. You can increase your focus and definition with practice. Right now, you are probably getting a lot of different sensations all at once. You can be more selective with what you see in time," Marla said.

"It's like I'm pouring the paint on, but you're selectively brushing in exactly what you want to see?" Vincent said. He was struggling to find a way to describe it. Marla laughed.

"Never heard it described like that, but that's fairly accurate."

"Whatever you're doing to your vision must be extremely potent, because I still can't see anything," Lara said. She started to walk off.

"Lara, trust me they're coming. Just stay close please," Vincent said. Lara slowed down and waited a few paces beyond Vincent. She was peering into the distance.

Minutes passed. Agonising minutes. Vincent looked again and again, and had trouble discerning any features on the shapes that were advancing.

"I think they're purposefully approaching slowly. Maybe they're wary of traps," he said.

"I think you're right. We know he's coming," Lara said.

"We did account for that in our planning. We had to assume that by having Freyda, he would be wise to our usual defensive mechanisms," Marla said.

"I can see now. Wraith is at the front," Vincent said. It was mixed feelings. Relief that the enemy had finally been identified and spotted. But dread at the ensuing confrontation. It had been a long and bloody fight at the temple, and most of that was before Wraith had even shown up. Now he was leading the group. He would not be sitting back.

"Makes sense. He would survive any traps, so he's going first," Lara said.

"Do you need to alert anyone about anything?" Vincent said.

"Not until he's closer," she said.

"Don't wait too long," Marla said. Vincent could hear the concern in her voice. He had to assume that she could see Wraith clearly now, and was starting to finally get an idea of what he actually was.

"Just a bit further," Lara said. She continued to stare off into the distance. Vincent was not sure what she was looking for exactly.

"That should be enough. I'll be back soon, just need to set something in motion," Lara said. She took off at great speed through the snow.

"How are you feeling?" Vincent said.

"I'm fine. Ready to rescue our sister."

"Good. Just keep a cool head. It looks like there's probably quite a few Shade Wizards there."

"I know. Don't worry about me," Marla said. But her voice was strained. Vincent didn't press the issue. He had to trust that they could protect themselves. He still didn't fully understand all they could do, although he had seen lots of potential.

"I'm here!" Wraith shouted. He was almost upon them, and his voice thundered through the space. It had to be amplified through magical means. It still carried that harsh, stinging tone. The sound brought back memories for Vincent.

I can't believe Alrion has had to deal with this, inside his head, he thought with horror. It sounded bad enough in theory, but hearing this reminder of what it would actually be like was scary. Vincent drew his sword and held it ready.

"Are you sure you want to welcome it with a weapon?" Marla said.

"Wraith won't be at ease otherwise. He will suspect something," Vincent said.

"I won't argue with that. Let's see what this thing looks like up close." Marla stayed in a neutral pose, but she looked alert and ready. Vincent peered out, trying to see Wraith's final approach.

This time, he looked different. His height, physique, and skin were all the same. But he was dressed in a black cloak. And he held a staff. It was wooden and ornamental with a jet-black orb at the top.

"Vincent! So nice to see you again. I'm touched that you chose to welcome me," Wraith said. Vincent looked past Wraith, trying to see what else he needed to deal with.

"There'll be plenty of time for introductions later. Why don't you start with the woman?" Wraith said.

"Marla, one of the Mystics. And you are?"

"Wraith. First amongst the Shade Wizards, and leader of the Blight."

"Funny that, I've never heard of you until today."

"Because I work in the shadows, your ignorance is testament to my power."

"Hardly," Vincent said. He adjusted his stance and stayed in the ready position.

"You only had half a chance with that blade last time, you have no chance this time. Where's Alrion? Hiding away?"

"He's waiting for you, and completing his preparations," Vincent said.

"Oh, that's nice. Are you going to start the fight now? Or can we start off with a civil chat?" Wraith said. He clicked his fingers and four similarly dressed figures broke out from single file and stood next to Wraith.

Shade Wizards.

He looked over at Marla and pretended like he was considering his next move. But they knew what to do. Marla nodded at him. Vincent sheathed his sword.

"I suppose we can try that first, she said it was fine. But keep your manners," Vincent said. Wraith laughed, the evil sound causing Marla to flinch.

You don't know the half of it, Vincent thought. But they had met Wraith and convinced him to waltz in like he owned the place. That was all they needed to do for now. The rest would happen soon enough.

30

FIRST STRIKE

Vincent couldn't decide whether it was better to know or not know what was coming. He was tense because he knew something would happen. But at least he had no way of tipping off Wraith accidentally. Vincent looked around as they walked, and spotted nobody.

"I expected more of a welcoming party," Wraith said.

"Why would they be here, when they could be with Alrion?" Vincent said.

"I'm the one you need to appease here. You all live by my whim alone. As soon as I decide otherwise, it's over for you." Wraith snapped his fingers to demonstrate how easy he considered it.

I can't wait for Alrion to take you down a notch.

But Vincent held his tongue. It was not the right time to antagonise Wraith. The walk was slow and considered. Vincent wanted to look back and see who else Wraith had brought. But the odd glances he had risked earlier showed only the Shade Wizards. They were flanking Wraith and trailing behind him. Vincent had to assume that Freyda was back there somewhere. But now was not the time to verify that.

A flash of light startled Vincent and he stopped suddenly. Before he could even empower his eyesight, he noticed a group of Mystics had attacked. They had come in pairs. Four groups were there now. The front Mystic in each pairing was streaking forward with a glowing hand. They had each singled out one of the Shade Wizards.

Before their enemies could react, the Mystics landed their attacks. An explosion of light enveloped each Shade Wizard and almost in unison they clutched at their chests.

That's amazing. But it's a suicide strike. Wraith won't let them get away, Vincent thought. But then he saw the purpose of the second Mystic. Before the lead Mystics had even finished moving, the rear ones were gathering their Soul power and pushing it to their legs. Their role was now clear. As the pieces connected in Vincent's mind he saw them streak away from danger, taking their partner with them.

Wraith had cottoned on, but the wave of fire he unleashed was too slow. The Mystics were all gone.

"Take advantage of my leniency, do you? What a foolish decision!" Wraith roared. He whirled around and faced Vincent.

"And now we leave," Marla said. She grabbed Vincent's hand and the two of them sped away before Vincent could say anything. The terrain flew by like a dream, and before Vincent could get his bearings he was standing in front of the great hall.

"Inside. We have no time," Marla said. Vincent opened the doors and stepped inside. He looked for Alrion and saw him at the end of the room with Jovana. The rest of the room was filled with Mystics. He spotted what he assumed were the eight that had just attacked. They were all crouched down and meditating. Marla seemed tired already. She walked past Vincent and took a position meditating as well.

"Well done," Vincent said.

"I'm quite impressed," Lara said. Vincent hadn't spotted her in the corner.

"So, we're all here then. This is the final stand?" Vincent said.

"That's the one. Once our visitors have arrived nobody is allowed to leave," Lara said.

"Sounds like quite a party," Vincent said. He understood that much of the plan. But he didn't like the thought of how it was going to work. Clearly that sneak attack had expended the full power of eight Mystics. And it wasn't likely to work again.

"It'll work. We don't have a choice," Lara said. Vincent nodded. She was right about that. But for now, his priority was Alrion. He walked up and joined his son.

Alrion looked up at the noise. He noticed a lot of people entering the hall. First it was a group of eight Mystics. And then his father and Marla.

Wraith must already be here. I feel like I'm ready as I'll ever be, but at the same time it doesn't seem like enough, he thought. But he felt reassured seeing his father there.

Lara entered soon after, and Vincent walked over.

"Are you ready?" Jovana said.

"Yes. I've done what I can," Alrion said.

"Good. Now you must remain calm and push through at the appropriate time. The clock starts then."

"I know," Alrion said. He was not looking forward to that. The intense pressure having to regather his power to cure Wraith. It would take a lot of restraint to focus on his task, rather than on whatever fight was there.

"I can see that you're ready. Wraith is here, and in fine form. He's already had a taste of the Mystics, and let's just say they wiped the smile off his ugly face," Vincent said. Alrion grinned.

"Good. So, he'll be here soon. I noticed that Lara is here."

"He can't be far behind. I'll give you the signal when you can complete activation."

"I'm waiting." Alrion could feel the tension in the room, and he himself couldn't sit still. He stood and tried to remain calm.

The giant doors to the hall flew off their hinges and embedded into the nearby walls. Wraith strode through the open doorway, a short procession trailing him closely.

"He certainly looks angry," Alrion said. Wraith looked the same as he remembered, but the addition of a black cloak and staff was interesting.

Maybe he has more completely mastered his transformation?

But he decided not to jump to any conclusions. For now, he just had to watch and wait.

"You ignorant insects! You dare attack me? I thought you were interested in avoiding unnecessary death and destruction. Now, you will pay!" Wraith shouted. Jovana motioned for Vincent and Alrion to stand aside. She rose to her full height slowly from the throne.

"Abominations should know their place. Show some respect before I throw you out," Jovana said. Her voice rang loud and clear throughout the hall. Wraith looked so angry that his eyes were about to pop out.

"What did you say to me?" Wraith roared.

"Come closer if you're hard of hearing." Jovana maintained her calm demeanour and poise, which seemed to annoy Wraith even more. He whirled around, looking at his retinue. After a few moments he signalled to them to hold and he walked slowly through the room. Wraith glared at the Mystics as he walked.

"That is far enough," Jovana said once Wraith had reached the midpoint of the room. "State your business."

"I'm here for Alrion. He has evaded me long enough. If you hand him over now, I will show some leniency when dealing with your Mystics."

"Alrion is my grandson. He will not be leaving with you," Jovana said.

"Start the process Alrion," Vincent whispered. Alrion nodded and closed his eyes. He started checking on each of the gateways within his body. Each one had been bolstered and filled with Soul power. All except one. But he knew what he had to do.

One by one he transferred the available Soul power to his heart. He wasn't sure how much could be contained in a single point, but nobody had cautioned him against it. He had a strange feeling of being full, and yet more and more power accumulated. He could already feel a strange resonance in his neck. Like the Blight could feel something was happening.

"What's going on over there? What's Alrion doing?" Wraith said. It sounded so distant, but Alrion could sense the fear within it. He could tell something was changing. But Alrion maintained his focus.

He took all his gathered Soul power and started to move it up, on a familiar path. At first a stroke of panic entered his mind. He remembered how hard it was to move so much energy at once. But his concerns were unfounded. It was not as bad as when he was dealing with the pool's energy. There was a weight and momentum to contend with, but the energy seemed to do a better job of staying on the path.

He pushed it along, building up pace. He could feel the inevitability of it. Such a large and dense mass of Soul power. The Blight could not stand by and resist that. Suddenly, the two forces collided within him.

As before, the Blight put up resistance. But Alrion knew it could not survive. He didn't panic, he just pushed gently. He knew it would falter, and give in to the overwhelming light. So, he kept up the pressure. And the Blight began to give way. But as it did so, the light kept going. It overran the infection and took up all the space within Alrion's body. He could feel the Blight bending, breaking, and then with one final explosion it was gone completely. Alrion experienced a moment of tranquillity, then blackness.

Alrion awoke in a haze. He was lying on the cold floor. As he dragged himself up he could hear commotion around him. Memories started to flood back.

Wraith's here. I cured myself. Didn't I?

He sat up and tested himself for any signs of the Blight. There was nothing. But he didn't feel different. The Soul power was not there. He started to panic. Something was wrong.

A warm hand settled down on his shoulder.

"You didn't finish the activation. Nothing is wrong," Jovana said. Alrion felt embarrassed first, then relieved.

"Thank you. I'm still catching up," he said. He looked at her. The stern look on her features had softened a little.

"Don't dilly dally. Time has not frozen for you." Jovana pointed at the room. Alrion looked over and saw a battle raging. That was the source of commotion. His father was fighting side by side with Marla, and Lara was backing them up. There were other Mystics in the battle too. Wraith was largely unengaged, but observing. He seemed to be waiting for something. Alrion spotted some Trackers in the fight too.

"Don't get distracted. Finish the activation and start gathering your power," Jovana said. This time it was harsher and it shocked Alrion out of his stupor.

"Of course," he said. He remembered the exercise when his father did it. He just needed to connect all his internal gateways just once. He reached out and felt his heart point. It was weak but there.

This may be harder, because I've expended all my power.

But that was no excuse. He just had to keep at it.

"I thought you'd gone and killed yourself. But I see you didn't have the nerve!" Wraith shouted. He stepped past the fight and started walking closer.

"Keep going," Jovana said. Alrion tried to focus, but he couldn't take his eyes off Wraith.

"I did the impossible. It was a little more taxing than I expected," Alrion said. Wraith stopped walking and looked at him with a curious look. Alrion closed his eyes and made another connection.

"I thought that perhaps you had done it. My pet Mystic told me that was what you were trying to do. I told her you couldn't do it, but look at this. You proved me wrong. But I don't want you getting any ideas. Come here pet," Wraith said. He beckoned without turning around. A woman stepped out from the back of the room and slowly approached. She was too far to identify properly.

Another connection. Don't lose focus.

Alrion looked out again and recognised Freyda. She wore a cloak with the arms exposed, and long black tattoos covered much of her skin. Another pattern criss-crossed her forehead. She kept her head down a little, and shuffled along like she was broken.

"Here she comes now. She is a wielder of this Soul power you seem to be after now. But look at her. She's been infected. It doesn't protect you, it just makes us have to work a bit harder." Wraith started laughing. He forcibly pulled up Freyda's face so she could look Alrion in the eyes. He could see her fear, and realised that whatever had been done, she was still aware of it. In some fashion. Alrion closed his eyes, and forced himself to connect another gateway. He was almost there.

"Too much to look at, is it? Well, that there is your fate Alrion. No matter what tricks you think you have up your sleeve," Wraith said. Alrion ignored him, he needed to finish up. Just a bit further.

"He's not listening to me. What's he doing?" Wraith said to Freyda.

"I cannot sense that, you have blocked me," she said. Wraith smacked her over the head.

"What do you think he's doing then?"

"Activating his Soul power," she said.

"Oh, this will be good. How long does that take?"

"The sequence shouldn't take longer than a minute if uninterrupted."

"And then?"

"Then ... he can use his new power," Freyda said. She trailed off at the end. Wraith lifted her head up and stared into her face.

"I can sense you are holding back. What do you want to share with me?"

"Because he passed out, he probably expended all his stored Soul power curing himself," Freyda said.

"I don't care about that. He's a wizard, that's what he will use,"

Wraith said. Alrion closed his eyes; he just had to concentrate one last time.

"Go ahead, Alrion, do your thing. It won't make a difference!" Wraith said. Alrion did as instructed, making the last link. A sudden surge of power within him took his breath again. He coughed suddenly, then felt like the wind had been taken out from him. He started to fall forward but Jovana grabbed him and hauled him back.

"It's a bit disorientating with your power drained like that. Not as it is meant to be. But welcome back," she said.

"Thank you. I will never be able to thank you enough," Alrion said.

"Don't let that stop you trying. But for now, you better start with that pool," she said. Jovana gave Alrion a short shove and he rose unsteadily. He stepped over and leaned over the pool of water, hovering his right hand above it. It was easier now, to start to harness the power. And it felt great to be restored. Like he was thirsty but in a different way.

"It's like another sense. It's incredible," Alrion said. He tried diverting some to his eyes, like his father had done. The room blazed with colour, and he had to immediately close them. But he opened his eyes again carefully and started to see. Jovana had a strong core of blue, and a powerful aura. Marla was the same, but the strength seemed different.

Next, he looked over at Wraith. He was a seething mess of black and purple energy. His core was a purple flame.

Makes sense, Alrion thought. He looked over the room, trying to find Alyx. He spotted her in the corner, sitting down. She was filled with black energy, scarily so. But there seemed to be blue and white orbs of energy breaking up what he assumed to be the Blight.

You're so close, I have to cure you, he thought. But he couldn't. Not yet Not with Wraith right in front of him.

"You look like you need a minute, Alrion. I'll let the others fight for now, and then step in myself. I want you to watch me crush you again. Only this time, you won't be able to drop me into a pit of sand."

Wraith started to laugh and walked back to the main fray. Freyda followed close behind. She glimpsed one soulful look back at Alrion.

She must have guessed what we are doing, but held back. Good, I just need a bit more time, he thought. Hopefully they could pull it off. He had no idea how to cure Wraith, but that was something he could ponder as he built his power. It wasn't like he could do anything else while the fighting continued.

31

ELDER INTERVENTION

Vincent placed a reassuring hand on Alrion's shoulder, then walked off. He needed to return to the fighting. After the initial excitement, the Shade Wizards had been cautious and had been keeping themselves alive. One by one the Mystics had been dangerously injured or forced to retire.

We need to press hard while Wraith is not fully engaged in the battle, Vincent thought. He headed straight over to Alyx. The weapon master was sitting at the edge of the room, watching the battle play out.

"It's time to whittle down the enemy forces," he said.

"I'm surprised you waited this long. I'm ready."

"Will you know when you've pushed too far?" Vincent looked at her again with Soul power infused eyes. The infection was rampant in her body. It was a miracle that she hadn't turned yet.

"You'll see it. Whatever they did to me to give me strength, also keeps the Blight at bay."

"Well, try not to get there. Conserve your energy. But we need you out there now." Vincent handed her Alrion's sword.

"Are you sure about this?"

"I need to know you can efficiently take out the Shade Wizards."

"Consider it done."

"Good. Let's not waste any more time then." Vincent strode off to re-engage with the enemy. He experimented with the Soul power a little. He decided to try and divert some to his legs. He was hoping it would give him better strength and mobility. But he would have to see if it worked.

Vincent tried to remain inconspicuous as he approached the fighting. If he played his cards right there would be some opening he could exploit. He heard a loud scream and quickly turned around. Alyx was charging in with two swords held out in front of her. She immediately grabbed the attention of all the Shade Wizards nearby.

That'll do nicely.

He used the distraction to slip past the front lines and flank. He could see Freyda had retreated and was surrounded by four Trackers.

"I can do this," Vincent told himself. He instantly increased his speed and dashed towards the nearest Tracker. His legs moved with uncharacteristic speed, which he wasn't used to. He almost tripped over himself after the fifth step, but managed to rein in the speed a little. The Trackers were on alert, but didn't seem to expect an attack so swiftly or for Vincent to close the distance so fast. He managed to get the jump on one, and had launched a deadly strike before the Tracker could even react. It tried to move out of the way but Vincent had anticipated the movement and had already accounted for it. He cut the Tracker down and whirled into another strike, putting the next Tracker on the back foot.

One down. Keep pushing.

Another Tracker stepped around and launched at Vincent from his blind spot. Sensing the movement Vincent swung his sword out and turned to get a better look. The Tracker dropped down into a slide, heading for Vincent's legs. Vincent pushed more Soul power into his legs and kicked out at the Tracker. He connected with its head, sending the Tracker skidding along the ground and smashing into the wall.

I could get used to this, Vincent thought. He ran over to the two remaining Trackers. One Tracker grabbed Freyda and retreated to the back of the room. Vincent decided to let that go for now, and turned his attention to the last one. It pulled out a crossbow and started firing.

"Quickly now," Vincent said to himself. He ducked low and ran as fast as he could. The Tracker lined up another shot. Vincent weaved, but the bolt caught him in the shoulder. The searing pain and force almost caused Vincent to tumble to the ground. But he pushed some Soul power to the area to support the wound and regained his balance. As the Tracker prepared another shot Vincent threw his sword. It flew straight and true, piercing the Tracker in the chest before it could get off another shot. Vincent dropped to the ground over the Tracker, retrieving his sword and taking a moment to rest.

We can't keep up this intensity.

The crossbow bolt thrummed in his shoulder and he turned his attention to removing it. He tried pulling it out, but the bolt was barbed and was catching.

Great.

He looked around and it seemed as though everyone's attention was elsewhere for the moment. He turned his focus back to the wound.

I need to try something else, he thought. He gathered the Soul power he had diverted to his shoulder and tried to imagine it healing his shoulder and forcing out the bolt. At first it was like trying to grab a handful of water. But the more he tried, the more the Soul power responded to his attempts and seemed to actually interact with the bolt.

Vincent felt an intense heat in his shoulder, and the crossbow bolt started to emerge. He grabbed the shaft to help it along, and after a few more seconds of concerted effort it came free and clattered onto the floor. There was an intense stinging pain, but it quickly subsided.

That could have gone worse. I better get back into it, he thought. He crept back around, keeping an eye on Wraith and the other combatants.

Alyx was proving a handful for them. She had already taken out one Shade Wizard, and was putting pressure on two more. If Wraith wasn't sending out the occasional fireball or stone javelin she would have taken out another. But whilst Wraith wasn't fully contributing to the fight, he wasn't sitting it out either. Lara was darting in and out, trying to bait them into attacking and providing an opening for Alyx. But they seemed to be wising up to that tactic and were more restrained.

I need to tip the balance.

There were three more Shade Wizards left. The other one was fighting off a handful of Mystics. But rather than help them, he decided to tip the scales for Alyx and Lara. After assessing the situation, Vincent charged in. But he picked a route that kept him as far away from Wraith as possible. It wasn't worth tempting fate.

The Shade Wizard turned to see who was attacking, and studied Vincent. It quickly threw out a wave of Force. Vincent tried to shield himself with his sword, but was thrown backwards. But he resumed his attack immediately. The Shade Wizard cast a wave of fire, forcing Alyx and Lara to retreat. His companion pressed the attack, a wave of rolling earth taking up the floor and threatening to throw them to the ground.

It's now or never.

Vincent gathered a large chunk of Soul power and again empowered his legs. But he held nothing back. The speed he attained was unbelievable, and he had trouble seeing what was ahead. But he readied his sword in an outstretched stance and hoped to impale the nearest Shade Wizard.

The enemy turned with a frustrated look on its face. But it seemed to be unable to comprehend Vincent's speed. It raised its hands and started to unleash a fire spell. But an attack from behind stopped the spell. The Shade Wizard slumped slightly. The delay was enough for Vincent to reach his target, and he plunged the Runesteel deep into the creature's heart. Together they fell, and Vincent scrambled to pick himself up again.

"Thanks for joining us," Lara said. She was crouched down next to him, checking to make sure the Shade Wizard was down.

"Only two left," Vincent said.

"Soon to be one," Lara said. Vincent looked over and could see she was right. Now that the Shade Wizard was more or less alone, Alyx was all over it. It was all the enemy could do to block the relentless assault. It seemed to be enhancing its arm to prevent the Runesteel from slicing through, and the benefit to Alyx was that the Shade Wizard seemed unable to find the time to bring out an offensive spell.

"Too easy," Wraith said, holding up a hand. A powerful wave of force knocked Alyx's weapons from her hands. She shouted with pain, but didn't stop. She retrieved the leather whip from her belt, and with almost no loss in momentum unfurled it and lashed out at the Shade Wizard.

It didn't expect the arc of the attack, and the whip wrapped around the Shade Wizard's leg. She yanked it closer, the creature toppling quickly and sliding along the ground desperately trying to regain control.

"Here!" Lara said, throwing her Runesteel dagger. Alyx plucked it out of the air and in a smooth motion slammed it into the Shade Wizard. It went limp and completely still on the floor. Alyx started to slump down, but caught herself. She looked exhausted.

That's too much, Vincent thought. He stood and decided to rush over and help her.

"Enough!" Wraith shouted. He generated a massive wave of force that radiated out from his body. It swept along at tremendous speed, knocking everyone back. No matter how Vincent tried to brace himself, he was suddenly on the floor.

"I didn't come all the way here to serve up my followers like this. No more stalling for time. Alrion, it is time to face me." Wraith pointed at Alrion and started advancing.

"I'm not ready yet. Curing myself drained too much of my power. I need time before we fight. That way it can be a fair fight," Alrion said.

"I don't care. Fight, don't fight. Use your Spark, don't. Either way, you're coming with me. It's over now. No more running, no more escape."

"Why are you so obsessed with me? Because I almost killed you?"

"You don't understand, do you? This isn't just about me, and it's not just about you. Yes, I'm a monster now. I can't pretend that I'm not. But there is worse than me out there. Join me now, and prevent a worse evil. If you come willingly I will stop attacking your friends." Wraith swept his staff out, gesturing at the rest of the room. Vincent's gaze followed. He could see a lot of injured, tired, and broken people. Despite their success at taking out Wraith's followers, it had been at a great cost.

Alrion closed his eyes. Vincent wondered what his son was thinking.

Surely, he won't give up now. Not when we've come so far.

Vincent noticed the last Tracker dragging Freyda closer to Wraith.

"This one knows something," the Tracker said.

"I doubt it's important," Wraith said.

"She thinks it is."

"More time wasting," Wraith said. He reached out and hauled Freyda up with one hand. She struggled weakly in his grasp.

"What is it you're hiding? Spit it out before I lose my temper."

"Soul power. It is the key to curing the Blight," Freya said. She looked terrified.

"Yes, yes I just saw him heal himself. What's so important?" Wraith shook Freyda like she was a rag doll.

"A wizard can use that power to cure others. Granthion proved that." Freyda looked like she was torn between talking, and trying to remain quiet.

"Look at what they are doing. They're stalling for time while the wizard prepares to heal you," the Tracker said. Wraith tossed Freyda to the ground. Her body hit the ground with a thud and she whimpered as she tried to sit up.

"It's starting to make sense now. Inviting me in, curing yourself with me here. Trying to buy time until you are ready. All to sneak in and take my power away. No, I won't stand for that. I've worked too hard, come too far for you to steal away my advantage now." Wraith looked livid. He started to stomp towards Alrion.

We can't let this happen. He needs more time, Vincent thought. He tried to sense his Soul power. It seemed low.

I'll just have to make do.

Speed would be his best bet now. He could surprise Wraith and get an attack in. Vincent gathered all his remaining Soul power, and as before directed it into his legs. He imagined it providing him with amazing speed. He took up an attacking stance and leapt forward.

He travelled much further than he expected with that initial surge, but managed to correct his course and not topple over. Wraith was continuing forward, not paying attention.

I have a chance.

As Vincent closed in he prepared a strike. His sword swung out, seeking its target. Wraith suddenly turned around, and caught the blade. With his other hand he drew a spear of earth from the ground and flung it at Vincent from close range. Vincent could do nothing. The spear sent him flying backwards, piercing his shoulder, and pinning him to the wall behind.

Great.

Vincent didn't have any Soul power left. And the pain was almost crippling. He saw Alyx standing, her legs wavering. Lara was by her side, helping her up.

"No," Vincent shouted. Alyx looked over at him, and shook her head. She picked up Alrion's sword and held it in both hands. Lara armed herself with the Runesteel dagger and dashed out first. Wraith waved his arm, and the ground rippled up into short pillars, blocking Lara's path. She vaulted over one and kept going. Wraith sent out waves of fire. Lara dodged between them, ignoring the intense heat.

It's not going to work.

Vincent struggled to remove the stone spear but it was tightly wedged into the wall. Lara threw some glass vials at Wraith. Two large plumes of smoke started spreading, blanketing the area. Wraith threw more waves of force, the spells dissipating the smoke and revealing Lara. She was right in front readying an attack. Wraith held up both hands.

"Die," he said. A wall of earth rose up before him, and he charged it with intense fire turning it into a wall of magma. As he was preparing to push it towards Lara, Alyx appeared behind Wraith. She had been using the attacks as a diversion to creep closer. She swung out with the Runesteel blade. It swung true and on target.

Wraith stuck out an arm and the Runesteel blade bit into it. But it didn't slice all the way through. With his other arm Wraith punched Alyx in the head and she fell to the ground in a heap. Wraith removed the sword from his arm and tossed it away.

Lara was already retreating, but Wraith saw her flee. He rotated his wall to be facing her and sent it flying at incredible speed. Lara looked back, and saw the massive wall of superheated rock heading towards her.

She can't get away, Vincent thought. He strained again at the spear holding him. It moved a little. With a blur of light, Marla streaked past and whisked Lara out of danger. They stopped next to Alrion. Marla dropped to her feet, panting. Lara looked worse for wear, but otherwise uninjured.

"No more games. It's over now," Wraith said. He dashed forward heading for Alrion.

No. Not now.

Vincent had to stop them somehow. He drew upon all his strength and surged forward, forcing himself off the stone spear and leaving it embedded in the wall. He stumbled and almost fell, the pain threatening to make him pass out.

I have to get to Alrion.

Things were not happening the right way. But Wraith was too far ahead, and too fast. He was moving with anger and determination.

"That's enough!" Jovana shouted. She stood from her throne and started walking towards Wraith.

"Sit down old woman, you'll only get yourself hurt," Wraith said, mocking her. He laughed. But Jovana wasn't backing down. She stepped between Wraith and Alrion.

"You'll have to get through me."

"As you wish." Wraith surged forward, a maniacal look on his face. Vincent moved forward as best he could, but wasn't going to catch up with them. Not before Wraith and Jovana collided. He feared the worst. Mystics weren't fighters, even though they had done admirably in the fight.

"It's time you stopped and considered your manners," Jovana said. As Wraith closed in she put her hands out in front of her and a bright light started to radiate out. Vincent was blinded; he couldn't see what was going on. He had to get closer, help out in some way. Whatever his mother was doing, it had to be some sort of last resort.

32

A TIMELY APPEARANCE

Alrion wasn't surprised when his grandmother stepped up. He had noticed her gathering Soul power as well. But he had no idea what she was thinking. She was still a complete mystery, and the extent of her power was also unknown.

The light blinded him but he could feel the surge of Soul power. It seemed so unusual feeling it from the outside. That shouldn't be possible from what he was told.

The initial flash was over, and Alrion's eyes started to recover. He could start to see what had happened. Wraith and Jovana were standing close together, just meters away from Alrion. A white dome of light surrounded them, and both were frozen in time.

"What have you done to me?" Wraith said. He was completely motionless.

"I have trapped you within my Soul power. You cannot move until I allow you to." Jovana was triumphant, but there was a weariness to her voice. Alrion couldn't even begin to comprehend what she had done. To extend her Soul power so far outside her body and do this, it was remarkable. And it was just what they needed.

Alrion looked across the room. His father was stumbling over, a major wound in his shoulder. Alyx had collapsed on the ground. Marla was off to the side, exhausted. Lara was with her, also exhausted and trying to catch her breath. The rest of the Mystics were either injured or trying to recover their power. It was a sorry sight. His grandmother had intervened just in time.

"I don't know what you're trying to achieve here. This barrier you have created will not last long," Wraith said.

"It will last long enough. Then Alrion can deal with you."

"No. I don't buy this at all. He may be able to do something, but he can't cure me. Not when he's just cured himself. I don't know exactly what he's going to try, but it's pointless."

"Then why the big rush to take me out?" Alrion said.

"I'm sick of your games. One lucky break in the temple and I've had to chase you across the world. All the while, trying to build up my forces. No more running. You will join me today, one way or another. And we will crush our enemies."

"Never. I'll stop you, as I have before. And you won't be able to hurt anyone else. You won't be able to create more monsters like yourself. Your time is over." Alrion couldn't understand Wraith's obsession with him. He clearly had worked with other wizards, although none of them seemed as powerful or as capable as Wraith. But Alrion didn't think he was that different. Not in ways that would be useful to Wraith.

"I can feel this barrier weakening already. It's just a matter of time. And you won't have enough for whatever it is you're trying. Just accept that it's going to happen." Wraith struggled more in the barrier. And Alrion could see Wraith's fingers moving a little. Time was definitely moving against them.

"Grandmother, how long do we have?" Alrion said quietly.

"Almost enough," she said. "Now's the time to speed things up."

"Sure." Alrion knew what she meant. He had to try and accelerate the absorption of the Soul power. He took his hand and slowly dipped it into the water. The rush of power was a shock, but he quickly adjusted.

Alrion focused carefully. He slowed the flow of Soul power to help direct it better. As he felt more comfortable, he relaxed his control and let it flow faster. It was an exhilarating feeling, like he was being carried down river rapids. But he also sensed the danger at the end.

"You're running out of time," Wraith said. He had some movement in his arms now.

"How did you let yourself become such an abomination?" Jovana said.

"We're all only one difficult choice away from this. I had to accept this form, or accept death."

"I know which one I would have taken," Jovana said.

"You're old, you've lived a full life. I have things yet to be achieved. I have wrongs that must be set right. I couldn't let death take me, so I did what needed to be done. And it's opened my eyes to much more. You'll all thank me when we're done here." Wraith sounded serious. But Alrion couldn't imagine a time in which he would thank that cursed man. He had been tormenting Alrion for as long as he had been a wizard. The very thought caused Alrion's blood to boil. He could feel his anger rising. It had been contained, but Wraith's presence and his insistence on being right was just too much.

I can't let him get away with this.

Alrion immediately started to consider using his Spark. If the barrier holding Wraith let spells through, he could potentially end the monster now.

"What are you doing?" Jovana said. She was giving Alrion a cold and distasteful look. His anger rose again, annoyed at her judgement. But then it suddenly dropped away. She was right. Everyone had sacrificed so much for this, and him getting angry could jeopardise it all.

"I'm sorry. He just has a way of making me so angry. I hate him," Alrion said. Wraith laughed. Jovana's eyes softened a little.

"He's not worth it. The more you become accustomed to your Soul power, the more you will understand how your emotions affect your body, and your energy. You may have used your anger as a tool in the past, but it's destructive. You need to leave it behind." Jovana went back into lecture mode. But Alrion knew she was right.

"Don't listen to that nonsense, use every tool at your disposal. You need it," Wraith said. Alrion looked at the creature. Wraith was an illustration of what could go wrong. He had taken the desperate options, he had kindled his rage. And he had been transformed into something obscene. And still didn't understand the extent of what he had done to himself, or was still finding a way to justify it.

"What made you like this? Why are you so intent on doing this at any cost?" Alrion said.

"Why do you care?" Wraith said. He looked wary.

"I don't understand why you could think this is acceptable. And you really seem to be obsessed with my family. Why?" Alrion genuinely wanted to know. He had to understand why Wraith had been so fixated on him this whole time.

"It's complicated. But I will say this. I lost my wife because of your father, and grandfather."

"How?" Vincent said. He was slowly staggering over. Wraith struggled more against the barrier. He was a bit more successful, but was still being held properly. Jovana stumbled, but managed to stand back up. Alrion could see the toll it was taking on her.

"It was my first assignment as a wizard. I was tasked with following and observing a young man who had run away. My wife was an accomplished archer and woodworker and decided to come with me." Wraith looked at Vincent with a look of intense hatred. Vincent stopped walking suddenly.

"Wait a minute," he said.

"Yes, you're getting the picture now. The young man was captured by some infected. My wife and I covered his escape by holding off a horde of Blighters and Tainted. But we were both infected in the process."

"Your wife lived then? When Granthion cured everyone?" Vincent said.

"No. She made me take her life. In order that she wouldn't get turned. It was her greatest fear, to lose control of her life. She opted to die with dignity." Wraith spoke the words with such venom Alrion could scarcely believe it. He watched his father look over in horror.

"What's going on?" Alrion said. He could see the intense toll this had taken on Wraith. But now his father was somehow involved.

"I was that young man. I ran from my father, to forge my own path. He had sent a wizard after me. Which must have been Branthor. And I assume the reason Branthor hates us so much, is because nobody told him that the Blight could be cured. So, his wife died for nothing, and Branthor was forced to live with that." Vincent's voice was quiet and almost breaking. Alrion could suddenly see what had happened. Branthor's life had been destroyed by his devotion to Granthion.

"You got it in one. Do you understand now? Or do we have to keep going over it again and again?" Wraith shouted at them. He renewed his struggling with additional purpose. Jovana collapsed down to her knees. Vincent continued staggering over, until he was next to Alrion.

"Your pain is my fault. Leave my son out of this," Vincent said.

"No. Never. I need his power. And I want you to suffer. It's the only way."

"You will never have him while I am still breathing," Vincent said.

"I'm only too happy to help you with that," Wraith roared. He lashed out with all his limbs at once, and the white barrier shattered. Sparing only a moment to ensure he was free, Wraith dashed forward aiming straight at Alrion.

Vincent held his ground, holding his sword out in front.

"I'll cut you down," Vincent said. He had a fierce determination in his eyes. Alrion had to think quickly. He wasn't ready, he could feel it. And he couldn't speed up at all. His grandmother was slowly getting up. She looked completely spent. He realised he had to do something himself. To buy them some time so he could finish things. Curing Wraith was the only way to stop him; that was certain. But Alrion realised that he couldn't keep passively waiting.

He noticed Lara by his side.

"Don't do it. Let us fight for you," she said. Alrion could see the exhaustion in her eyes. But there was still a steely glimmer of determination.

"Not at the cost of your lives. Not when I can do something."

"You must endure the pain of this fight, so that you can end it for good. Trust us." Lara had a tear in her eye and she quickly wiped it away.

"I can't lose you." Alrion reached out with his free hand and touched her cheek where the tear had fallen. Lara closed her eyes and leaned into his hand.

"You won't. Just stop him for good." She took his hand away and stood in front of him, her Runesteel dagger at the ready. With a crash Wraith and Vincent collided. Vincent swung hard and fast, but Wraith was too strong. He knocked the sword away and punished Vincent with a blow of force at close range. Vincent flew back and crashed against the wall again. He crumpled, and stayed down.

"No!" Alrion shouted. Wraith laughed again, and resumed his approach. Lara was next. Alrion furiously tested his Soul power. It wasn't there. He knew he couldn't risk attacking without having it all there. It was too risky. He had to make sure that the cure worked. But he was out of time.

Lara moved much faster than Alrion thought possible, given her exhaustion and her previous fighting. She evaded Wraith's strikes, and managed to sneak into a good position to strike at its heart. But Wraith had seen it coming. A burst of fire from his hands made Lara duck and roll. Wraith followed up with a cascade of stone, and the rising floor pummelled Lara over and over until she settled yards away. She just lay on the ground.

"And now, it's just you. Are you going to continue to sit there and wait for your fate?" Wraith said. He had a satisfied smile on his face. Alrion was torn. He needed more time, but he wouldn't go down without a fight. He debated what to do. He needed to do something. But what?"

"You really are a monster. It's time you were put down for good!"

Celes shouted. Wraith turned just in time to see a vial hurtling towards him. He shielded himself with his arm, the contact smashing the vial and unleashing an explosion of epic proportions. Alrion ducked down behind the water fountain and felt the heat wash over him.

"I'm here Alrion, as promised. Let's finish this," Celes said.

33

THE PRICE OF LIGHT

Alrion stood and surveyed the scene. His mother was standing there, readying another explosive vial. Wraith stood there looking confused but was otherwise unhurt. Nobody else seemed to be injured by the blast, but they were all already in bad shape.

"Nice trick, won't work again, so don't even bother," Wraith said. He turned to Alrion.

"No more delays. You're mine." Wraith didn't wait around, and leapt forward once more. Alrion was trapped. He couldn't leave the water fountain, and he couldn't fight back. His time was out, but he wasn't ready. It hadn't worked. He froze.

Wraith continued forward, a wicked grin on his face. He discarded his staff and reached out with his hand. Alrion knew what was coming. But he couldn't act. Wraith reached him and grabbed his shoulder. Alrion could feel the claw-like hand trying to burrow within. He could feel the injection of the Blight. A piercing scream shocked him out of his state.

Alyx was writhing around. And she started to change colour.

"Oh no," Alrion whispered. It was happening. She was finally turning. He was too late.

"Watch her transform. You will be next," Wraith said. Alrion looked on in horror. Alyx's body contorted in every direction, her skin hardening and becoming like black stone. She was turning into a Shade. One final unearthly scream and it was over. Alyx looked around in confusion then sped out of the room.

"It's quite a traumatic experience, I'm afraid to say. But you will be with her soon," Wraith said. He had an intense look of concentration on his face.

Alrion didn't know what to do. Alyx had turned, Marla and Jovana were spent. His father and Lara were knocked out or too injured. It was just him, and he was being infected again.

There has to be a way.

Then Alrion had a realisation. His body was fighting the infection. And he was still taking on Soul power from the well.

Maybe I can fight back, he thought. He reached for his Spark. It was a strange sensation now, with the Soul power in the mix. He grabbed his Spark and sent out a wave of force.

Wraith didn't expect it and was knocked back. He looked at Alrion suspiciously. Alrion inspected his wound, and it was already healing.

The Soul power, he thought. It was protecting him, and he was refilling it at a high rate. He threw out another wave of force. Wraith swatted it away with minimal effort. But Alrion noticed something strange. He enhanced his eyes with Soul power and sent another wave of force. And then a small wave of fire. Wraith was more annoyed than anything else and not hurt. But that's not what Alrion was trying to do.

His eyes confirmed what he was feeling. Each time he drew and used his Spark, Soul power mixed in at the same time. He couldn't seem to create a spell without using both.

"Soul power is the key to curing him. Mystics can't use it outside their body, well not ordinarily. But I can with my Spark. I have a chance." Alrion came up with a plan.

"I was using a light touch, like last time. But since that's not working you're going to get the full treatment," Wraith said. He held up his hand and it started to transform. His fingers turned into razor-sharp claws, and they started dripping with a thick, black substance.

"You won't resist this." Wraith laughed and started to close in.

Alrion saw the Shade Wizard approaching and he thought back to one of his earlier encounters with a Shade. How he had created a ball of fire so hot it could penetrate the skin of the Shade. With a bit of tweaking, that could do the trick.

Alrion gathered his Spark and tried to limit the amount of Soul power that went into it. As Wraith approached Alrion created a small ball of red-hot fire. He pushed it forward straight at Wraith's chest. The Shade Wizard didn't even flinch and let it hit him.

As expected the ball of fire started to penetrate through Wraith's skin. But he seemed more focused on getting his claws on Alrion.

I've got him.

Alrion could see a small trail of Soul power linking him and the ball of fire. This was his chance. He took one more influx of Soul power from the pool, then channelled everything he had into that ball of fire. Using his Spark as a conduit, the Soul power had a path to travel. And it surged along. Alrion could see it travel like a thick rope of golden fibres. The Soul power entered Wraith's body. He stopped abruptly and looked down.

"What have you done?" he said. Alrion didn't answer, but focused on the Soul power. He channelled it into the raging hot fireball, and smothered it. He converted the burning ball of fire within Wraith's body into a ball of pulsing Soul power. Slowly but surely it grew and grew. Wraith dropped to his knees and clutched at his chest. Alrion remembered the struggle he had dealt with, forcing out that one big blockage of Blight. He couldn't begin to understand what Wraith was now going through.

He probably deserves it, Alrion thought. But at the same time, he realised that there had to be a better way. He couldn't do this for everyone else.

"This is not possible!" Wraith shouted. Again, Alrion didn't respond. He just kept pouring more and more Soul power into Wraith. He had an established conduit now, and it wasn't much more difficult than moving it around within his own body. He hadn't reached his peak Soul power, but he had somehow managed to get enough into Wraith that he could keep adding to it and still keep Wraith at bay.

The Shade Wizard started to glow white. It was like the light from within was shining through his skin. The intensity increased, until Wraith was completely submerged in a cocoon of light. He screamed once more, then became quiet.

Alrion released the spell, and stopped the Soul power. His hand slipped out of the water and he slumped down to the ground. He felt so tired and drained. With great effort he dragged himself up and leaned on the fountain to look over at Wraith.

The light was subsiding now. Wraith was no more. Branthor lay naked on the ground, the black cloak acting like a blanket.

It worked.

He couldn't believe it. But there Branthor lay, living and breathing. There were no signs of the infection. Alrion used the little Soul power he had left to examine Branthor. He could not see any Blight left within the man.

"You're cured," Alrion said. Branthor opened his eyes and looked up. His face was a mixture of fear and wonder.

"I don't believe it," Branthor said. He seemed to jump a little at the sound of his voice, and he stared at his hands.

"There's not a speck of Blight left within you. I think this is the part where you say thanks?"

"I feel so displaced. My mind. They were manipulating me too. Only a little, but enough. I can't believe I didn't see it," Branthor said, muttering to himself. He looked back at Alrion.

"I am thankful. You have proven yourself to be far greater than I imagined. But you cannot understand the gravity of what you have just done."

"What do you mean? I stopped you."

"Yes, I was a thorn in your side and fixated on you. But that's partially because they wanted it. I can see that now. I was never your greatest threat. I was standing between you and them. You're no longer safe."

"You were keeping me safe?" Alrion couldn't believe what he was hearing.

"Now that I'm out of the picture, there's nothing stopping them from coming for you."

"Who's they?"

"The generals. They're rebuilding, and now you've shown how dangerous you are. They won't rest until they have you. And now me. I can't stay here, it's too dangerous." Branthor sat up and looked around.

"You're not leaving until I'm ready for you to leave," Alrion said. He needed to know more. He also didn't trust Branthor. Who knew what he would do now?

"My Spark is intact. And I hold all the wisdom from the Pool of Knowledge. You cannot hold me here. I am sorry for what happened, it was more than I should have done. You now know why. But there was no other way. And I would still make the same choices."

"Just stay. Explain what's going on."

"No, I have no way of knowing where they are now. I have to disappear. Goodbye Alrion, we will meet again." Branthor vanished. Alrion blinked and looked around the room. He couldn't see the wizard anywhere. Alrion plunged his arm into the pool of water and siphoned off some Soul power. He enhanced his vision and got a glimpse of a shape leaving the room. But he did notice that Branthor had left behind the staff that he had been using.

He's gone, I'm in no condition to follow, Alrion thought. Branthor had sounded scared, which was not a good sign. Celes ran over and hugged Alrion. He had forgotten she was there. He welcomed the hug.

"Alrion that was incredible! I realised that I couldn't do anything to help. I felt so helpless watching."

"You intervened at the right moment. And it all worked out." Alrion heard a groan from nearby.

"I need to check on everyone now." Alrion walked over to check on Jovana.

"What did you do?" he said.

"Something foolish. But it worked, as I knew it would. Check on the others, they seem to be injured." Jovana waved him away. Alrion thought she looked in bad shape herself, but he knew that he was dismissed. First, he found his father. Vincent was against the wall in a seated position. He lifted his head slightly as Alrion and Celes approached.

"What did I miss?" he said.

"It's over now. Wraith is no more, and Branthor has escaped. I'm just checking on everyone."

"Don't worry about me, I've been worse. Your mother can help me up. Where's Lara?"

"I'll go check," Alrion said. He spotted her at the other end of the room. She was still lying down.

Oh no.

He forced himself into an awkward jog. His muscles were tired and lethargic. The broken ground was hard to traverse, and he almost fell a few times. But he arrived next to her and quickly dropped down. She was lying still on her side, but seemed to be breathing. Alrion gently turned her so she was on her back, and put his hand on the side of her face.

"Lara. Lara can you hear me?" Alrion looked over her for signs of injury. There was nothing obvious. He noticed her eyes open slowly.

"I had a bit of a nap. What's going on?" she said.

"It's over now. Are you hurt?"

"Nothing life threatening. I'm sorry I couldn't protect you."

"Shh, don't worry. It was my fault; I wasn't strong enough to protect you all. But the plan worked. I'll help you up." Alrion reached down and gently eased Lara into a seated position. She winced in pain, but her breathing slowed and she looked comfortable.

"Everything hurts," she said. Alrion nodded and helped her up again. With significant effort they were both standing, leaning on each other. They staggered along until they were closer to the throne. The ground there was undisturbed and they sat together.

"I bet you regret stealing that ring from me now," Alrion said, trying to lighten the mood.

"It was the best thing I ever stole," Lara said with a smile. A look of concern quickly passed over her face.

"Where's Alyx?" Lara said. Alrion looked away.

"What happened?"

"She turned into a Shade right as Wraith attacked me. There was nothing I could do."

"Where is she now?"

"I have no idea. She ran away. Wraith said something about the turning process being traumatic. I failed her."

"But you stopped Wraith. You cured yourself!"

"I did. But I promised I would cure her, and I failed. She's a monster now, and I don't know where she is."

"Don't worry, we'll find her together. And we'll bring her back. That's a promise." Lara leaned against him and he put his arms around her. It felt good to have her close. They had come so far together and finally defeated the man who had been hounding them the whole way. But the victory felt hollow. He couldn't enjoy it.

34

AFTERMATH

"I told you I would come," Celes said.

"I should have known you would come at the last minute. You have impeccable timing," Vincent said.

"Always. How's your injury?" Celes crouched down and examined it. She seemed concerned.

"I'll live. For now, I'm more worried about my mother."

"Then let's go to her. Although I wish I was meeting her under better circumstances." Celes helped Vincent stand, and supported him with an arm around his back.

Together they walked forward, one step at a time. Vincent could see his mother was struggling, which was alarming. In the short time he had known her she had always projected herself as strong. Showing any weakness was not a good sign.

What has she done? Vincent thought. He knelt next to her. "How are you feeling?"

"I've been better."

"I'll help you up." Vincent gently eased her up into the throne. She settled back into it with a sigh. Celes stood quietly off to the side of the throne.

"Something's not right. Do you need to use the water?" Vincent was really worried now.

"That won't help. I believe you have someone to introduce?"

"Yes. This is Celes, my wife." Vincent beckoned for Celes to come over. She walked over and crouched down to kiss Jovana's hand.

"Jovana. I'm your mother-in-law. Aren't you lucky that you haven't had to deal with me all this time?" Jovana laughed which turned into a cough.

"I would have loved for you to be in our lives. I'm truly sorry that it took so long."

"I think we are very alike, you and I. It takes a certain person to follow their family to the ends of the earth. You have a good fire, and he's needed that kind of person to challenge him. I feel comfortable that he has you looking after him."

"Thank you so much for your kind words. Don't worry, I'll keep him in line. I look forward to getting to know you better."

"You won't I'm afraid. It was lovely to meet you. Andar, make sure everyone else is fine then come back." Jovana dismissed Vincent, then closed her eyes.

"Lovely to meet you too," Celes said. She gave Vincent a questioning look. He shook his head and she started walking out.

I have a bad feeling about this.

He slowly did the rounds. Alrion and Lara were fine. Marla was just exhausted, but uninjured. The rest of the Mystics were in various states of injury, but nothing life threatening. He spotted Freyda sitting against the wall, rocking back and forth.

"Freyda. Are you alright?"

"No. Yes. They ran off when Wraith was defeated." Her voice was quiet and shaky.

"I don't know what he did to you. But Alrion can cure you and remove the Blight."

"That will be good. But he can't cure me, not truly." Freyda's voice cracked and she stared out of the open door.

"Everything will be fine, you'll see." Vincent looked around and saw no signs of any enemies. It was not worth pursuing them now. Satisfied that he had checked on everyone he returned to his mother.

She had slumped in the chair, and her breathing was now laboured.

"What's happening? Please tell me."

"I'm dying, Andar."

"How? Alrion can help you. Or Marla." Vincent was in a panic. "Alrion get over here!" he shouted. Alrion said something to Lara, and rushed back.

"It's no use. I did it to myself. I overextended myself, I burned myself out. Too much Soul power, and expending it the way I did. It's like burning the candle at both ends with two infernos." Jovana's eyes closed and she reopened them moments later.

"This can't be happening. We're finally reunited. And you saved Alrion."

"I knew this would happen, I saw it in the waters. But I went ahead anyway. It was my turn." Jovana let out a weak smile.

"What's going on?" Alrion said. He looked over Jovana. "You're hurt?"

"Dying. It was my turn to sacrifice myself. That's our lot I suppose. Your grandfather started it all."

"Why?" Alrion said. He looked distraught. Vincent put a reassuring hand on his son's shoulder.

"It was her choice. Sometimes you need to choose between two choices, neither good. But this, can't we do something?"

"No, you can't. All you can do is take the gifts you have, and use them well. You both have an important legacy to live up to. You are the descendants of the greatest wizard and greatest Mystic to ever live. You must succeed in your quest."

"I will. I promise. Can't I do something for you?" Alrion said.

"No, there's no going back. I've fulfilled my purpose, and I finally met you. As much as I wanted things to be different, there was no other way. I've had a good run. It's been a long and full life. And I didn't just drift away in my sleep. I went out with a bang." Jovana slumped down on her side, lying on the throne. After a few moments she opened her eyes again.

"Everyone must leave. I want to be alone with my son." Jovana closed her eyes again. Her chest rose and fell with difficulty. Vincent turned to Alrion.

"Please respect her wishes. Go find your mother, I'll come get you," he said. Alrion nodded.

"I'll take this, so we can study it," Alrion said, picking up Branthor's staff. Then with Lara they found Marla and escorted everyone out slowly.

"We're alone now," Vincent said. He tried to choke back the emotion, but it was rushing out.

"Good. I forgive you, Andar. And I know the burden you have been carrying. You are a foolish man, but I understand."

"I'm sorry. I've let everyone down, one way or another."

"But not him," Jovana said. Vincent was silent.

"He will understand when the time comes." Jovana gave Vincent a knowing look. Vincent didn't know how to respond.

"Come now, did you think you could hide from your mother?"

"I suppose not. You have a few tricks up your sleeve."

"More than you know. Hopefully, you'll learn a few. There's a book in my private quarters. It is a manual to the power of Soul. You and Alrion must study it carefully. Mastery will take a lifetime, but you need the knowledge to be on the path. This, you understand."

"I do. What can I do for you now?" Vincent held back his tears with great difficulty.

"Hold my hand and stay with me. It will remind me of when you were a sweet young boy. A simpler time, before all this madness." Jovana closed her eyes and Vincent held her hand. Her breathing slowed and he could see the life slowly fading from her. The tears broke free and streamed down his face. There was no more holding back. And, like that, her life drifted away.

∾

Vincent emerged from the great hall into the blistering wind. He noticed Marla standing just outside.

"I will go to her now. You are not familiar with our customs."

"I'm sorry."

"I know. We will talk later." Marla walked back into the building with purpose. Vincent watched her leave, and had to decide where to go next.

I'll try our room. Maybe the others are there.

He trudged through the snow, putting one foot before the other. His mother's passing had hit him harder than he realised. He had spent his whole life treating her as a fact, and not a person. He thought he was immune to those feelings, due to the separation and the passing of time. But he was wrong. Being there, seeing her, even for a limited time had brought everything back. Memories of feelings from their short time together. And the selflessness of all she had done to help, to her final act of sacrifice.

Vincent stopped his train of thought. It was just going to end in more tears, and he had to be strong for Alrion. His son had just gone through so much. Every trial and injury that Alrion had to suffer was like a dagger through Vincent. He should have spared his son all this. But he could not. All he could do was support him as best as he could. But even that was not enough. At least they were together.

Vincent arrived at the small quarters they had been staying in and paused before opening the door. He sighed, then entered. He saw Alrion, Lara, and Celes inside all conversing. They stopped suddenly when they saw him.

"Is she ...?" Alrion said.

"Yes. Marla is attending to her now." Vincent sat down on one of the beds. Celes rushed over and gave him a hug.

"I'm sorry," she said.

"Thanks. I think she understood the separation we had. But it shouldn't have been that way. It's my fault."

"Don't beat yourself up. Didn't your father take you away at a young age? Your mother didn't exactly live around the corner either," Celes said.

"True, but it just doesn't feel like I did enough."

"You need to be kind to yourself," Alrion said. Vincent looked up, surprised. Alrion continued.

"I've been thinking the same way. Blaming myself for what I could have done differently. But that was just the journey that led us here. All we can do is learn to be better." Alrion paused and looked at Vincent. Vincent was stunned. He didn't expect this maturity from his son. He felt so conflicted. Incredible pride at how Alrion had grown and matured. And also, a little guilty that recent events had accelerated this growth, and perhaps he could have shielded his son better.

"It's going to be hard, but you're right. Thank you Alrion."

"I could just see you doing the same thing, and we need to snap out of it. That's how the Blight controls people. It plays on their negative emotions and keeps them from breaking free."

"Something interesting to consider. What do we do now?" Vincent said. There was silence.

"We need to honour my grandmother. Then, we need to find Alyx. I have a promise to keep," Alrion said.

"Don't forget Freyda," Vincent said. Alrion nodded.

"When we're ready for that, I'll look for Alyx. If I find her, I'll bring her to you. And you can help Freyda in the meantime," Lara said.

"That's probably for the best."

"I'll help you. I don't know who Alyx is, but I witnessed her transformation. I'll do anything I can to help," Celes said.

"So, we have a plan. There's just one thing we need to take care of now," Vincent said. He let out a deep sigh. He wasn't looking forward to this. And not just because his mother had sacrificed herself for them. He realised that he had never done this for his father. He had never held a proper memorial.

I'm sorry, he thought and left, looking for Marla.

∽

"Thank you for your patience, please come now," Marla said. She walked serenely through the settled snow, leading them to a smaller building they had never entered before. Marla opened the heavy metal door, and held it open for Vincent. Once he was inside she went ahead.

It took a minute for Vincent's eyes to adjust, as it was a lot darker. He saw steps before them going down.

"Be careful, there's lots of steps," he said. He heard murmurs of acknowledgment behind him, and pressed on. There was the occasional torch to light the way, but it wasn't enough. He descended carefully, wondering where they were going. As he reached the bottom he let out a gasp.

Before him was a small stone structure like a tiny house, and beyond it was a vast lake. But it was no ordinary water. It shone like a star, bright and white. He could feel his skin tingling from just being near it. Surrounding the edge were all the Mystics. They stood with their heads bowed.

This is something else.

"This is the source. The most concentrated collection of Soul power in the whole world," Marla said. Vincent could believe that. It seemed so immense; he was actually scared of it. Marla must have noticed his reaction.

"Yes, it is something to be treated with care and respect. The water that you have used in your training is only a diluted feed from this source."

"Incredible," Vincent said. He couldn't believe something like this existed. No wonder his grandmother had lived here.

"We are ready now. Please take a position," Marla said. Vincent found a place to stand near the edge of the lake. Alrion and Celes stood on either side of him and Lara stood next to Alrion. Vincent noticed them holding hands.

Good.

"We gather here today, to recognise the passing of our eldest, Jovana. She was the guiding light that we have all followed, and her wisdom has kept us all safe and given us purpose. We owe everything we have to her." Marla paused before speaking.

"As is the custom, we will return her Soul to the source, so that she can continue to guide and assist us forever more." Marla walked over to the stone structure. Marla's hand glowed and she placed it on one of the walls. The structure began to glow white, and resonate with a strange sound. It was like something was building and building within.

A bright light suddenly burst from the top of the structure, then as it rose it began to bend. It rushed into the middle of the lake with immense force. A giant peak of water rose up, like a giant stone had been tossed into the lake. It gradually subsided and the waters settled down. But Vincent was sure it looked brighter than before.

He knelt, and reached down to touch the water. Marla rushed over to stop him, but he waved her off. He carefully put his hand into the water. The Soul power was intense and overwhelming. It was nothing like he had experienced before.

Farewell mother. I will strive to live up to your memory and will forever cherish the gifts you have given me, Vincent thought. He slowly removed his hand from the water.

"That was incredibly dangerous. You know now how potent the waters are," Marla said.

"I had to, to bring a piece of my mother with me," Vincent said. He rose and slowly walked out. He didn't want anyone else to see the tears.

35

GONE

Lara slowed her steps and eventually stopped.

"I think we need a break," she said. Sitting on a nearby rock Lara stretched her legs. Celes sat down next to her.

"We've been all over this mountain today. I'm not sure we will find anything," Celes said.

"We have to. Alrion really needs to set this right."

"He does seem rather attached to Alyx from what you said. Is there something going on there?"

"No." Lara almost shouted the words and reined herself in.

"I seem to have touched on something," Celes said with a smile. "Don't worry, I've seen you two together. I approve."

"This just seems awkward, discussing it with you."

"It doesn't need to be. Just promise me that you won't hurt him." Celes looked Lara directly in the eyes. Lara held her gaze.

"I promise."

"Good." Celes looked away. "You think his obsession with Alyx is just his sense of responsibility?"

"Mostly. The only reason she was infected was because she saved us. But I think it's more than that. I think he admires her, and her fighting ability. And her fierce independence. She's done amazing things all by herself. But that's all been taken away from her, because she's infected."

"That does seem like a big responsibility for him. We need to find something. I don't want to go back empty handed." Celes rose and looked around the area.

"We could try over here. It's not a proper track, but that wouldn't stop her. Especially in the state she's in." Lara pointed at what was little more than a gap between rocks. But it extended further than they could see.

"Worth a try. After you," Celes said. Lara took the initiative and pushed forward. The ground sloped up quickly, and they almost had to climb up in sections.

"I'm really not sure about this," Lara said.

"I know what you mean. But can you head back knowing you hadn't checked this?"

"Absolutely not. We have to exhaust all the possibilities."

"I thought the same."

"I just hope we find something, even if it's not her." Lara was desperate to find Alyx. Alrion seemed so lost in his thoughts. But he didn't want to talk about it.

"Ooh, look at this," Lara said. She stopped and let Celes catch up. Then she pointed at some markings just ahead.

"Looks like signs of a struggle. Look how torn up the ground is," Celes said.

"My thoughts exactly. This isn't what I would call a heavily frequented area. We could be on to something."

"I sure hope so." Celes signalled forward with her eyes and Lara pushed ahead. She took care following the trail, but also trying not to step on it or damage it in any way. The search took them around the corner and off on another small trail. It ended in a dead end. But there was something waiting for them.

"Is that a Tracker?" Lara said.

"Definitely. I wonder what happened?" Celes crept closer to inspect. Lara could tell from the way the Tracker was lying that it was dead. It was in an unnatural position.

"Look at this." Celes waved Lara over. With care Lara stepped around the body to see what Celes was pointing at.

"The neck?"

"Yes. It looks like it has been crushed. That's unusual." Celes ran her fingers over the skin.

"It's horrible. What could do this?"

"A Shade could do this." Celes looked at Lara.

"You don't think ..."

"This guy escaped. Alyx escaped. She had just been transformed, a lot was going on. Maybe she chased it down and killed it. Do you have a better explanation?"

"Not really."

"I travelled extensively with a Tracker. He was a bit different I think, but they're incredibly resourceful, tricky, and quite strong. I don't see what else could have happened." Celes stood and looked over the rest of the area.

"You're probably right. But where would Alyx go next?"

"If she hasn't come back ..." Celes trailed off and looked at Lara.

"Then she's gone away? To protect us?"

"Or for some other reason. But I think we're out of luck. And we're almost out of daylight. We need to head back."

"I wish I had more than this. Let me look around here one last time." Lara gingerly turned over the Tracker, looking for any other clues. There was nothing at all. She looked over at Celes and shook her head.

"We're done here, let's head back." Celes marched forward and Lara rushed to catch up with her.

Alrion was not in their room when they returned.

"Let's try the great hall," Lara said. Celes nodded. They walked quickly and with purpose to see if he was there.

"How do you think he will react?" Celes said.

"To the news of Alyx? I think it will rekindle his disappointment in himself. I really wanted to get him something more concrete."

"He was always terrified of failure. I think it's been holding him back for a long time. Vincent used to always say that he knew Alrion was capable of more in the workshop, but never tried."

"He's been trying pretty hard here."

"I can see that. It's hard to explain, but as a parent it's so difficult to see your child go through things like this. You want them to succeed, and learn the lesson. But you don't want them to suffer anything. So, I'm glad that he's found something to care about. But you'd never want it under these circumstances."

"I can understand that. I can't even begin to imagine that sort of responsibility." Lara shook her head.

"It grows on you," Celes said, and flashed her a smile. Lara returned the smile and stepped through the giant doorway.

She spotted Alrion instantly. He was at the back of the room, standing over the water fountain that Jovana always used. Next to him was Freyda. He looked up when they entered.

"Good timing, come over," Alrion shouted. Lara headed right over, with Celes at her side.

"I'm about to cure Freyda. I've been thinking about it a lot, and talking it through with Marla. I think I have a way that will be kinder than what Branthor went through."

"Sounds good, I hope it works well," Lara said.

"Me too," Freyda said. She still looked out of sorts.

"Before I start, do you have any good news for me?" Alrion said.

"Well, we have some news," Celes said. She looked at Lara.

"We found evidence of Alyx. Off the main trail we found the Tracker that fled. His throat had been crushed."

"And you think Alyx did that?"

"Looking at the injury, I don't think a person of average strength could have done that. It's our best explanation." Lara looked over at Celes and she nodded. Alrion looked thoughtful.

"That's good in that she seems to have retained her mind, even if only a little. Did you find anything else?"

"No, that was all. She's gone." Lara looked down.

"But we'll find a way to track her. It's important," Celes said. Lara looked over at her and nodded along.

"I know we will, I have a promise to fulfil. But first, I have to help Freyda." Alrion waved Freyda closer. She closed the distance with hesitation.

"I am so sorry for what you went through. I can never fully atone for that, but I will set things right."

"You are not accountable for the actions of a monster." Freyda's voice was quiet, yet defiant.

"I failed to stop him before, which I am responsible for. I'll have to find a way to balance that out. But at least, this is something I can do for now." Alrion put his right hand slowly into the water, so it was touching the surface. With this left hand he placed it on Freyda's chest.

"I'm amazed they managed to get the Blight to take hold. But I believe I can fix that right now." Alrion closed his eyes. His left hand glowed white, and Freyda's body seemed to respond. She gasped and almost stumbled, but she held her footing. A bright light soon surrounded her. It suddenly exploded and vanished, leaving Freyda stumbling forward. Alrion managed to catch her in time and ease her back onto the throne.

Lara couldn't believe it. He had made it look so easy.

It's really happening.

Sure, Wraith and Freyda had been special cases. But if Alrion could cure them, he could cure anyone. It was incredible. Freyda opened her eyes after a minute and looked around. Her eyes flashed quickly.

She must be using her power, Lara thought. Tears streamed down Freyda's face.

"You did it. You drove it away. I can't thank you enough." She clutched Alrion and sobbed into his chest. Alrion looked shocked, but held the woman tenderly. Freyda recovered and wiped her face.

"I'm sorry, I didn't mean to do that. I felt like my life had been taken away. It was so horrible!" Freyda visibly shuddered.

"I understand completely. And I am glad that I could help you."

"I feel renewed." Freyda stood quickly. There was a new spring and energy to her that hadn't been there just minutes ago.

This really is the stuff of miracles, Lara thought.

"What will you do now?" Alrion said.

"First, I will return home. But I'm not sure if I can stay. This whole experience, it's been like returning from the dead. I can't settle into my old life, well not straight away."

"Journey as far as you need. We will always be here to help," Marla said. Freyda bowed.

"Lara, let's go for a walk," Alrion said. He walked over and offered her his hand. Lara's heart skipped a beat and she held on tight.

What's going on?

In all the time they had been travelling together, not once had Alrion taken her aside. Her mind raced, wondering what might be the cause of it. But the realist in her shot down any fanciful thoughts.

Alrion just has no clue. He'll just want to grill you about Alyx.

They walked in silence across the snow, heading towards a building Lara had not yet explored. Alrion opened the door and motioned for her to enter. She stepped inside and looked around. It was a sparse, empty room but had what looked like a large pool in the middle.

"This is where we did our training. It's nice and quiet here," he said.

"Don't worry, I'll find Alyx," Lara blurted out. She didn't want him to be disappointed in her again.

"I know. This is not about Alyx, forget her for a minute." Alrion paused and look to be gathering his thoughts.

"This has been a really tough time. Being infected and on the run, fearing each day if we would be attacked and feeling like I couldn't even defend myself. I haven't exactly been the easiest person to be around during all that."

"I don't blame you. But you got through it."

"I did, well we all did. Together. But I've learned something through all this. I've got a different perspective now. We can't use destructive things as a crutch, not anymore. I used my anger, my frustration to fuel myself and push forward. But that's their way, that's what the Blight does. And we need to be better than that." Alrion seemed to be building up to a point.

"I understand." Lara didn't know what he was getting at though. It was all very confusing.

"And it's so easy to focus on those emotions, and neglect the other parts. It's not just about what we're doing, it also has to be how we do it. We have to embrace the better way." Alrion shifted uncomfortably and looked around the room.

Why is he philosophising so much? Lara thought. She remained quiet and let him continue speaking.

"It's our connection that helps us succeed. It's love being the opposite to all the hate that they thrive on." Alrion swallowed hard. Lara was starting to get a sense of what he was trying to say.

"I love you," he said abruptly. His face started to turn red, and he looked like he was trying to turn away. But he looked her directly in the eyes. She could see the sincerity of his words.

"I know," she said, almost laughing. He started to say something else but she just leaned in and kissed him. It was lovely and warm and felt so right after so long. She withdrew, and looked at him. He looked equal parts happy, and surprised, and relieved.

"I love you too. You're stuck with me now."

"I could think of worse things," Alrion gave her a smile. It was a real smile, one that she hadn't seen for a long time. That warmed her heart. His old self was coming back, from before being infected.

"You had me worried for a while there with Alyx." Lara gave him a pointed look and Alrion looked sheepish.

"I'm sorry about that. It was just respect and admiration. And I wanted to treat her like a human being. All that talk of being a weapon and a tool, that wasn't right."

"I thought that might be the case. But we worked that all out."

"You ... talked about me?" Alrion looked surprised.

"Of course we did. I care about her too, so don't be surprised about that. We'll find her. We just need to figure out a way to do that."

"It's of absolute importance. I can't move forward until we do. She's the one person I swore I would cure, and I won't be able to focus on what I need to do until she's found and cured."

"So, everything else is on hold?"

"Things can still continue to happen. But my entire focus from now on will be learning how I can find and save her. The quest is on hold." Alrion had a fierce determination to him. Lara loved that; that he cared so much. But it was also worrying.

"Are you sure that's the right thing? I'll support you, but it's a big thing to put everything else on hold."

"I'm sure. I can't be the hope people need, if I can't even save one person."

"Then I guess we need to step up our game." Lara shook her head. Things were different but also the same. But there was a gentle relief in her heart. She felt like she knew how he felt, but she didn't know if he realised it. Or if she had been mistaken. But his words today had lifted a great weight off her, one that was heavier than she had realised.

36

SPARK OF TRUTH

Alrion stepped through a hallway, the sounds of his footsteps echoing strangely around the space. He looked around and had a sudden realisation.

"I'm in a dream. One of those dreams." He stepped through the doorway and saw his grandfather sitting at a desk, writing away.

"Here we are again," Alrion said. He pulled up a chair and sat next to his grandfather.

"Here we are. You are nearing the end of your quest."

"How do you know?"

"Because you have completed the three trials. Don't forget, I'm just a part of you that is interpreting your knowledge and your memory."

"I realise that. Each time you show me something. Or I'm showing myself something. What is it this time?"

"Very well." Granthion stood slowly and walked over to a heavy stone doorway. He opened it slowly and it revealed a scene behind. Alrion walked over and looked closely.

A much younger Granthion held an orb of light in front of him as he walked through a dark cavern. The walls were worn down, as if by the wind and rain. Which seemed odd for what seemed like a deep cave. There was the occasional stalactite, but otherwise the cave was unadorned.

The young wizard walked forward without fear or hesitation. He trekked further and further down, like he knew what he was looking for. Finally, he reached the end of the cave. It was a wall. The cave just ended abruptly. Granthion slowed and approached the wall carefully. He held up his light and gasped. Alrion could see why.

The wall wasn't like the rest of the cavern. It looked like it was oozing and fluid. It pulsed and moved with a strange rhythm. It was alive.

"Is this really it?" Granthion said. He peered closer at the surface. He stepped back and took in the whole of the wall.

"This can't be it," Granthion muttered. He walked around the small space inspecting all of the walls. But he returned all the same to the strange oozing wall. He brought the light closer and closer. The wall seemed to react to it, shrinking away from the light ever so slightly. Granthion reached out with his other hand, slowly and tentatively. Closer. Closer. Finally, his hand touched the wall. For an instant nothing happened. Then the wall came alive, swallowing his hand. Granthion yanked it back in horror, thick black tendrils of oozing substance clinging to his fingers. He couldn't shake them off.

A stream of fire erupted from his hand, encasing the black goo, and burning it. The flames leapt onto the wall itself. But once they transferred they fizzled out instantly.

"What have I done?" Granthion said. He hurled more and more spells at the oozing wall, and struggled harder to free his hand. Eventually he managed to yank it back, the black substance that had been on him retracting back into the wall. But it had left a mark. Black streaks lined his hand.

The vision quickly collapsed and all that was left was blackness. Alrion closed the door and turned back to the now seated Granthion.

"That was you! Where was that?"

"That was the source of the Blight."

"You found it? And you touched it?"

"Yes, I became infected. And I always suspected that it had greater repercussions than just that." Granthion looked back down at the book before him. Alrion thought through the statement.

"What do you mean?" Alrion said. Granthion looked up again.

"In the time since that moment, there have been two rather major turning points in the existence of the Blight. The widespread creation of Shades. And the turning of the four generals." Granthion returned to his book.

"Oh no. That explains your obsession. You sought out and found the source of the Blight. But not only were you infected, you think that it somehow grew and changed because of its contact with you?"

"That is correct."

"That explains so much." Alrion was stunned. His mind was buzzing with all the potential of that revelation.

"That ruined your life."

"I have to assume so, looking at the other information available. Although, a great many things were achieved because of that."

"I wish I could stay here and talk to you. Why can't I do that?"

"Because your mind is not open or strong enough to join too much information together at once. There are protections in place."

"How do I overcome that?"

"I cannot tell you."

"Because you don't know, or you won't?"

"Who takes care of the Pool of Knowledge?" Granthion said. Alrion paused then answered.

"Nominated guardians. They also drink from the pool."

"And would these guardians know how to expertly access the available knowledge?"

"They should."

"And what happens when they drink from the pool?"

"Their knowledge is added to the rest. So, I must have the knowledge myself. You're just having fun with me, aren't you?"

"You're asking the wrong person." Granthion smiled.

"Fine, I get it. I can't rush this. Surely you can give me something else." Alrion was desperate. He needed to know more. This revelation by itself opened up too many questions. Which was probably why he wasn't being shown more. Granthion looked thoughtful, and finally spoke.

"The crystal amulet that you wear. You should figure out what's inside." Granthion smiled once more, then vanished. The room itself started to break up and Alrion was swallowed by blackness.

Alrion awoke with a start, thrashing his arms around. He realised he was in bed, and it was still dark. But that was just because nobody had lit any lamps, he couldn't tell what time of day it was. As his eyes adjusted he looked over at everyone else. His parents were asleep, as was Lara. He couldn't sleep again, so he crept out of bed, pulled on a coat and boots, and left the quarters.

The first light was breaking across the mountain, the bright rays and pink sky looked stunning. Alrion realised how much natural beauty he was surrounded by. He felt like he understood why his grandmother had lived here for so long. It wasn't just access to the source of Soul power. It was the beauty, quiet, and isolation. Something that made sense to him now.

Without a direction he wandered, but found himself standing before the great hall. Temporary doors had been built from wood and placed there without any decoration. He pushed one aside and stepped inside the room. There were a few candles lit, and the minimal glow from the water fountain helped illuminate the throne. Marla was sitting there.

"What brings you here so early?" she said. Her voice carried through the hall.

"I couldn't sleep, and found myself here."

"It must be for a reason." Marla seemed to stare at him as he approached.

"Are you their leader now?"

"I am not the eldest, but I feel as though I was meant to be her successor. I will gather all the Mystics and we will vote. Together we will reach a decision."

"You have my vote, if that counts." Alrion stopped just in front of the fountain of water. He peered into it, wondering how his grandmother had used it to see visions. The slight glow of the water reminded him of something.

He pulled out his crystal amulet and looked at it. It was the same as always, a thin black tendril stuck within it. He remembered the final words from his dream. There was something to discover.

"I've never seen a Soul crystal like that." Marla walked over to get a better look. Alrion removed it carefully and handed it to her. She turned it over in her hands, inspecting it. Alrion saw her eyes flash as she used her Soul power.

"As expected. And there's a strand of Blight in there too. This is incredible. Where did you get this?"

"My grandfather made it. Every wizard gets one as part of the initiation ritual."

"A wizard made this? That's unbelievable. To think that a wizard could manipulate Soul power." Marla handed the crystal back, and Alrion put it back over his head.

"It's strange, but I noticed that before when I was fighting. The Spark seemed to attract the Soul power and drag it along. I'm guessing that is why it worked."

"I still haven't learned how to put Soul power into vessels like that. It is a difficult and restricted skill. The eldest never taught it to me."

"But did she have it written down?" Vincent said as he approached. Alrion hadn't even heard his father enter the room.

"Possibly. Why?"

"She told me that Alrion and I must learn as much as we can. There's a manual of some kind in her quarters."

"The forbidden tome. Very few of us were even told of its existence, but I never thought it would be so accessible. I assumed it would have been hidden away somewhere else." Marla looked shocked.

"What safer place than under her watchful eye?" Vincent said.

"Very true. Well, we must honour her wishes."

"If you're to lead, you must lead from the front. You must learn with us," Alrion said.

"Of course, you're right. It's time I stopped fearing the unknown. The eldest spent so much time instilling in us the dangers of other techniques."

"She must have known that she would not be around to guide you in them," Vincent said. Marla grew very still and quiet.

"I must learn everything there is about storing Soul power in objects. It's the key somehow." Alrion started peering into the water fountain.

"I'm sure everything we need will be in that book. The eldest was always prepared."

"Good. I have a few ideas already, but I need to think them over."

"Such as?" Vincent gave Alrion a suspicious look.

"Why ruin the surprise now? Let me figure it out more, then I can show you instead of just telling you."

"Fair enough. We'll just have to wear protective clothing." Vincent laughed and even Marla smiled a little. Alrion looked at his father, thinking of the key revelation he received from his dream. He considered asking the question, but thought better of it. For now, there were more important things to focus on.

"I need to go for a walk. Can we all look at the book together later today?"

"Of course. I will coordinate with your father," Marla said.

"Thank you." Alrion turned and started walking away. He realised that he still hadn't achieve the whole purpose of his initial walk. He had to think through what he had learned in his dream.

Each time, he had been shown his objective. First it was the vault of silence, then it was his grandmother, and the power of Soul. This time it was a little different.

But what if it's not?

If he took the information on as presented, then he needed to find the source of the Blight and cure it from there. As his grandfather had so foolishly tried many years ago.

He also knew that wizard spells would not work. And since the dream had showed him his grandfather, he had to suspect something else as well.

"My grandfather sacrificed himself to cure Avaria. What will this do to me curing the whole world? Especially if I'm doing it at the source of the Blight?" The thought sent cold shivers down Alrion's spine. He felt his stomach churning at the idea of it all.

Whatever the situation is, you need to expect that it will end in sacrifice. It's worth it, isn't it? Alrion thought carefully. His life was still so young, and he had so much more to do. But he couldn't live on knowing that he had a chance to stop the Blight and he had not taken it. What had happened to Alyx was tearing him up. He had no choice.

Plan for a better way, but know that if it comes to it, you can do this.

"You have that look on your face," Lara said. Alrion looked up in surprise.

"What do you mean?"

"I haven't seen that look since you last had one of those dreams. Do you know how to end this?"

"I only know the location. You're not going to like it."

"Where?" Lara's face was a picture of concern.

"The source of the Blight." Alrion watched her face go ashen.

For her sake, be strong, he thought and put on a brave face. Lara said nothing, and when Alrion started off again she joined him. It was a difficult path ahead, and for now at least, it was a relief to know that he would not need to walk it alone.

THE STORY CONTINUES

SOUL OF LIGHT

BOOK FOUR OF THE HIDDEN WIZARD

The final exciting chapter in Alrion's story.

A wizard like no other.

An uneasy alliance.

An impossible choice.

Can Alrion fulfil his destiny, and at what cost?

ABOUT THE AUTHOR

Vaughan W. Smith is a fiction writer from Sydney, Australia, who explores big life questions through story. His favourite genres are Fantasy, Mystery, Science Fiction and Thrillers.

www.vaughanwsmith.com

www.ingramcontent.com/pod-product-compliance
Lightning Source LLC
Chambersburg PA
CBHW021406110726
47901CB00008B/2075